Praise for Ally Blue's
Demon Dog

"Ally Blue has had a long string of success in this paranormal genre and this story is certainly worthy of being added to that illustrious list. [...] ...if paranormal is your delight—then Ally Blue is one of the best in the genre."

~ *Reviews by Jessewave*

"*Demon Dog* is an intriguing suspense. I found this thriller to be exceptionally enjoyable."

~ *Literary Nymphs*

D1289997

Look for these titles by
Ally Blue

Now Available:

Willow Bend
Eros Rising
Catching a Buzz
Fireflies
Untamed Heart
The Happy Onion
Adder
Dragon's Kiss
Graceland

Love's Evolution
Love's Evolution
Life, Love and Lemon
Cookies

Mother Earth
Dragon's Kiss
Shenandoah
Convergence

*Bay City Paranormal
Investigations*
Oleander House
What Hides Inside
Twilight
Closer
An Inner Darkness
Where the Heart Is
Love, Like Ghosts

Hellscape
Hell's End

Print Anthologies
Hearts from the Ashes
Temperature's Rising

Demon Dog

Ally Blue

SAMHAIN PUBLISHING

Samhain Publishing, Ltd.
11821 Mason Montgomery Road, 4B
Cincinnati, OH 45249
www.samhainpublishing.com

Editing by Sasha Knight
Cover by Kanaxa

First Samhain Publishing, Ltd. electronic publication: December 2012
First Samhain Publishing, Ltd. print publication: November 2013

Dedication

For my husband's friend M., whose true (maybe) tales of the strange and unusual inspired this particular adventure...

Chapter One

Greg Woodhall burst through the employee entrance of DogOpolis, Chapel Hill's one and only gourmet hot dog palace—as the proud owners called it—five minutes late. "Traffic," he explained before the daytime manager could turn around from her inspection of the refrigerator's thermostat. "Sorry." He clocked in and sprinted for the break room to change into his uniform.

"Traffic, my tired feet. There's bike paths all the way from your place." The manager, Elena Sims, followed him. She leaned against the doorframe, arms crossed and forehead creased in a fierce frown. "Besides, I've personally seen you ride up on the sidewalk to go around a traffic jam, so don't give me that."

Busted. He opened his locker, peeled off his tank top and threw it inside. The sandals came off next, then the shorts, both adding to the pile on the floor of the locker. He turned to face her, giving her the full-frontal force of his very best puppy-dog face plus his boyfriend's favorite tiger-print thong. "I just got going a little late this morning, Len. I'm really sorry. It won't happen again, I promise."

She pursed her lips, but he knew she wasn't actually mad. "Okay. Seriously, though, make sure you're on time from now on. You *know* lunch is our busiest time."

"I know." He lifted his dark green uniform pants out of the locker and stepped into them, shooting Len a wide smile. "Thanks for understanding."

"Oh, yeah, I understand, all right." She aimed a pointed stare at his chest, which bore several purple marks courtesy of that morning's mattress romp. "Which reminds me, say hi to Adrian for me."

"I'll do that. Thank you." Grinning, he fastened his pants and reached for the matching green-and-white shirt.

She rolled her eyes. "You're on the register today. C'mon out when you're done changing." She turned to leave, stifling a yawn behind her hand.

As Greg shrugged into his shirt, he heard a shuffling sound behind him. He pivoted, expecting to see Len coming back into the room.

She wasn't there. Neither was anyone else.

He frowned. Was he hearing things, or what?

Not that he had time to worry about it right now.

Shoving the uncomfortable thought to the back of his mind, he finished buttoning his shirt, pulled on the socks and shoes he kept in his locker for work and hurried after his manager.

It happened again while Greg was ringing up one of his former UNC professors, although he didn't realize it at first. After all, it was a busy afternoon. His fellow employees dashed back and forth behind him all the time. It took him a few seconds to notice that neither Denise nor Malachi had moved from the registers on either side of him.

He glanced around as subtly as he could. Everyone else was in the back. So whose footsteps had he heard right behind him just now?

On the other side of the counter, Dr. Clark let out a loud sigh. "Still with the attention span of a gnat, I see. Did you get my order, or do I need to repeat it?"

Behind the sweetest smile in the history of smiling, Greg smothered the urge to say things that were completely inappropriate in the workplace. "Two turkey dogs with mustard and coleslaw, an order of O chips and a large unsweetened tea." He added gratuitous eyelash-batting when the professor's nose scrunched as if he was disappointed that Greg had heard him the first time. "That'll be ten-eighty, sir."

Dr. Clark handed him a credit card. He swiped it, gave it back and set the pad on the counter for a thumbprint.

He heard the footsteps again as he was handing Dr. Clark his tray. This time, Greg didn't look. He didn't want to know.

By the time his shift ended at five, the combination of an unusually busy afternoon and too many sounds without people attached to them had Greg jumpy and worn out. He changed back into his T-shirt and shorts before getting his and Adrian's dinner dogs together so no one could keep him working. Damn, he'd never been so ready to go home in his life.

"Hey, G. Your O chips." Malachi handed Greg a large bag of homemade kettle chips fresh out of the fryer. "I put in a thing of that chipotle ranch dip Adrian likes."

"Awesome. Thanks." Greg tucked the chips into the big plastic bag along with Adrian's salsa verde dogs and his own mustard and cole slaw ones. "See you at rehearsal, yeah?" He had a part as a chorus member in the current PlayMakers Repertory Company production—job number two, though it didn't pay as well as DogO—and Mal ran the lights and sound.

"I'll be there." Mal saluted him with a grin, brown eyes sparkling.

Greg laughed as he made his way to the employee entrance in back. "Bye, Len," he called to his manager, who was ringing up a customer at the drive-through. "See you tomorrow."

Ally Blue

She glanced at him. "Bye, Greg."

Between the office and the break room, a dark shape moved at the limit of Greg's peripheral vision.

He turned, goose bumps rising on his arms. Malachi, Eden and Crystal continued at their respective tasks up front. Len had moved out of the drive-through window to gather the order. She gave him a curious look. "Greg? Did you need something?"

He looked around. He could've sworn whoever he'd seen was bigger than Len, who practically had to stand on a box to work the drive-through, but no one else was there, so it must've been her.

It *had* to have been her. Had to have been a person. Something real he saw and his brain misinterpreted. Creepy black shapes were a whole level up from footsteps, and dammit, he did *not* want to play that game.

"Naw. Thought I forgot something, but I have it." He answered her frown with a grin that hopefully hid the way his pulse suddenly raced. "See you."

He strode outside, sliding his shades over his eyes, and went to unlock his bike from the rack. Forget about weird sounds and shapes and stuff. He *really* wanted to eat dinner with Adrian before rehearsal tonight, and he had to hurry if he wanted to make that happen.

Dinner secured in the basket on the front of his bike, Greg swung himself aboard and started up the bike trail toward his and Adrian's cozy little apartment a couple of miles away.

He smiled to himself as he rode. Sure, he bitched about his low-wage wiener-slinging job and not-exactly-starring role in the play, but that was all hot air. He knew how lucky he was. Especially when it came to the best part of his life—Adrian Broussard.

12

The thought of Adrian in bed that morning—tousled black hair, big dark eyes, sexy, kiss-swollen mouth, and oh *God* that gorgeous, naked body—spurred Greg to pedal faster. If he made it home in time, maybe they'd have a chance for more than dinner.

Greg arrived at the PlayMakers Theater for the scheduled all-day rehearsal on Saturday tired, grumpy and with the smell of frying oil permanently lodged in his nose.

Myah Sandoval, a fellow generic singing-and-dancing townsperson in the PlayMakers production of *A Tar Heel Born*, stopped halfway through her warm-up routine to stare at Greg as he stomped across the stage. "What the hell's wrong with you?"

"I had to work a double shift yesterday because Denise called in sick. Adrian was already asleep when I got home last night, and all we had time for this morning was coffee and a hello in passing because he had to be at the physics lab early." Greg let out a deep sigh. "I'm ready to be rich now. Why aren't I rich?"

Myah laughed. "I feel your pain. Wouldn't we all love to have more money?" She lifted one foot up onto the prop table and stretched sideways across her leg.

"No kidding." Greg yawned. "All right, I'm gonna go get changed. See you in a few." He waved at Myah and headed offstage.

In the dressing room—the newest part of the building, added during the 2016 renovations of the backstage area—Jon Hudson and Omar Nejem were talking while they changed from street clothes into light, comfortable things better suited for dancing onstage all day. They both looked up when Greg came in.

Jon stared at Greg with his usual uncomfortable mixture of resentment and fascination. "Hello, Greg."

"Jon." Greg didn't understand Jon's whole deal with him—insults one day, weirdly intense stares the next—but he wasn't about to waste any time worrying about it since Jon had never been his favorite person. Instead, he turned his best dazzling smile to Omar, who he actually got along with. "Hi, Omar. You're looking awfully chipper this fine morning." Greg toed off his sandals and dug his jazz shoes out of his bag. "That date with Enrique must've gone pretty good, huh?"

Omar blushed to the roots of his neat black hair, an interesting effect with his dark complexion. "It did, yes. We had a nice time." He studied Greg with unnerving intensity. "So, how's Adrian? I haven't seen him for a while."

Which was Omar-speak for *I can tell something's wrong but I can't tell if it's something wrong at work or at home and I know you don't want me to ask in so many words, especially in front of Jon, who we both know will be a giant dick about it.*

Yeah, Greg hadn't known Omar for long, but he'd learned a lot about him very quickly.

Unlike Jon, who remained a mystery. Not the least because a mutual acquaintance asking about Adrian apparently pissed him off enough to make him turn interesting shades of red and stalk out of the room.

Greg shook his head as Jon disappeared out the door with his jazz shoes in one hand and a sense of the wounded victim following him in a nearly visible cloud. "Swear to God, he's fucking nuts."

Omar nodded, his expression solemn. "All is definitely not well in the state of Jon. But that's neither here nor there, really." He leaned against the wall, arms crossed and every bit of his considerable attention focused on Greg. "Is everything all right?"

Greg wasn't about to tell Omar about the strange shadows and noises that had plagued him for the last couple of days at DogO. Omar wouldn't laugh like some people, but he'd worry about Greg hallucinating.

Not that the thought hadn't crossed Greg's mind. Which was more than a little scary.

"Yeah, fine." Greg shrugged. "Adrian and I are both really busy lately, so we haven't gotten to spend as much time together as usual, that's all." He flashed the evil grin he used to steer people away from serious subjects. "Overwork and undersex makes me cranky."

"Ah. I see." Omar pushed away from the wall, cheeks pink and his usual shy smile back in place. "Let's get out there before Noemi comes after us."

Greg laughed. Their director was a wonderful woman, calm and patient to an almost saintly degree, but she hated her cast loitering in the dressing rooms and would not hesitate to fetch them out and drag them onto the stage half-naked if she felt it necessary.

A shove of his foot stashed Greg's bag out of the way under the makeup table. He followed Omar out of the dressing room and onto the stage just as Noemi called to them.

As Greg took his place onstage, something fluttered in the shadows between the curtains at the tail of his eye. He resisted the urge to turn and look, because it was obviously nothing. Just the movement of the fabric as someone brushed past.

Except that no one had been near that spot. And the shape seemed awfully human.

Rehearsal went well, though Greg personally thought they'd have to spend less time going over the final song-and-dance number if Jon would stop sneaking glances at the chorus and pay more attention to his leading lady. Isabella DeSoto—a pro if ever there was one—agreed, judging by the increasingly frustrated way she glared at Jon.

"All right. It's nearly seven. Let's call a halt for today." Noemi rose from her seat in the theater's front row and stretched, both hands on the small of her back. "All-day rehearsal tomorrow, children. Be here at nine, ready to work. Now off with you." She made a shooing motion with her hands.

Theo Smathers fell into step with Greg on the way offstage. "Maybe Jon should pretend he's proposing to you instead of Isabella."

Greg stared. "What? Have you lost what little of your mind you had left?"

"Oh, Gregorio." Theo shook his head. "You're so clueless sometimes. Dude, he was staring *right at you* during the proposal scene."

"He was not." Greg thought about it. In fact, Jon *had* been looking in his direction. *Shit...* "He was probably staring at nothing, you know. Did it occur to you that his attention might've been wandering because he's about as professional as a seventh grader? The only reason he got this part is 'cause no one else who auditioned could sing it."

Like me.

He kept that bit to himself. No need to sound any more bitter than necessary.

"No argument on that point." Theo scratched his short, sandy beard, watching with a thoughtful expression as Jon walked toward the dressing room with his brows drawn together and his mouth set in a grim line. He might as well have had a sign on his back reading *stay away.* "Did it occur to *you* that your dance shorts are really tight and you have a great body?"

Greg sighed. "Oh, my God. I give up." He'd known Theo ever since freshman year, but he thought he'd never get used to a straight guy being so un-shy about speaking up on the matter of another man's assets.

He nearly ran into Theo when the man stopped in his tracks, turned and peered into the shadows formed by the curtains at the sides of the stage. Greg followed his gaze, but didn't see anything. "Theo? What the hell are you looking at?"

Theo said nothing. Greg waited, ignoring the other cast members skirting around them and shooting Theo cautious glances. Theo was a great guy who would walk through fire for his friends, but he lived in his own world. Greg was no longer fazed by his occasionally weird behavior.

After a few seconds, Theo sighed and rolled his shoulders. "I think that was a kid."

Greg laughed. "Um. What?"

"The ghost I just saw." Theo looked at him like he'd said something stupid. "It was little, so it must've been a kid." He ran a hand through his unruly curls. "I mean, I guess it could've been some other ghost, but the only other one *I've* seen is the flapper lady. I see her all the time."

In a blinding flash of insight, the figure Greg had seen in the curtains made sense. A ghost. Of *course.* Every theater had a ghost. He'd graduated from UNC with a degree in Dramatic Arts, for fuck's sake, he *knew* that.

It didn't explain the shit going on at DogO, but hell, he'd take what he could get.

17

Excited now, Greg let go of Theo's arm and turned in a circle, as if he could spot the flapper ghost right then and there. "Where have you seen her?"

"In the lobby, mostly. I've seen her in the audience too though a couple of times."

Myah emerged from the women's dressing room at that moment. "What, the flapper ghost? Yeah, I've seen her before. Only in the lobby, though." She tilted her head sideways. "You've seen her in the seats?"

Greg couldn't help feeling this wasn't fair, since *he* was the one with the boyfriend who could talk to the dead. He planted his hands on his hips. "Okay, I'm starting to feel left out here. All I've seen is a shadow. It didn't look like anyone in particular."

"Hey, count yourself lucky you saw *that* much. Most people never see any of the PlayMakers' spirits." Myah hauled her enormous purse higher up on her shoulder and pinned Greg with a curious look. "Why are you trying to spot a ghost?"

Theo laughed. "Hell, Greg's been on the lookout for ghosts ever since Adrian brought him around to the dark side back in sophomore year."

Greg glared at Theo, who grinned back at him. "I'm not *on the lookout*. I just think it's cool that the stories about this place might be real, that's all."

"There aren't that many stories," Myah pointed out. "The only one I ever heard was about Professor Koch, who founded the place. He's supposed to haunt the theater."

"Oh, hey." Theo's eyes took on an unholy gleam. "You should get Adrian to talk to his dads about getting BCPI out here to investigate the place!"

Myah's forehead creased. "BCPI?"

"Bay City Paranormal Investigations. Adrian's dad and stepdad own it." Greg met Theo's gaze, excitement building as the idea grabbed hold of him. "I like that, Theo. I like that a lot. I wonder if Noemi would go for it?"

"Or the university. It'd be cool if they did." Myah bounced in place. "I had no idea Adrian's dads owned a paranormal investigations company. That is *awesome.*"

Greg beamed. "I know, right? I bet they'd love to investigate this place."

"What are you children still doing here?" Noemi crossed the stage toward them, her low heels clicking on the wide boards. "I thought you'd be anxious to go."

Greg, Theo and Myah all shared a questioning look. Theo shrugged, as if to say, *whatever you think.* Typical. Myah gave him a thumbs-up. Squaring his shoulders, Greg faced Noemi's curious expression. "My boyfriend's dads own a company that investigates hauntings. We were just talking about how cool it would be if they could come investigate the PlayMakers."

Understanding dawned on Noemi's face. "Ah, yes. I remember reading about that when you and he solved the mystery of the Groome Castle haunting a few years ago."

"Yeah." Greg was surprised she knew about that. He raked his sweaty hair from his forehead. "So. What do you think?"

She ran a thumb over the stones of the bracelet on her opposite wrist. "Actually, I think it's a good idea. Proceeds for the Repertory Company have been dropping over the last year or so, in all our venues. Perhaps an official investigation into this theater's alleged haunting would be good for business." She smiled. "I'll talk to the school about it. Now you children go home."

Greg barely stifled an excited squeal as Noemi walked away. "Come on, let's get our stuff and get out of here. I have to go home and tell Adrian."

Myah left, calling goodbye to Greg and Theo. Greg hurried into the dressing room, with Theo hot on his heels. The two of them changed, grabbed their things and went on their way, exchanging goodbyes with the tech crew on their way out.

As he left the theater, Greg did his best to spot the ghost child, or the flapper, or one of the other spirits. But he couldn't, no matter how hard he tried.

Chapter Two

"Adrian. It's wonderful to see your face." Dr. Bo Broussard smiled. "You too, Greg. It's been too long since we had a chance to talk."

Adrian returned his father's smile, marveling at the perfection of the ImmersionSpace projections. If he hadn't known for a fact that his body was in the recliner in his and Greg's apartment, he would've sworn he sat opposite his dad and stepfather, Sam Raintree, at a picnic table in the Gulf State Park in Gulf Shores, Alabama. "It's good to see both of you too."

"Same here." Greg leaned his virtual elbows against the weathered wood and lifted his face to the computer-generated sky. Adrian couldn't help noticing that in ImmersionSpace, the recent tightness around Greg's eyes and the tension in his shoulders had vanished. Which was good, though Adrian remained intensely curious regarding why some people looked exactly the same while Immersed as they did in real life and others showed subtle differences. "Man, I wish this was real. It's *awesome.* I love hanging out here."

Sam laughed, gray eyes crinkling at the corners just like they did in actuality. "If you two ever had time to visit us, you could come to the beach with us for real."

"Believe me, I wish we could." Adrian laid a hand on Greg's thigh under the table and squeezed. Maybe it wasn't real, but it made him feel anchored to reality anyway. "So, did the school contact you about investigating the PlayMakers Theater?"

Bo and Sam glanced at each other. Something unspoken passed between them, as it often did—as it had ever since they'd first gotten together when Adrian was a child—and Sam nodded. "They did, yes. Just this morning, actually."

"A woman named Noemi Turon called us," Adrian's father added. "The director of your current play, I believe, Greg, is that right?"

"Yeah." Greg bumped his shoulder against Adrian's, his face alight with excitement. "So, y'all are on board?"

"Yes, we are." Bo rubbed his chin. "We can't bring everyone, of course, but we'll put a team together and be up there in two or three days."

"We're really looking forward to it." Sam slid an arm around Bo's shoulders. "It's been way too long since we've had a chance to visit Chapel Hill. This'll be a great excuse to come up there."

A light, happy warmth filled Adrian's chest. As much as he loved Greg, his doctorate work and his whole life here, he still missed Mobile and his family sometimes. Spending time with his dads would be wonderful. He was anxious to see the rest of the Bay City Paranormal crew as well. He'd grown up around them and thought of them as part of his extended family. If only his mom, his brother and his other stepdad were here, they could have a regular reunion.

"I can't wait to see all of you." Adrian leaned into Greg's shoulder, rubbing the back of Greg's thumb with his. "How're Mom and Lee? And Sean?"

"They're all good. Excited about seeing you both for Thanksgiving." His dad smiled and raked a strand of salt-and-pepper hair out of his eyes. "Though Sean may be late, depending on Auburn's game schedule."

Adrian grinned. His brother's football schedule often conflicted with family get-togethers, but that didn't keep Adrian from being proud of his younger brother's status as starting quarterback for Auburn University. "I just hope they televise the game, if he has to play."

"Greg, your parents are more than welcome to come stay with us as well," Sam added. "The invitation's still open if they change their minds about coming down. Bo and I have plenty of room."

Greg shook his head. "Thanks, but it's really all right. My great-aunt Marilyn's been wanting them to come to her place for Thanksgiving, so they're going to stay with her in Dayton."

Adrian tensed because he knew what was coming next. He and Greg had already talked about it, and he'd listened while Greg called his aunt names that would probably shock her into her grave if she ever heard them, then mourned the fact that his parents would even consider spending the holiday with a bitter old woman who still thought gays ought to be outlawed— no exceptions for great-nephews. Adrian gripped Greg's leg harder, and Greg shot him a grateful look.

Bo's brow furrowed. "Greg, you don't have to answer if you'd rather not, but...are you coming to stay with us in Mobile because you want to, or because of family issues?"

"Um. Both." Greg stared at the table, shoulders hunched.

He didn't say anything else. He didn't need to. Adrian knew his dads understood. They'd been through worse in their time.

Sam watched Greg with sympathy in his eyes. "You know you're welcome in our home anytime, for any reason. Bo and I consider you family."

Even in ImmersionSpace, Greg's cheeks flushed a faint pink to frame the shy smile he still wore around Adrian's father and stepfather. "I really appreciate that. Thank you."

Across the table, Adrian's dad started and grabbed at his hip. The muscle in Greg's leg jumped beneath Adrian's palm.

Adrian darted a concerned glance at Greg, who ignored it. Adrian stifled a sigh. Greg had been on edge lately, and Adrian had no idea why. He rubbed his hand up and down Greg's thigh.

"Damn. That's the..." Bo circled his hand in the air, as if looking for the right word. "The buzzer. We have a bit of a time-sensitive case in progress right now. That's Danny buzzing me to let me know that Andre needs to speak to Sam and me."

A jolt of fear ran up Adrian's spine. Neither of his dads seemed particularly stressed, but after all the danger they'd been through in the past with the interdimensional portal cases, Adrian couldn't help worrying. "Is everything all right, Dad?"

"Oh, yes, it's fine." His father leaned forward. "Don't worry, son. It's nothing dangerous. Just a scheduling issue with the owners of the home we're investigating."

The tension melted from Adrian's shoulders. "Okay. Good. Well, say hi to everyone for me. We'll see you in a few days."

"We can't wait to see you." Sam smiled. "Good night, boys. Love you."

"You too, Sam." Adrian reached across the table to touch his father's hand. He still marveled that he could actually *feel* it, though he knew the whole thing came from tweaking nerve centers in his brain. "I love you, Dad."

"I love you too, son." Bo gave Adrian's fingers a squeeze. "See you both soon. Good night."

"Good night," Greg echoed. "See you."

Bo and Sam vanished from their side of the virtual picnic table. Adrian shook his head. "I understand the physics, but I'll never, ever get used to that."

"You would if you Immersed all the time like everyone else does."

"You don't."

"I'm special. You know this." Grinning, Greg reached beneath the table and patted Adrian's hand where it still rested on his thigh. "Go ahead and blink out first. I know it freaks you out when you see me go."

"You have a smart mouth," Adrian said, but he couldn't argue the point. It really did bother him to see Greg vanish in front of his eyes. Knowing it was only Greg leaving ImmersionSpace didn't help. They'd never managed to blink out at the same time either, probably because Greg was faster. He narrowed his eyes at Greg. "You okay?"

Greg did a good innocent look, no doubt about it. His fair brows rose toward his hairline. "Yeah, I'm fine. Go on, I'll see you back in reality."

Adrian wasn't sure he believed Greg was as fine as he claimed, but ImmersionSpace didn't seem like the right place to argue about it. And really, *was* there anything to argue about? Maybe he was being too sensitive.

He squeezed his right eye shut until the visual menu popped up in front of his left eye, then blinked his way to the *exit* command and emerged from the virtual world back into the real one. He concentrated on removing his headset during the short time it took Greg to blink out. He hated looking at Greg's slack face and limp body while his mind was still in the Space almost as much as he hated watching him disappear from it.

Greg emerged with a jerk and a startled noise. Yanking off his headset, he turned a wide-eyed stare on Adrian. "What was that?"

Mystified, Adrian shook his head. "What was what? I didn't hear anything."

"Oh." Greg's gaze dropped to his lap. "Must've just been some Immersion glitch."

Adrian nodded. "It happens. Especially with this newest software. People have reported lots of strange experiences when blinking out."

"Yeah. I've heard that too." Greg put his headset on the table beside the sofa. When he looked up again, the smile he used to mask his worries and fears was firmly in place. "So. Pretty cool, huh?"

"Well, it's all right, but it's not like we've never Immersed before." Setting his headset on the coffee table, Adrian pulled Greg up to straddle his lap. "Is everything okay?"

"Everything's fine. And I can see you turning into a worrywart, so stop it." Greg wound his arms around Adrian's neck. "Anyway, I wasn't talking about Immersing. I was talking about the gang coming up to check out the PlayMakers."

"Oh." Adrian slipped his hands under the back of Greg's T-shirt to touch his smooth, warm skin. The muscles beneath felt tense. Maybe Greg was just a little overworked. "Yeah, it's cool. I'm excited about it. The investigation, and the visit. It'll be great to see everybody."

"It really will." Greg slid his fingers into Adrian's hair, tilted his head down and brushed a light, teasing kiss across his lips. "Do you think they'll let us help?"

"I don't know. Why, do you want to?"

"Shut up."

Adrian laughed because they both knew damn well Greg was *dying* to help. Had been ever since Groome Castle had opened his eyes to the reality of ghosts and the paranormal. Tilting his head up, Adrian covered Greg's smiling lips with his own. Greg opened to him with a soft, happy hum, one hand clutching a fistful of Adrian's hair and the other caressing his cheek.

After nearly three years together, the taste of Greg's mouth and the feel of his body pressed close still had the power to send Adrian's pulse racing and his powers swelling inside him. He spread both palms flat on Greg's back, the better to enjoy the flex of firm muscles as the kiss went deep.

Greg broke the kiss several long, glorious minutes later. He rubbed his cheek against Adrian's. "Is there any lube in here?"

"No. I'll get it, though, hang on." Adrian held his hand above his head and concentrated his psychokinetic energy toward the open door of the bedroom behind him. It took a few seconds, but the lube sailed off the bedside table where he'd left it the last time they'd made love—God, had it really been almost a week ago? Maybe Greg's jumpiness lately meant he simply needed to get laid—and hit his open palm with a solid smack. He held it up, grinning. "Lube. We're ready to go."

Greg shook his head. "It's seriously creepy-cool when you do that shit."

Adrian rested his head in the curve of Greg's neck. "I'm glad it's at least partly cool to you. I felt like I was nothing but creepy most of my life."

"I know." Greg raked his fingers through Adrian's hair, hugged him close and laid his cheek on the top of his head. "I'm only teasing about the creepy part, you know. You'll never be creepy to me." Greg shifted to kiss Adrian's brow. His fingertips traced slow circles on the back of Adrian's neck. "I love you. I love everything about you. *Especially* your mojo. I feel like you really ought to know that by now."

"I do know. Believe me. And I love you too." Adrian moved one hand downward to cup Greg's butt. "Stand up so I can undress you."

The way Greg's chest hitched against Adrian's spoke volumes. Adrian smiled. Greg had a serious kink for Adrian stripping him with psychokinesis.

Greg climbed off Adrian's lap and stood in front of him, trembling from head to foot, cheeks flushed and kiss-swollen lower lip caught between his teeth. His hands clenched and opened at his sides, over and over again.

God, he's perfect. And he's mine.

Vowing to never again let a whole week go by without worshiping Greg's body the way it deserved, Adrian reached out with his mind and flipped open the button on Greg's shorts.

Afterward, lying cuddled together on the sofa, Adrian dragged his fingertips through the dew of sweat on Greg's spine and thanked whoever might be listening for the rare joy of an evening without the demands of hot dogs, physics or the damn play. Lately it seemed like he and Greg hardly ever got to take their time making love then snuggling naked in each other's arms while the summer sunset blazed through the western window.

"Mm." Winding his body tighter around Adrian's, Greg nuzzled Adrian's throat. "This is nice."

Adrian smiled, his face buried in Greg's tangled hair. "I was just thinking the same thing." He molded his palm to the curve of Greg's bare ass. "Seems like we haven't gotten to spend much time together lately. Screwing on the couch without at least one of us having to jump up and go somewhere afterward feels like a huge luxury."

Greg laughed, the sound soft and lazy. "You're not wrong. Gotta say, DogO isn't a bad job, all things considered, and of course I love being in *A Tar Heel Born*, but I'm seriously glad I don't have to do either one tonight."

"Me too." Adrian stroked a hand over Greg's arm where it lay tucked around Adrian's middle. "I should probably be getting ahead on grading, but hell, I need a night off."

"What, you can't work on doctorate research *and* assistant teaching without having to take time off once a month or so?" Lifting his head from Adrian's chest, Greg gave him a reproachful look. "Idle hands are the devil's playthings, said my great-grandfather."

"I'll show *you* idle hands." Grinning, Adrian grabbed Greg's rear in both hands and squeezed.

"Hey! If you're gonna molest me, at least make me dinner."

"Is that your way of saying you're hungry?"

"Maybe." Greg yawned, his head dropping back onto Adrian's chest. "On second thought, why don't you mojo your phone over here and call for pizza delivery? I don't think I want you to cook, since it would involve you getting up."

"In a minute." Adrian lifted Greg's chin before he could get too comfortable. The tension had returned to Greg's expression and the tone of his voice, which meant Adrian's worry was back too. "You've been awfully tired and jumpy the last few days. Is there anything going on other than you working way too hard?"

A hint of something unidentifiable fleeted through Greg's eyes and vanished before Adrian could make sense of it. Greg shook his head. "Not really. Just overdoing it, I think." The teasing light Adrian knew well sparked in Greg's eyes. "You know me, I'm allergic to hard work. I was born to be a gentleman of leisure, but life's just not cooperating with me."

After more than three years together, Adrian wasn't so easily fooled. He smacked Greg's butt. "Greg, it's me, remember? I know better."

The corners of Greg's mouth tipped up. "Look, it's nothing. I promise." He rubbed the pad of his thumb over Adrian's lower lip. "You've been as busy as I have. You know how all that work can mess with your head."

"I certainly do." The nagging little voice in his brain made Adrian wind his fingers in Greg's hair and hold him still to study his face. Lack of sleep had left his gray eyes reddened around the edges. "You'd tell me if anything was wrong, wouldn't you?"

"Of course I would. We went down the keeping-secrets road three years ago. Didn't work out very well."

Adrian gave him a wry smile. "Truer words were never spoken."

"Uh-huh. You're not the only one in this relationship with brains *and* beauty." Greg stretched forward enough to kiss Adrian's lips before he could retort. "Now, since you super-smart types apparently lose the thread of conversations really fast, let me put you back on track." He poked Adrian in the chest. "I'm hungry. Buy me pizza."

Part of Adrian wanted to argue because he couldn't help feeling deep in his bones that Greg was holding something back. Not anything big, maybe, but still. After the way keeping things from each other had almost destroyed their relationship before it truly began, Adrian hated the idea of Greg not telling him something, no matter how small.

On the other hand, he might be imagining the whole thing. It wouldn't be the first time he'd worried about nothing since they'd been together.

In the end, the trust they'd built over the years won out. Holding up his hand, Adrian concentrated on his phone until it came sailing through the air into his palm. "Veggie with tomato, or pepperoni and pineapple?"

Greg smiled. This time, Adrian knew the relief he saw on Greg's face wasn't his imagination.

Greg's plan that Sunday was to leave work right on time at four o'clock. Maybe even a little early. The Bay City Paranormal crew were supposed to meet Greg and Adrian at their place at five, and Greg would rather not make them stand in the hall if he could help it. Adrian was supposed to be home from the lab by one, so he ought to be there, but banking on it would not be a good idea. He'd gotten caught up in his work and come home late too many times to count.

Of course, Greg's intention to call Adrian and remind him had fallen through for the same reason his leaving-work-early-maybe idea fell through—too many hot dog fans.

Damn DogOpolis and their awesome dogs.

"Three Demon Dogs and a double order of O chips," Greg called, sliding the three hot-sauce-and-jalapeño-covered hot dogs through to the front, along with a sturdy paper tray loaded with chips fresh out of the fryer. He untied his apron and pulled off the plastic gloves before Crystal could throw any more orders at him. "Okay, people. I'm already fifteen minutes overtime here. I'm going home. See y'all tomorrow."

He made his way to the break room followed by a chorus of goodbyes from his coworkers. To his surprise, Len sat slumped at the small plastic table with her head resting on her folded arms. She seemed to be asleep.

Greg edged through the doorway toward his locker, trying to decide what to do. He hated to wake Len when she was obviously exhausted in spite of how often and vigorously she denied it. On the other hand, if anyone told her higher-ups she'd been sleeping on the job, she might get fired.

As it happened, Len took the decision out of his hands by jerking awake as soon as he opened his locker. "What? Who's there?" She blinked at Greg and turned away, her face flushing red. "Oh. Greg. I... Um..."

"It's okay, Len. I won't tell anyone." He stripped off his uniform shirt, one eye on her. "Are you okay?"

"I'm fine. I have an exam tomorrow and I stayed up practically all night studying." She scrubbed both hands over her face in an obvious—and unsuccessful—attempt to hide her yawn. "Are you heading home now?"

"Yeah. My shift's over, and Adrian and his dads are waiting for me." Greg shimmied out of his pants, hung them in his locker with his shirt and grabbed his shorts. "They're coming up to investigate the PlayMakers Theater. Pretty cool, huh?"

"It is, yeah." Len aimed a keen look at Greg. Her forehead creased. For a second, Greg thought she was about to say something. Then she pushed to her feet, and the moment passed. "Well. I hope the investigation goes well. Say hi to Adrian and his dads for me."

"Sure. See you."

Len gave him a tired smile and a wave. Greg finished dressing, his thoughts turning to the upcoming investigation. He knew he wouldn't be able to participate very much because of all the demands he already had on his time, but they'd *have* to involve him in some way. After all, he was the link between the theater world and the paranormal investigation world. He couldn't very well be left out of things. Right?

Something clattered behind him. Startled, he spun and stared around the room. The magnet Crystal's artist boyfriend had made for her lay on the floor below her locker.

Greg let out an irritated breath, turned and dug his sneakers out of the bottom of his locker. God, he'd been jumpy all week, for no particularly good reason. Just annoying crap, like Crystal's magnet, or less identifiable noises. Or odd shadows he caught from the corner of his eye. Nothing he could put his finger on and say *this* is something real happening. Adrian had noticed, of course. Nothing got past him. But what the hell was there to say? Greg wasn't about to tell his fact-grounded lover that he'd been spooked by falling magnets, corner-of-the-eye shadows and things that weren't there.

He'd gotten his shoes on and shut his locker when someone touched his back. He yelped in surprise. "Shit! What the—"

He stopped and stared when he saw no one there. Crossing the room, he peered out into the narrow hallway. No one there either. Dex stood at the fryer, and Crystal and Len were working the registers. None of the kitchen crew had left their stations either. While Greg stood there, his heart hammering in his throat, Denise walked through the employee entrance. She smiled at him on the way to the office to clock in. "Hey, Greg."

"Hey, Denise."

With one last, dark glance toward his locker, Greg hurried outside. "That did *not* just happen in there. I did *not* feel that."

His hand strayed to his back as he approached the bike rack. The brush of his own fingers felt no different from whatever had touched him in the break room.

He scowled beneath his shades. It looked like ignoring this whole thing was about to get damn difficult.

Adrian had just finished picking up the last of Greg's dirty clothes off the bedroom floor and had wandered out to the living room, wondering if he should call Greg, when the man himself burst through the door. Sweat dripped from his hair and blood ran down his left leg from a scrape on his knee.

"I fell off my bike where the tree root buckles the pavement a little bit," Greg answered the question Adrian hadn't asked. He stripped off his shirt and used it to mop the beaded moisture from his flushed face. "And yeah, I'm fine other than the skinned knee. But damn, I need a shower. I had to ride hard to get back here in time. *Please* tell me I have time for a shower."

"You have time for a shower." Adrian glanced at the clock. "Better make it fast, though, if you want to be out before they get here."

"Cool. I can do that." Greg kicked his shoes off, dropped his sweaty T-shirt on the tiles by the door and headed for the bathroom.

Shaking his head, Adrian gathered Greg's dirty things and trailed behind him. "I just got finished cleaning up, you know."

"Oh. Sorry." Greg stepped over the crumpled pile of his shorts and socks on the floor and leaned toward Adrian, not quite touching because he was smart enough to know Adrian would not appreciate getting Greg's sweat all over his clean clothes mere minutes before their guests were due to arrive. "I promise I'll leave the bathroom clean enough to lick the floor." Greg angled his head for a quick kiss, then another, longer one. "Now get out of here before I drag you into the shower with me. I know your dads understand, but I'm sure they don't want to know."

"And I'd rather not have the visual of my *dads* showering together in my head, thanks all the same." Adrian covered Greg's mouth with one hand before the evil grin could turn into words. "I know you don't agree. Spare me."

One fair eyebrow arched, but Greg said nothing. He raised both hands in surrender. Adrian stepped back, letting his palm fall away from Greg's mouth. "Okay, I'll be out in the living room. Don't forget to wash your knee with *soap*, okay, and put a bandage on it."

"Yes, Mommy." Greg sidestepped out of reach before Adrian could land a smack on his bare butt and leaned into the shower to turn on the water.

Adrian was out the door and about to close it when Greg called to him. "Hey, Adrian?"

He turned. "Yeah?"

Greg stepped into the shower. "Your dads are hot." He shut the curtain, hiding his smiling face.

For a moment, Adrian contemplated the possibility of dragging his annoying, playful, delicious man out of the shower and giving him the spanking he obviously wanted. Or using his mojo—as Greg always called Adrian's psychokinesis—to make Greg *feel* like his ass was getting the whipping of a lifetime.

In the end, though, Adrian decided either course of action would inevitably lead to sex, and they didn't have time for sex before the Bay City Paranormal team arrived. Not even the quickest quickie ever.

"You are *so* getting it later," Adrian muttered to the bathroom door as he shut it on his way out.

The buzzer announcing the arrival of visitors sounded while Greg was in the bedroom getting dressed. Adrian's father swept him into a hug the second he opened the apartment door. "God, it's great to see you, Adrian."

"You too, Dad." Adrian drew back, grinning ear to ear. "How was the drive up?"

"Fine. We ran into some road work in Montgomery, but other than that there was no real holdup." Smiling, Bo clapped

Adrian on the back and moved to hug Greg, who walked out of the bedroom at that moment. "Greg! Hi."

While his father and Greg talked, Adrian turned to Sam as he came through the door. "Hi, Sam."

"Adrian." Sam wrapped Adrian in the warm hug that never failed to bring back memories of childhood. "How's everything?"

"Pretty good. Busy. You know how it is."

"I do, yes." Sam pulled away with a smile. "I hope you and Greg are taking care of yourselves, and each other."

"We're trying. Though we have days when we barely see each other."

"You're not just kidding about that." Greg nudged Adrian aside to claim a hug of his own from Sam. "Hey, Sam."

"Hi, Greg." Sam ruffled Greg's hair, like he always did. A crease dug between his eyes as he drew back. "How're you doing?"

It sounded like an innocent-enough question on the surface, but Adrian knew his stepdad well. Sam had been the one to spend endless, frustrating hours helping Adrian learn to control his telekinesis during his hellish preteen and teenage years. Along with Adrian's father, Sam had taught Adrian to conquer his fear of his power enough to harness and direct it. You didn't live through that sort of thing with a person and not learn to catch the sound of skillfully masked concern in his voice.

Not that Adrian didn't agree with him. Greg still insisted nothing was bothering him, in spite of the shadows beneath his eyes and his increasing tendency to jump at every unexpected noise. Or sometimes at nothing Adrian could identify. The idea of a direct confrontation with Greg didn't appeal, but Adrian had about reached the point where his worry for Greg's well-being topped his desire to not start a fight.

As he'd expected, Greg brushed off Sam's question with a smile and a shrug. "Oh, I'm doing fine. Busy almost earning a living and paying my acting dues in the chorus." He made a show of leaning sideways to peer behind Sam. "Where's the rest of the gang?"

"They're looking for a place to park," Bo answered. "They let us out so we could come on up."

Greg snickered. "Good thing. The parking around here's a nightmare."

A knock sounded on the door, and Adrian grinned. "Hey, they're already here. They must've found one pretty close by." He jogged to the door and flung it open.

Dean Delapore greeted him with a wide smile and a hug hard enough to squeeze the breath out of him. "Oh my God, Adrian, *look* at you! Just as handsome as your dad." Grabbing Adrian's head in both hands, Dean planted a kiss on one cheek, then the other, before letting him go.

"He's been going around kissing everyone like that ever since he and Sommer went to Italy last spring," Cecile Langlois said, edging around Dean into the apartment. Smiling, she rose on tiptoe to hug Greg. "It's so good to see the two of you again."

"You too." Greg kissed her cheek, clasped both her hands in his and held her at arm's length. "You're just as beautiful as ever. I don't know how David manages to hold on to you."

She laughed. "Sweet talk just like that, probably." Turning, she gave Adrian a hug as well. "Wow, you look more like your father every time I see you, Adrian."

"I consider that a compliment. Thanks." Adrian squeezed her narrow shoulders. "Come on in and sit down, everyone. Would you like a drink? We have orange juice, water, beer, chardonnay and iced tea."

"I'd love a beer." Dean wandered into the kitchen. "What kind you got?"

"Carolina Pale and Brown, straight from the brewery." Greg grinned. "Nothing but the best."

"No damn kidding." Opening the fridge, Dean grabbed a bottle of pale ale and another of brown. "Cecile. Heads up."

She caught the bottle of Carolina Pale Ale Dean tossed her. "Thanks." A quick twist removed the top. She took a long swallow. "Mmm. That's good."

"Brown's better." Dean held up his bottle in a silent toast, then drank. "Damn, I needed that after driving all day. Thanks for sharing, guys." He left the cramped kitchen area and plopped onto one of the four chairs clustered around their small round table. Cecile claimed the one beside him.

"No problem." Adrian aimed questioning looks at his dads. "What about y'all? Anything?"

"I'll take a Brown Ale too if you have any more." Sam sank into a recliner with a long sigh. "Bo?"

"Just a glass of juice for me. Thanks."

"Coming up." Adrian opened the refrigerator, grabbed the juice and a beer for Sam and went to fetch a couple of glasses from the cabinet.

While Adrian opened the beer and poured the orange juice, his father perched on the arm of the chair beside Sam and draped one arm across his shoulders. "Greg, I hope you won't mind if we ask you some questions about the haunting. What you've seen, and reports of what others have seen."

A pleased expression crossed Greg's face. He darted a sidelong look at Adrian. "No, I don't mind. I mean, I doubt I can tell you a lot, really, but I'd love to help however I can."

Adrian slid the beer and glass of juice across the counter toward Greg. "Here, hand these to Dad and Sam, will you?"

"Sure." Greg carried the drinks to Adrian's dads, who took them with smiles and thank-yous.

"We don't expect you to have all the answers, so don't worry about that." Sam leaned forward, one hand coming up to rest on Bo's knee. "We just need a starting point, that's all. You're bright, you're observant and you're inquisitive. And most importantly, you're not only interested in the paranormal, you've also encountered it before. That means you may have noticed a lot more than you think you have." He took a long drink of brown ale. "Damn, that's good. Remind me to buy some to bring home with us."

Adrian laughed. "I'll do that."

Greg crossed back to the counter to get the glass of wine Adrian handed him. "I haven't actually seen anything myself, as far as ghosts or anything at the theater. But I know several people who have. I can tell you what they've told me, and I can tell you what I know about the theater's history and the local stories about the haunting."

"That'll be perfect. From there, we can figure out who to talk to next and what we need to ask them." Bo drank deeply from his juice then rested the glass on his thigh. "I know you're aware that we'll be meeting with your director this evening, partly to talk about the haunting and partly to discuss an investigation schedule that won't interfere with rehearsals. The two of you are welcome to join us if you'd like."

"Seriously? That'd be awesome. I'd love to come. Thank you." Greg glanced at Adrian, excitement written all over his face. "What about it, Adrian? Are you in?"

Truthfully, Adrian had work to do. But it was nothing that couldn't wait another day, and he'd missed spending time with his father and Sam these last few months. Not to mention Dean and Cecile, who he hadn't even had a chance to visit with the last time he went home.

He smiled at Greg's nearly palpable excitement. "Sure, I'll come along. It'll be great to sit in on the initial phase of an investigation. I haven't done that in ages."

"Wonderful!" Smiling, Cecile reached across the table and grasped Greg's hand. "So, Greg, tell us all about this play you're in."

Greg's face lit up. "Oh, it's *amazing*. It's a musical romantic comedy set in the eighteen hundreds, and it's about these two people who meet and fall in love on campus here in Chapel Hill. They're both con artists, see, and they're both pretending to be Chapel Hill natives but they're not, and..."

Adrian let his mind drift, having heard it all before more than once. He poured himself a glass of water from the filter attachment on the tap and sipped it, looking on with a smile while Greg enchanted everyone in the room just like he always did.

As if he felt Adrian watching him, Greg glanced over. His gaze locked with Adrian's. Adrian grinned at him. Greg smiled back, and Adrian felt the warmth of it all the way to his toes.

He would've enjoyed it more if it weren't for the odd cautiousness that had crept behind Greg's eyes lately.

Standing there and studying the tension that never quite left Greg's shoulders these days and the way his gaze cut this way and that like a nervous fly, Adrian decided an honest discussion needed to be had. Greg would probably hate it—hell, Adrian hated having to force the issue—but too bad. After the mistakes they'd each made in those first fumbling months of their relationship, they'd sworn honesty to one another. Adrian would by God make sure they each lived up to that promise. Greg would thank him for it in the end.

Right?

Chapter Three

Adrian was watching him. Had been all through dinner, all through drinks at the town's hottest new wine bar, and especially through the tour of the theater Noemi gave the group, after Bo asked when they'd be able to see the place.

The whole thing irritated Greg worse than an itch on the bottom of your foot when you can't take off your shoe and scratch it. Especially since he felt Adrian ought to be concentrating on ghost-finding, not boyfriend-annoying. Sure, Sam and Cecile would both have their own psychic radios tuned in, but it wasn't the same. Greg had talked to Adrian and Sam both about this, and he knew for a solid fact that no one but Adrian could actually *talk* to ghosts.

Well, no one in this group, anyway. Other people in the world could probably do it, but they weren't here.

For his own part, Greg couldn't help feeling disappointed that they didn't run across the PlayMakers' one frequently rumored spirit during the tour. Not so much as a mysterious moan or a sinister shadow. He wasn't ashamed to admit—to himself, anyway—that he felt much braver facing the strange and unexplainable in the proper spooky environment with a crew of pros by his side than alone in an otherwise perfectly ordinary fast-food-joint break room. Weird shit had no business happening in places like that.

But no, they saw nothing. Heard nothing. Felt nothing, according to Adrian, Sam and Cecile, though the group's enthusiasm for the case didn't seem dimmed in the least. Which was good. Still, Greg couldn't help wishing they'd seen/heard/felt/otherwise experienced *something*, if only to give him another focus for all the paranormal shit haunting him—so to speak—lately.

Noemi said good night at the theater, promising to meet the group there the next day for their investigative session. Greg and Adrian escorted the BCPI crew to their van and hugged them all good night, then began the short walk to their apartment hand in hand.

They strolled in silence for a while, broken only to greet people they knew as they passed. Greg waited, determined not to ask Adrian what the hell he'd been staring at the whole night. If Adrian had something to say, Greg wished he'd go ahead and say it.

"The tour was cool," Adrian said eventually, once they entered their apartment-complex grounds. "Strange as it sounds, I've never been in the PlayMakers Theater before. It's really beautiful."

"Yeah, it is. I love it. I'm glad the Repertory Company started using it again." Greg leaned closer to Adrian as they navigated the winding sidewalk along the edge of the small parking lot to their building. "Too bad we didn't see anything tonight."

The smile Greg loved curved Adrian's lips. "Don't worry too much about it. If that place is really haunted, BCPI'll find the evidence."

"I know they will. Everybody's excited they're here."

He and Adrian fell silent again. Adrian kept his not-so-sneaky glances to himself now, but Greg felt the building tension in the grip of Adrian's fingers around his. It came as no surprise when Adrian turned to him once inside their apartment with shoulders squared and face set in battle mode. "Greg, I think we need to talk."

"I was afraid you were gonna say that." Smiling in spite of himself at Adrian's grim expression, Greg slipped both arms around his man's waist and planted a kiss on his tightly closed lips. Did it again, and again, soft little pecks and flicks of his tongue until Adrian's mouth softened, relaxed and opened up for a *real* kiss. Greg only stopped when he felt some of Adrian's tension melt away. "It's me, Adrian. I love you. Whatever you have to say, I promise I'll listen, okay? No need to look like you're about to face a firing squad." He grinned and patted Adrian's butt.

Adrian let out a halfhearted laugh. "You're right, of course." He kissed the tip of Greg's nose, then stepped out of his embrace and took his hand once more. "Let's sit."

Greg followed Adrian to the sofa, resigned to the inevitable. Adrian looked way more relaxed than he had a couple of minutes ago, but a certain wary thoughtfulness lingered on his face. It made Greg nervous, even though he was pretty sure he knew what was coming.

Or maybe he was nervous *because* he knew what was coming.

He sank onto the couch beside Adrian, their fingers still laced together. "Okay, Mr. Mojo. What's up?"

Adrian chewed on his bottom lip, his forehead furrowed. "Please don't joke right now. I feel like this is kind of serious—or it *could* be—and I'm already a little nervous about bringing it up, so I'd appreciate it if you could be serious."

Greg frowned. "Okay, what the hell? What's with all the *I'd appreciate it* shit? Normally you'd just tell me to stop fucking around and be serious. Why are you so damn nervous that you're tiptoeing around me like I'm unstable or something?"

"I don't mean to." Adrian's shoulders hunched. He looked miserable. "I'm just worried about you, I don't really know what to do and I'm afraid of saying the wrong thing."

Yep. That's about it.

Sighing, Greg leaned against Adrian's shoulder. "I'll help you out, huh?" He turned Adrian's hand in his and ran his free thumb over Adrian's bitten-short nails. "You've been worried because I've seemed tired and jumpy to you, but I've kept on telling you nothing's wrong. You know something's going on, though, and you want to know what it is because you're worried about me, but at the same time you don't want to keep bugging me about it because you don't want to seem like you don't trust me." He wove the fingers of his left hand through those of his right, trapping Adrian's hand between both of his own. "Does that sound about right?"

"Yes." Adrian's answer sounded both relieved and scared. He shifted enough to rest his cheek against Greg's head. "I guess you probably don't want to talk about it. But I wish you would. I wish you'd at least let me know you're really all right. I know *something* is happening to you lately. I can sense it, almost like I can sense ghosts. It's a...an energy, almost. I can't quite put my finger on it, but I can *feel* that something's different about you, and I need to know if you're really okay." He swallowed, the movement of his throat a faint shift in the corner of Greg's eye. "You know I'm here for you. Anything you need. Always. Any time." He sat silent for a moment, his breath stirring Greg's hair. "I love you, Greg. Let me help."

What was Greg supposed to say to that?

At least Adrian wouldn't tell him he was crazy.

Kicking off his sandals, Greg tucked his feet under Adrian's thigh and snuggled as close as humanly possible. "There's been some weird things happening lately. At...um...DogOpolis." He thought about it. "Or. Well. Mostly. I guess."

"DogOpolis? *Mostly?*" Adrian straightened up, dislodging Greg's head from his shoulder, and pinned Greg with an intense stare. "What do you mean? What's going on?"

Gazing into Adrian's concerned eyes full of a familiar, keen interest, Greg felt better about sharing the things he'd experienced over the past week or so. "I've heard strange noises. Seen things out of the corner of my eye. Um. At DogO and the theater. But the theater's haunted, right?" He let out a laugh that sounded completely out of place. "And earlier today at DogO, I actually felt someone touch my back when no one was there." He shrugged. "It's just little things, really. It might be my imagination. But it's sort of creeping me out, to tell you the truth. Especially the stuff at DogO. I mean, that's not supposed to happen at a fast-food place."

"You've never been one to imagine things, so I'm not inclined to think you're imagining it now. I know a person's eyes and ears can play tricks on them, but that doesn't mean what you're experiencing is all in your head." Adrian studied Greg's face as if he was trying to read the truth of the situation in the shadows under Greg's eyes. "BCPI is already investigating the theater. I'd really like to come out to DogO sometime soon and feel it out, if that's all right with you. If there's any kind of presence or unusual energy there, I should be able to sense it."

Greg's shoulders sagged with relief. "That would be awesome. Thank you."

"Hey, you know I'd do anything to help you." Taking his hand from Greg's, Adrian touched Greg's cheek. "I can come by tomorrow. Does that work for you?"

"That works great." Greg grinned and hooked an arm around Adrian's neck. "C'mere."

Adrian laughed and let Greg pull him close. Greg put all his love and gratitude into a slow, deep kiss. He hadn't believed for a second that Adrian would laugh at him or dismiss his fears. But it hadn't even occurred to him to ask Adrian to come check out DogOpolis. Now he could find out for sure whether anything out of the ordinary was going on there.

As usual, Adrian knew exactly what Greg needed before he knew it himself.

Adrian arrived at DogOpolis at four thirty the next afternoon. He smiled at the girl on the other side of the counter. "Hi, I'm Adrian Broussard. I'm here to pick up Greg. Is he ready?"

"Oh, yeah, he's just back in the break room changing." She turned to point toward the rear of the kitchen. "He said for you to come on back if you showed up."

Adrian managed not to laugh, but it was a near thing. He'd known coming in that Greg would be waiting for him in the back because they'd arranged it that way beforehand.

Understandably, Greg didn't want his coworkers to know he'd been seeing, hearing and feeling strange things here lately, so he'd asked Adrian to text him before leaving campus to pick him up from work today. That way, Greg could make sure he was waiting in the break room, and Adrian would have an excuse to feel out the rest of the restaurant directly rather than doing it from the dining area. He always got better results that way.

It was all very cloak-and-dagger, which Adrian found a bit silly. It was also important to Greg, which meant Adrian agreed to do it anyway.

"Thank you very much…" He glanced at the girl's name tag. "Crystal. Nice to meet you."

"You too, finally. I never seem to be here when you come by." She grinned. "Oh, and Greg ordered some dogs and chips for y'all to take home. Denise is working on those now. You can pick 'em up on your way out."

This time, Adrian *did* laugh. They ended up with hot dogs and O chips for dinner a lot these days. "Sounds good. Thanks again."

Crystal opened the employee gate at the end of the counter for him, and he walked into the kitchen. The life force of a building full of people flowed all around him, but he'd learned to tune that out long ago, especially when trying to sense the more subtle energy of the dead and other paranormal entities. As he moved past the fryers, the work stations, refrigerators and stoves, nodding and greeting Greg's friends on the way, he let his power reach out like psychic tentacles, groping its way into the unseen dimensions of the restaurant to root out anything dark that might be hiding there.

He found nothing. Felt nothing at all out of the ordinary. Which didn't entirely silence the warning whispering in the back of his brain, though he was at a loss to explain why.

Maybe you just don't want to tell Greg he's imagining things after all.

It was sure as hell a daunting prospect. The lack of a paranormal explanation didn't have to mean the things Greg had experienced were in his head, though. There could be perfectly ordinary explanations for all of them.

Adrian nodded, as if to cement the idea in his brain. Greg would be relieved to know he hadn't suddenly become the target of a mischievous or malignant spirit.

Greg had already changed out of his uniform and into his usual T-shirt, shorts and sandals when Adrian entered the break room. A mix of eagerness and apprehension flooded Greg's face as soon as Adrian walked in. "Hi, Adrian. Thanks for coming to pick me up. Not good bike-riding weather today."

Adrian forced himself not to roll his eyes at Greg's loud-enough-to-be-sure-everyone-hears-me tone. As if anyone would think twice about Greg's boyfriend driving him home from work, even if it *hadn't* been pouring buckets all day. "Not a problem. You ready to go?"

"Yeah." Greg crossed to Adrian's side in a few hurried strides, took his hand and kissed him. "So? What about it? What'd you feel?"

Here goes. Adrian slipped an arm around Greg's waist and put his lips close to Greg's ear. "Nothing unusual at all. It feels completely normal to me."

Greg drew back and stared, disbelief carved all over his face. "You're kidding."

"No, I'm not. There's nothing but life energy here, which is as it should be with a room full of people." Adrian caressed the curve of Greg's back. "Look, this doesn't mean you imagined anything. It only means there's a non-paranormal explanation for it all. We just need to find out what it is."

"Oh. Yeah, I guess so." Greg's forehead furrowed, as if he couldn't decide whether to feel hopeful or put out. He glanced over his shoulder. "Do you feel anything in here?"

"No. It feels the same as the rest of the place. Except..." He leaned closer to Greg. Buried his face in Greg's hair and breathed deep. Which was nuts, since he couldn't literally sniff out whatever it was niggling at his senses right now, but he'd learned to do what his gut told him, however odd it might seem. "I don't know. You still have that kind of almost-energy lingering around you. It's bothering me because I don't know what to call it."

"Hm." Greg rubbed his cheek against Adrian's, for all the world like a big cat, then drew back to look him in the eye. "Whatever it is, it's just me, though, huh?"

"Yeah." Not liking the wary, borderline-frightened expression his words put on Greg's face, Adrian grinned and squeezed Greg's ass. "It's probably the power of your sexiness. Attraction has its own mojo, you know."

The familiar arch of Greg's eyebrow said he wasn't buying it, but his lips hitched into a halfhearted smile anyway. "If you're trying to make me feel better, it's working." He took Adrian's hand, lacing their fingers together. "I guess the point is, DogO isn't haunted. That's a good thing, because a haunted hot dog joint would just be weird."

Adrian laughed. "I suppose it would be, huh?" He followed Greg back to his locker and leaned against the other lockers while Greg hung up his uniform and stuffed his wallet in his back pocket. "Seriously, Greg, don't worry, okay? There doesn't seem to be anything sinister here, as far as I can tell, but there's certainly nothing wrong with *you*. Next time you hear something, or feel someone touch you, or see something strange from the corner of your eye, stop and take a second to try and figure out what it really is. That gives you all the power over the situation and not only takes away your fear, but takes away the mystery of it by helping you work out what's really going on."

Greg closed his locker, clicked the padlock shut and turned to touch Adrian's cheek. His eyes shone with sympathy. He was one of the very few people in the world who knew how many years and how much work it had taken Adrian to learn that not every sound or shadow meant a monster waiting to break through the barrier between worlds.

"You'd know too. So thank you." Leaning forward, Greg pecked Adrian on the lips. "C'mon, I gotta clock out." He stepped around Adrian and headed for the door.

Adrian followed Greg to the office. While Greg clocked out on the small screen set into the wall beside the door, Adrian watched the green-and-white clad workers rushing around the kitchen. He shook his head. "Seems like every time I come over here y'all have a whole different crew."

"You say that as if you come here a lot." Greg laughed at the blush Adrian felt climbing into his cheeks. "I'm only kidding. I hope you know I don't expect you to come visit me at work all the time."

"I know. I can't help feeling kind of bad about it, though. It seems like you and Mal are the only ones I ever see more than once." He peered around the kitchen as he and Greg headed for the front of the restaurant. "Wait, he *does* still work here, right?"

"Yeah, he's just in class today. Most of the staff here are students, you know, which means they're part-time." Greg poked him in the ribs. "Forget about all that. You don't need to worry about it, I promise. Okay?"

Adrian laughed. "All right. It's forgotten."

"Good." Greg stopped at the counter to pick up the bag Crystal had left them and held it up. "I got dogs with mustard and relish for both of us. And O chips, of course. I hope that's okay."

"Sounds great."

Greg strode toward the exit, calling goodbye to his coworkers as he left. Adrian trailed behind him. He kept his psychic senses wide open in case he'd missed something earlier, but he still felt nothing.

That was a good thing. Of course it was.

So why did he leave the place with a vague uneasiness lodged in the pit of his stomach?

Chapter Four

Unfortunately—to Greg's mind, at least—BCPI had to do their investigating during the day, since the Carolina PlayMakers took the place over from late afternoon until well after midnight most days, between actors, costuming, the tech people and the stage crew. Not that nighttime would've been any better for Greg, since he could hardly play ghost hunter all night then spend the better part of the day at DogO without nodding off and accidentally deep-frying his hand or something, but still. Keeping his attention on his work took every bit of self-control he had, when all he could think about was infrared cameras and EMF detectors and all the cool ghosts the team had probably spotted while he was stuck here slinging wieners and chips.

He tried not to let himself consider the shadows, the weird noises and the occasional unexplained touches he'd experienced right here at DogO. That was nothing but his imagination. It *had* to be.

"It's not fair," he complained to Mal on day two while they worked hot dog assembly. "Adrian gets to go."

"God, you're right. *So* unfair." Mal squirted mustard on two dogs and slid them to Greg for relish and sauerkraut. "They really ought to appreciate how your acting skill could contribute to the investigation."

Greg rolled his eyes. "Shut up." He reached a gloved hand into the relish bin and sprinkled a generous helping on both wieners.

Unsurprisingly, Mal didn't shut up. "And your hot dog assembly skills? Don't even get me started." He plucked two more paper hot dog trays out of the holder and laid them out on the assembly board. "Those *bastards*. You should call the ACLU or something, man."

Laughing, Greg whipped a long strand of sauerkraut at Mal. "Jesus, shut *up*, asshole. I get your point, I'm being stupid." Something tugged at his hair. He glanced over his shoulder. Len stood at the frying station, too far away to have touched him. She didn't turn to look at him.

He frowned. It was a draft from the air-conditioning. That's all.

Right.

Mal was still talking, oblivious. "Don't forget about your constant complaining. This is like the fourth time today you've bitched about being left out of the damned investigation. And I get to hear it here *and* at the PlayMakers. *That's* fun."

Greg shot him a dark look. "Yeah. I got it. Thanks." He piled sauerkraut on the two hot dogs then set them on the order shelf for the workers out front. "Denise! Order up."

She turned around and peered through the opening, her face set in a scowl. "You guys keep it down, the customers might hear you."

"Sorry, D. We'll be quieter." Malachi smiled, all big soulful eyes and sincerity.

Denise blinked and looked away, like she always did when Mal paid attention to her. "Well. Good. Thanks." She took her order and went back to work, her cheeks distinctly pink.

As soon as she was out of earshot, Greg dug an elbow into Mal's ribs, almost making him drop the wiener he'd just plucked from the warming oven. "You shouldn't play with her like that. It's mean."

"C'mon, you know I need validation. Besides, she's the one with a boyfriend. I'm single." Mal settled the tofu wiener into a bun and reached the tongs into the oven for an all-beef one. "Hey, you know what you should do?"

"About what?"

"About your investigation problem, man. Keep up." Mal peered at the computerized order screen in front of their workstation. "Steak sauce? Seriously?" He shrugged and poured the required sauce on the tofu dog.

"Gross." Taking the dog from Mal, Greg loaded it with tomatoes, onions and green olives as specified in the order. *Ew.* "So, what should I do?"

Mal grinned. "Get 'em to order some DogO delivery for lunch."

"I don't see how—" Then Greg did. His eyes widened. "Ooooh. I can deliver it." He frowned. "Well, *then* what? It's not like I can stay there when I'm supposed to be working."

The look he got suggested that Mal would've slapped his forehead if he wouldn't have had to change his glove afterward. "G. You're an *actor.* Audition for the part of ghost-hunting helper, okay? Take the time you have and show them what you can do, and they'll invite you to help them investigate for real. See?"

It was a tempting idea. A *good* idea, even. Greg took the next dog and stared at it without seeing it. "But I—"

"You don't work every day, you know," Mal interrupted, displaying a previously unknown ability to read Greg's mind. "Get them to invite you to help investigate on your day off. Good grief, I thought you were smart." He nudged Greg's arm. "This one's coleslaw only. Get with it before Denise decides we need a lecture."

No one wanted *that*, least of all Greg. He scooped up coleslaw, spread it on top of the beef wiener and set both hot dogs on the shelf while Mal scooped O chips into a large-size tray. "Order up!" Greg called, setting the chips on the shelf beside the hot dogs.

A touch like an icy finger dragged down the back of his neck. The cold was so intense it burned. He whirled around with a startled yelp.

"Whoa, what the hell?" Mal actually backed up a step, eyes wide. "Greg? What's wrong?"

Greg darted a hunted look around the kitchen. Like before, nobody was close enough to have touched him.

Except one person.

He eyed Malachi. The man was a well-known practical joker, but this wasn't his style. Too subtle. Still...

"Mal, did you just touch the back of my neck?"

"No." Mal studied him as if he might attack any minute. "Are you all right, G?"

Greg thought about that. *Really* thought about it, for the first time. If DogO was haunted—unlikely as that scenario seemed from the get-go—Adrian would've picked up the energy. If the weird shit going on had some ordinary explanation, surely Greg would've figured it out by now.

He'd never seriously believed that imagining the things he'd seen and felt and heard lately meant he was cracking up, but hell, he was starting to run out of options.

Except that the back of his neck still stung. Which meant whatever had touched him was real. He didn't know if that made him feel better or worse.

He plastered on his best fake smile. "Yeah, I'm fine. It must've just been a draft or something."

"Probably so, yeah." Mal smiled back, though the concerned crease between his eyes stayed put. "We need more hot dog buns. You mind grabbing some?"

"Sure."

Greg stripped off his gloves and dropped them in the trash can on the way to the pantry. He felt Mal's stare on the back of his skull the whole way. Returning with a bag of buns in hand, he caught Len watching him. She dropped her gaze to the fryer as soon as he looked at her.

He kept his expression neutral. The way he figured it, the only thing worse than having his boss suspect he was losing it would be letting on that he'd noticed.

Sometimes a theater degree came in handy in the real world. This was one of those times.

Adrian was in the middle of cooking dinner that evening when the apartment door opened and slammed shut. Greg wandered into view from the tiny foyer, already stripping off his clothes. "Oh, my God, what smells good?" He walked into the kitchen, breathing deep.

"Stir-fry. Just frozen vegetables and some spices, but I was getting tired of hot dogs and I figured you were too." Smiling, Adrian slipped an arm around Greg and kissed him. He tasted like sweat, the result of a mostly uphill bike ride in the September heat. "How was work?"

An odd expression fleeted across Greg's face and was gone before Adrian could make any sense of it. Greg wrinkled his nose. "It sucks to have to make fucking hot dogs all day when there's ghost hunting going on, dammit."

So *that* was it. Not that Adrian was surprised. Greg hadn't exactly made a secret of his enthusiasm for all things paranormal since the whole thing with Groome Castle and seeing the ghost of Lyndon Groome for himself.

Grinning, Adrian let go of Greg so he could stir the vegetables. "I know you wanted to help out. I'm sorry."

"Yeah, well, it wouldn't've been so hard to deal with if you hadn't gotten to go, you know." Greg went to the refrigerator, took out the orange juice and gulped several long swallows straight from the carton.

"I didn't get to stay the whole time," Adrian reminded him. "I had to spend some quality time in the physics lab working on my research project, and I still need to grade papers tonight." He frowned as Greg put the juice back and bumped the refrigerator door shut with his hip. "Why can't you use a glass?"

"Oh, what, are you gonna get my germs or something?" Greg gave Adrian's butt a smack on the way out of the kitchen. He flopped into one of the chairs around the dining table and rested his elbows on it. "So how'd everything go?"

Adrian shrugged. "So-so, I guess. I'm still not getting the waveforms I'm looking for on my multidimensional simulations, so I'm thinking I must've made a mistake in the equations somewhere. I mean, I *know* I'm on the right track in a general sense, but the equations get pretty horrific when you get down to the quantum level, and just from the way the waveforms look that must be where I went wrong. It's going to be a headache to find which one needs fixing, even with the program I created, but—"

"Whoa, hey, time-out." Greg held up one hand to silence Adrian. "I have absolutely no idea what any of that was right now."

"I was talking about my research into multidimensional space-time. For my doctorate?" Adrian shook his head. "You were asking about the theater investigation, weren't you?"

"Well. Yeah." Greg had the decency to look shamefaced. "Sorry your research got set back, though. You're *so* smart, I know you'll figure out what went wrong and fix it."

Affection warmed Adrian to his toes. Greg could be thoughtless sometimes—*just like the rest of us, I guess*—but he had a generous, giving nature, and he loved Adrian with all his heart. What more could a person ask for?

"Thank you. I hope you're right." Adrian stirred the vegetables again, then judging them done, switched off the heat and went to the cabinet to fetch plates. "To answer your question, the investigation went fine. Or at least the part of it I saw went fine, and when I talked to Dad later he said the rest of it went really well too. They didn't actually experience anything, but Sam, Cecile and I all picked up on what felt like residual energy, and of course there's still all the files of video and audio evidence to go through."

Greg sat up straighter. "Hey, maybe I can help do that."

Adrian laughed. "You'd have to ask Dean, he's in charge of tech on this trip." Setting the plates next to the stove, Adrian divided the spicy, steaming vegetables between them.

"Hm." Greg jumped up to pour water for himself and Adrian from the spigot in the refrigerator door. "Listen, Mal had a great idea today for how I can get in with the investigation."

"*Mal* did?" Adrian fetched forks from the silverware drawer and stuck them on the plates. "Oh, I can't wait to hear this."

"Shut up, he has good ideas sometimes." Picking up his plate and water glass, Greg headed back to the table, shooting a thunderous look at Adrian on the way.

Adrian took his plate and glass and sat beside Greg, fighting a smile. "Sorry. Tell me."

With a narrow-eyed glance at Adrian, Greg forked up a mouthful of food. "Oh shit, that's good." He chewed and swallowed. "Okay. Mal said I should get the BCPI team to order hot dogs delivered for lunch, then I could make the delivery and impress everyone with my investigative skills while I'm there. Then they'll all say, hey, Greg, why don't you help us out next time you're off?" Greg shoveled a heaping forkful of stir-fry into his mouth. "So what do you think?"

It was all Adrian could do to keep from laughing. Only Malachi would come up with that plan, and only Greg would have the self-confidence to actually believe it would work. Adrian chewed his vegetables to give himself time to get his reactions under control.

"I think it's...interesting." Adrian reached across the table to touch Greg's hand. "But I don't think you need to jump through all those hoops. We can just tell Dad and Sam you'd like to help out and ask them if there's something you can do." He rubbed his thumb over Greg's knuckles. "Come on, you didn't really think you needed to do all that stuff, did you?"

Greg hitched up one shoulder, his smile sheepish. "Naw, I guess not. You're gonna think this is stupid, but I still kind of idolize your dads. I mean, they're the best in the business when it comes to paranormal investigation, and all I really have to offer is enthusiasm. I feel weird asking them to let me help, you know?"

Adrian's heart melted. Scooting his chair closer to Greg's, he cupped Greg's cheek in one hand. "Dad would say that's what every paranormal investigator starts out with—that fire in the belly, the need to know more. That's exactly why they'll not only *let* you help, they'll *want* you to."

Greg laid his hand over Adrian's. "Thank you."

Adrian didn't need psychic powers to read the look in Greg's eyes. Leaning closer, he angled his head to cover Greg's lips with his own.

Greg's mouth opened for Adrian's tongue. A low, rough moan rose from Greg's throat. He fisted one hand in Adrian's hair. The other hand went straight for Adrian's crotch, rubbing him through his shorts.

Oh sweet Jesus. Shoving Greg's left thigh sideways, Adrian wormed a hand inside Greg's shorts to caress his balls. He loved the way the touch made Greg *uh-uh-uh* and move his hips in obvious desperation. An easy twist of Adrian's psychokinesis pinched both of Greg's nipples just hard enough to force his back into an arch that broke the kiss and turned Greg's wordless noises into curses and pleas.

Shaking with the sudden rush of need, Adrian slid his fingers into the hair at Greg's nape and bent to kiss his throat. Greg yelped and jerked away, his hand hovering over his neck without touching. "Ow. Shit."

Concern cut through the desire fogging Adrian's brain. "What's wrong?"

"It burned when you touched the back of my neck." The corners of Greg's mouth hitched up. "Sorry to ruin the mood."

"Don't worry about it." Adrian touched Greg's shoulder. "Here, let me look at it."

Greg turned in his chair and bent his head. Adrian lifted Greg's sweaty curls out of the way, taking care not to touch the painful spot. He whistled when he saw it. "Good God, Greg, what happened?"

"Why?" Greg glanced at Adrian over his shoulder. "What is it?"

"I'm not sure." Nudging Greg's head back into its previous position, Adrian peered at the inch-long stripe of red, raw skin. "It looks like a burn. Not a bad one or anything, but yeah, that's what it looks like to me." He dropped Greg's hair and sat back, frowning. "How in the hell did you manage to burn the back of your neck?"

He didn't expect Greg's tense silence or the wide eyes and dead-white face when Greg turned to face him again. Worried, Adrian took Greg's hand in his. "Something happened. What was it?"

Greg licked his lips. His fingers locked through Adrian's and hung on. "Mal and I were working at the hot dog assembly station, and something touched the back of my neck. It felt like a finger, only it was really, really cold, like dry ice." He stared into Adrian's eyes. "I turned around, but there was nobody there. I thought I'd imagined it."

Adrian fought the wild urge to laugh. It wouldn't help matters. "Looks like you didn't."

They regarded one another in thoughtful silence for a while. Adrian knew they were thinking the same thing—what now?

Chapter Five

In the end, Adrian decided to go back to DogOpolis for a recheck, since he'd obviously missed something the first time. He wanted to bring Sam with him as well, but Greg was adamant that any psychic investigation be done in stealth.

"Nothing's happened to anyone else," Greg said over breakfast the next morning. "If you and Sam go in there poking around and talking about ghosts and psychic energy and shit, everybody's gonna think I'm losing it."

"I don't know why they'd think that." Adrian split the last of the coffee between Greg's mug and his own. "That burn on your neck wasn't caused by your imagination."

Greg favored him with a dark look. "The mind is a powerful thing, you know."

"Yeah, I know." Better than most people, Adrian figured. He studied Greg's thoughtful expression with a dawning suspicion. "You're afraid we'll go back and not find anything."

Greg shrugged. "You didn't find anything before, and you're just as powerful as Sam."

Adrian watched Greg staring into his coffee and didn't know what to say. He understood how it felt to fear for your sanity.

But the burn on Greg's neck was there. It was real. So if Adrian and Sam went back to DogOpolis and sensed nothing, that meant...what, exactly?

None of the possibilities were comforting.

"Anybody can miss something," Adrian said after a few seconds spent fumbling for the right words. "And I know my abilities are strong, but Sam has *way* more experience with it than I do. He might be able to pick up something I didn't, especially if it's something subtle."

"Yeah, I guess so." Greg sipped his coffee. "I still don't want everyone to know."

"There's nothing wrong with your mind." Adrian rolled his eyes at Greg's skeptical look. "Greg. You're fine. I really believe that. But listen, I'll talk to Sam and we'll work out a way to get in there and check the place out together without anyone knowing why we're there. Okay?"

"Okay." Greg gave him an anemic smile. "Thanks."

"You're welcome." Adrian popped the last bite of waffle into his mouth. "You want me to see if Sam can go out there with me today?"

Greg's eyes went wide. "No! Oh my *God*, no. I'm off today. It would be weird if y'all went there and I'm not there."

Adrian disagreed, but he didn't push it. He saw no reason to believe Greg was in any real danger, despite the mark on his neck. With no immediate urgency to the situation, he'd just as soon not waste time arguing the point. "Okay, we'll wait. No big deal."

Across the room, Greg's pod started thumping out Papa Bear's latest hit, "My Cub". Adrian snickered into his coffee mug while Greg jumped up and bounded over to the cluttered catch-all table by the door.

"You could've mojoed my pod over, if you hate that song so much," Greg grumbled, shooting Adrian an amused look as he thumbed in the passcode to check his incoming message.

"Naw. I spoil you too much as it is."

"Replace 'too much' with 'not nearly enough' and you'll have it right." A wide grin spread over Greg's face. "Hey, BCPI can't get into the theater to investigate today because there's apparently some kind of big-shot VIPs on campus and they're touring the place. The school's hoping to get some private funding for the dramatic arts programs, so they're touring all the theaters." He keyed in an obviously short message and Adrian heard the over-the-top orgasm noise Greg used for his message-sent sound.

"That's great. For the school, I mean. I hope they get the money. Not so great for the investigation, though." Adrian rested his elbows on the table and studied Greg's inexplicably glowing face. "Not to rain on the parade you're evidently having over there, but what are you so excited about?"

Laughing, Greg crossed the room, plopped himself down on Adrian's lap and planted an enthusiastic kiss on his mouth. He set his pod on the table. "That was Dean. He was asking if I had any time free to help him do some research today into the history of the theater and the stories of the hauntings there."

"Oh, I see." Adrian grinned. "I guess they knew you wanted to help without either of us even having to say anything. That's great."

"Yeah. I mean, it's not exactly the same as getting in there with the equipment and all, but hey, I'll still be helping out. And I always liked the research part of doing papers in school." Greg bounced on Adrian's lap. "I think this'll really be fun. I can't wait to get started. And since it's my day off, I can devote the whole day to it. Well, until I have to go to rehearsal, but that's not until five."

Unable to help himself, Adrian wound his arms tight around Greg's waist and buried his face in Greg's throat. God, but Greg caught up in a fervor for something—a cause, a project, whatever—was irresistible. The spark and buzz of his life force amped up by passion always kicked Adrian's psychokinesis into high gear. Humming, he bit Greg's neck.

"Hey! Stop that." In direct contrast to his words, Greg grabbed Adrian by the hair to hold him in place. "*I'm* off today, but *you're* not." Greg arched his neck, baring more skin to Adrian's lips, tongue and teeth. "Don't you have to be on campus to torture the baby scientists soon?"

"I have a whole hour." Adrian dug his tongue into the spot where Greg's pulse thudded strong and fast. "Come shower with me."

Greg snickered. "I'll make you late."

"Oh, I don't think so. You're not gonna last that long."

"Is that a challenge? Did you just challenge me?"

Lifting his head, Adrian met Greg's gaze. The gray eyes gleamed with the zeal for battle. In fact, Adrian hadn't issued any deliberate challenge, but what the hell. On the occasions when Greg's competitive streak bullied its way into the bedroom—or the floor, the sofa, or especially the shower—it made for some seriously intense sex.

Adrian stuck a hand between Greg's legs to cup his balls through his favorite ratty boxers. "You keep it going forty-five minutes, and next time I'll do you with just that dildo you like and my psychokinesis."

Greg's eyes fluttered shut, and Adrian grinned. Greg had been begging him to indulge that particular kink ever since Myah gave them a box of sex toys as an apartment-warming present last year.

Opening his eyes again, Greg pinned Adrian with a part lustful, part I'm-winning-this-shit stare. "You are *on*. Prepare yourself for the ride of your life, cowboy." He climbed off

Adrian's lap and strode toward the bathroom with the air of a man on a mission.

Adrian followed, not even trying to hold back his smirk. This was going to be fun.

Greg won, of course. Like there was any doubt. His back ached and his right knee sported an impressive bruise, but Adrian owed him a mojo-powered toy fuck, and that was what counted.

Luckily, Dean didn't ask about the shit-eating grin Greg couldn't keep off his face, or the marks Adrian had left all over his neck. Of course, Dean probably knew better. Watching him and his partner, Sommer Skye, together during that visit to Mobile on spring break in '17, Greg figured they got up to some pretty interesting things.

Greg had always thought it might be fun to hide in their bedroom closet and watch them going at it. Not that he'd ever tell Adrian that in this lifetime.

He glanced at his watch. To his surprise, three hours had passed since he and Dean returned from lunch, and it was now four forty. "Ah, damn. I need to go. Rehearsal starts in twenty minutes, and I still need to get changed."

"Oh, okay." At the interface next to Greg, Dean yawned and stretched. "I'll walk to the theater with you, if you don't mind. I need a break."

Greg grinned. "You said you needed a break from evidence review too. Said that's why you were doing the research thing today instead of Cecile."

"They say the attention span's the first thing to go."

"Nobody says that."

"Don't argue with your elders, young'un." Dean finished a download from the library's interface into his pod, disconnected, stuck the pod in his pocket and signed off. He pushed back his chair and rose. "You ready?"

"Yeah." Greg scrolled once more through the webpage on the founding of the University of North Carolina at Chapel Hill before he signed off. "I wish we didn't have to go. This has been awesome." Reaching beneath the table, he retrieved his bag, slung it over his shoulder and stood to follow Dean toward the library exit.

A darting shadow caught the corner of Greg's eye. He turned to look, his pulse rushing in his ears. At first, he saw nothing. Then a little girl ran out from between the stacks, followed by a young woman who bent down and swung the child onto her hip.

Greg let out a long breath. God, he really needed to get a grip before somebody decided to throw him in a rubber room. Not least because he wasn't convinced that the shadow he'd just seen could be explained by the child, or the woman.

He wasn't sure what that said about him, but he didn't like any of the possibilities.

Dean, oblivious to Greg's mini-drama, was continuing their conversation. "I hear you. Once you get a taste for research, it's hard to quit."

"Definitely." The newly installed sensor field triggered the door as they approached. Greg hung back so Dean could go first, then followed him across the bright vestibule and through the outside door into the warm, muggy afternoon. He lifted his face to the sky, eager to shake off the sense of foreboding the weird shadow inside had given him. "What did you find? Anything interesting?"

"Could be. No deaths in the theater that I could find, but I did dig up lots of firsthand accounts of your friends' flapper in the lobby, and also a few sightings of a small boy in the wings. Interestingly, I only found a couple of documented sightings of Professor Koch." Dean gave him a curious look. "What about you? You seemed pretty engrossed in the history pages."

Heat climbed up Greg's neck into his cheeks. God, he wished he'd quit doing that. He had absolutely no good reason to blush every time one of the BCPI crew asked him an investigation-related question. Or pointed out his obvious fascination with the case, for that matter. "Yeah, well. It's interesting, you know?"

"Oh, yes. I do." Dean nudged Greg with his elbow. "So, what'd you find out?"

"More than I thought I would." The sun emerged from behind a bank of thick gray clouds overhead. Squinting, Greg unhooked his shades from the collar of his T-shirt and slid them on. "I already knew the theater used to be a library when it was first built, and the rumor that Federal soldiers stabled their horses there during the Civil War was finally substantiated for good several years ago. But I had no idea the theater was a bathhouse for a while."

Dean's eyebrows rose. "Seriously?"

"Yeah. Well, not like *that*. At least, not that I could find anywhere." And Greg had tried his best. God, had he ever. Some of the vintage gay bathhouse porn he'd dug up a few years ago—after he'd learned what a bathhouse *was* in gay culture—was pretty hot. If the PlayMakers Theater had ever been that sort of place, though, the entire web was conspiring to keep it a secret. "But I guess you never know, huh?"

"Nope. Just because no one says it happened doesn't mean it never happened." Dean grinned. "I didn't find any sightings of hot gay ghost-on-ghost action. But I'm definitely gonna be on the lookout for that next time."

Greg laughed. He'd liked Dean from the first time they met, and hanging out with him today had done a lot to reduce the uncharacteristic shyness Greg still felt around the BCPI crew.

The conversation drifted into small talk about the Chapel Hill-Carrboro area nightlife as the two of them walked the short distance from Davis Library to the theater. "You should come in and say hi to everyone," Greg said when they reached the PlayMakers. "They'd love to meet you."

"I'd like that too, if you're sure it's okay."

"Yeah, we've got a few extra minutes. Besides, everyone keeps asking me when they get to meet you and the BCPI gang." Greg climbed the steps toward the door, glancing over his shoulder at Dean. "C'mon. It won't take long."

Dean followed Greg up the steps and into the lobby. Theo and his fiancée, Chelsea Rochester, stood inside, talking to Myah. "Hi, Greg," Chelsea greeted with a smile. "How are you?"

"I'm good. How about you? I haven't seen you in forever." Pushing his shades to the top of his head, he hugged her and pecked her on the cheek. "How's senior year going?"

"Not bad. Mostly I'm on pins and needles waiting to see if I'm accepted into the master's psych program." She held out a hand to Dean. "Hi, I'm Chelsea Rochester. I'm a friend of Greg and Adrian's."

Theo grabbed Dean's hand and shook as soon as Chelsea let go. "Dean, right? Theo Smathers. I follow the website. The LeBlanc House investigation last month was *insane*, man."

"Thanks." Dean grinned, clearly amused. He cut his gaze back to Chelsea, who was smiling at Theo with the practiced calm of a woman who'd long ago decided she knew exactly who he was and loved him in spite of it. Or maybe because of it.

"Yeah, I'm Dean Delapore. I work with Bay City Paranormal Investigations. We're up here investigating the theater."

Myah's face lit up as she took her turn shaking hands with Dean. "I'm Myah Sandoval. It's great to meet you, Dean. We're all so excited y'all are here."

"You found anything yet?" Theo asked in typical blunt Theo fashion.

Dean shrugged as if he got that kind of question all the time. Which he probably did, now that Greg thought about it. "We don't like to draw any conclusions until we've reviewed all the evidence."

Theo looked disappointed. Greg knew the feeling. Grinning, he slapped Theo on the back. "Don't worry, they'll tell us what they find out when the time comes."

The front door opened and Jon strode in, wearing a skintight vintage *Wicked* T-shirt and a pair of huge brown sunglasses that covered nearly half his face. His stride faltered when he spotted the group in the lobby. He pulled off the giant shades and approached, smiling. "Hello, all." His usual too-intense-for-comfort gaze landed on Greg. "Hi, Greg. Who's your friend?" He turned his polite smile to Dean.

"This is Dean Delapore, with Bay City Paranormal." Greg nodded in Dean's direction. "Dean, this is Jon Hudson. He's playing the male lead in *A Tar Heel Born*."

"Oh yeah?" Dean took Jon's hand with a smile and shook. "Greg was telling us all about the play the day we got here. It sounds fantastic."

"Oh, it is." Jon's smile warmed with the attention. "You and your coworkers should come see it if you're still here when we debut. Opening night is about three weeks away." He darted a sidelong look at Greg, for all the world as if he couldn't go two minutes without staring at him.

Greg pretended to notice something interesting outside. Jon's constant, borderline-stalker attention was really starting to get on his last nerve.

Dean's eyebrows went up. "Well, I'm not sure if we'll still be in town then, but if we are we'd love to go. I know Adrian'll be going."

The faint wrinkling of Jon's nose at the mention of Adrian's name was so obvious, he might as well have spit on the ground. "Yes, I'm sure." Straightening his shoulders, he sidestepped toward the open door leading from the lobby into the theater. "Well, people, we should get going. Dean, very nice to meet you."

"You too, Jon." Dean waved at him. Once he was out of sight, Dean leaned over to murmur in Greg's ear, "Does Adrian know he has competition?"

Theo snickered. "Told you."

Greg scowled. "Shut up."

Laughing, Chelsea kissed Greg's cheek. "I need to go. It was great to see you, Greg. Tell Adrian I said hi." She turned to kiss Theo, one arm around his shoulders. "See you at home, honey. Love you."

"Love you too, sweetpea." Theo gave her a pat on the rear before letting her go. "Bye."

Dean held out his arm. "Care for an escort, milady?"

"Oh my, a real gentleman." Chelsea slipped her hand through the crook of Dean's elbow. "Thank you, kind sir."

The two of them swept out the front door, Dean waving over his shoulder as they went. Greg shook his head. "C'mon, Theo. Let's get changed."

He hurried through the inner door and down the aisle between the rows of plush seats with Theo at his heels. Jon had changed into his dance shorts and was pulling on his jazz shoes as Greg and Theo piled into the men's dressing room. Jon stood and followed Omar out the door along with several of the other men. To Greg's relief, Jon seemed to have decided Greg deserved to be ignored. He strode through the door without so much as glancing in Greg's direction.

Theo kicked off his flip-flops and set them on the wooden bench along one wall. "Uh-oh. You're in trouble."

"Yeah, well, I'm gonna have to figure out how to get in trouble all the time, then." Putting his bag on a plastic chair, Greg kicked off his sandals, undid his cut-offs and wriggled out of them. "I like being ignored for a change."

"Can't blame you, man." Theo undid his button-fly jeans, took them off and set them on top of his sandals. He wore his dance shorts underneath the baggy pants. "So, what were you and Dean up to? Are they letting you help out with the investigation?"

While he pulled on his dance shorts, Greg thought about how to answer. On the one hand, Theo had some odd ideas about what it meant to keep something in confidence. Chelsea at the very least would know everything Greg said. In precise detail, since Theo had a dead-perfect memory when he chose to use it. On the other hand, Chelsea wouldn't tell another soul, and anyway, Greg hadn't done or learned anything that needed to be kept secret.

"I was helping Dean do research on the history of the PlayMakers Theater," Greg said after a moment. "Not as cool as helping do the actual investigation, and I didn't find out anything really crazy, but it was still pretty cool. And it was *fun* too. I'm gonna help out again next time I'm off."

Theo's eyes widened. "Oh man, that's *awesome!* What all did you find out?"

Greg started to tell him—because why not?—when Noemi stuck her head into the open door. "All right, children. Come along now, we are running behind."

"Be right there, Noemi." Greg dug his jazz shoes out of his bag and began pulling them on, hopping on first one foot then the other.

Noemi was back out the door before he finished talking. As she left, Greg heard her tell someone, "Stop loitering and get onstage immediately."

When he and Theo left the dressing room, Greg spotted Jon heading to the stage just ahead of them, back stiff. So he'd been hanging around listening to them talk. Not that he'd overheard anything juicy, but still. For Jon, information only gave him ammunition for poking at Greg in his weird middle-school-girl way.

Greg stifled a sigh. This was going to be a long night.

Forget it. Don't pay any attention to him. Do your job and don't let him bug you.

Easier said than done, maybe, but Greg was bound and determined to try.

As he and Theo headed for the stage, something moved in the periphery of Greg's vision. He stiffened, startled in spite of himself. Then he remembered why he shouldn't worry about anything he saw or heard here. The PlayMakers was a haunted theater. He'd seen a ghost, that's all. It wasn't the first time and it wouldn't be the last. And he wasn't the only one who'd seen spirits here.

Still, he couldn't help feeling relieved when the ghost—because that *must* be what it was—vanished as soon as he twisted around for a better look. He didn't like the ominous way the black shadow lurked at the very edge of his perception, or the hard chill the sight of it gave him.

He did his best to put it out of his mind and concentrate on performing, but the memory lingered. He couldn't shake the feeling of being followed by something sinister.

Adrian and the BCPI group were still gathered in Dean's hotel room that evening discussing where to go for dinner when Adrian's pod broke into "Ice Cream Truck" at full volume.

Cursing Greg under his breath, Adrian fished the pod from his shorts pocket and thumbed it on. "I really wish you'd stop reprogramming my tones, dammit." He walked to the other side of the room, not that he could avoid the amused looks or Dean's unapologetic snickering that way.

"Okay, number one, you knew it was me. Number two, and most importantly, you *heard* it instead of having it on vibrate or more likely silent. I got you the newest pod mostly because it has all these customizable features, and you're gonna by God use them even if I'm the one who has to program them for you."

Adrian sighed because Greg expected him to, but his mouth curved into a smile. "Fine. So what's up? Won't you get in trouble for calling during rehearsal?"

"All of us got sent home except for the leads."

"Seriously?"

"Yeah. Jon kept flubbing his lines. Boy, Noemi was *pissed*. I think if it hadn't been so close to opening night, she would've recast the part, but it's way too late now. She sent everyone else out and told Jon he'd stay right there and work one-on-one with her until he could get it right. She told Isabella she could leave too, but she said it would work better if she was there, so she stayed."

"Wow." Adrian shook his head. "Are you at home, then?"

"Naw, I just left the theater. I called 'cause I wasn't sure if you were at home or still doing ghost-hunting stuff."

"Actually, we're at the hotel. We've called a temporary halt on evidence review and were trying to figure out where to go eat." Adrian walked over to one of the beds and sat beside his father. "Where are you? We could come pick you up."

Bo patted Adrian's leg, smiled and nodded. From her perch beside Dean on the other bed, Cecile clapped her hands. Adrian grinned at her. They'd all missed Greg at their evening get-togethers almost as much as Adrian had.

"Tell you what, I'm not far from Franklin Street. I'll cross over and meet you at Franklin and Columbia. Where were you thinking of going?"

"Not positive, but Cecile really wanted to go to Panzanella."

Cecile nodded. "I'm with Cecile," Sam called from his spot leaning against the pillows on Bo's other side.

Greg laughed. "Tell Sam I'm with Cecile too. I'll see y'all in a little bit. Love you."

"Okay. Love you too." Adrian ended the call and stuck his pod back in his pocket. He looked around at his friends and family. "All right, we have one more for dinner. And I guess we're going to Panzanella."

"Awesome." Dean rose and stretched. "What's Greg doing out of rehearsal already? It's not even eight yet."

"The guy who plays the male lead, Jon, kept flubbing his lines. He and the female lead, Isabella, are staying on to work one-on-one with the director. She sent everyone else home."

To Adrian's surprise, Dean laughed. "That's probably a good thing."

"What do you mean?" Adrian got down on his knees to retrieve one of his sneakers, which had gotten shoved between the bed and the nightstand.

"What, you haven't noticed the way Mr. Hollywood Jon there goes all moony-eyed over your boy?" Dean shook his head. "It's kind of sad, really. I think the guy's socially stuck in ninth grade or something, the way he acts. Where'd I put the SUV keys?"

"The ice bucket tray, where you always put them." Adrian's father squeezed his shoulder. "Okay there, son?"

"Yeah, fine, just..." Adrian shrugged and forced a smile. "I've met Jon before. I didn't notice him acting like that toward Greg, but I do agree that he's socially immature." He gave his dad a grateful look. "I'm okay, Dad. Thanks."

Bo smiled and let his hand drop. He patted the front pocket of his jeans, his ritual to make sure his wallet was in its usual spot.

"Well, you know you don't have to worry about Greg paying this Jon person any attention." Cecile slung her purse over her shoulder, all the force of her considerable intelligence and insight focused on Adrian with squirm-inducing intensity. "That's precisely the sort of thing he hates."

"I know. He complains about Jon enough." Adrian frowned as a thought struck him. "Funny he's never mentioned Jon having this crush on him though."

"Maybe he didn't notice at first, or didn't want to think it was true," Sam suggested. "It can be pretty uncomfortable when someone you actively dislike takes an interest in you." He headed for the hotel room door. "Come on, guys. Let's head out."

They followed him out the door and into the still-warm evening, turning the corner of the concrete walkway toward the SUV parked a short distance away.

Dean fell into step beside Adrian, his expression thoughtful. "Maybe Greg didn't want to tell you because he was afraid it would upset you." He turned a guilty glance to Adrian. "I really shouldn't've said anything. I'm sorry."

"No, don't worry about it. I'm not upset."

Dean's eyes narrowed in obvious disbelief. Adrian plastered on his very best *no, really* smile.

"Fine. Pretend it doesn't bother you any." Dean grasped Adrian's arm. "Jon's a sad, arrogant man who doesn't stand a chance with Greg, and you know as well as I do that the only reason Greg didn't say anything to you was because he didn't think it was important. And it *isn't* important, so please don't let it get between you and Greg, okay?" He let go of Adrian's arm, slapped him on the back and skirted the SUV to climb into the driver's seat before Adrian could even think of what to say.

As Adrian crawled into the backseat between his dad and Sam, he told himself Dean was right. Why would Greg bring up Jon's crush on him, when it didn't affect their relationship one way or another? Contrary to what some people thought, Greg wasn't one to hold someone's feelings against them or make fun of them for it.

It all sounded perfectly logical in Adrian's head. Still, he couldn't help the streak of pure possessiveness he felt when he imagined that jackass Jon Hudson looking at Greg *that* way.

He'd have to tell Greg. He didn't look forward to confessing his irrational jealousy, but at least Greg would get a laugh out of it.

Greg *did* laugh, though Adrian saw his irritation in the tension around his eyes. "Wow, Adrian, I can't believe you'd actually get jealous over that idiot." He sipped the pinot noir he and Adrian had decided to share. "I wouldn't look twice at him even if I didn't already have the greatest guy on earth."

"I realize that. And I fully acknowledge that I'm being stupid. But whoever said emotions were logical?" He leaned over to nuzzle Greg's hair, something he probably wouldn't have done in the middle of a restaurant if he wasn't two glasses into the wine bottle, but what the hell. Anyone who didn't like it could fuck right off. "I don't want to talk about him anymore."

Greg laughed again, without the underlying exasperation this time. "Maybe you shouldn't've brought him up, then." He squeezed Adrian's thigh under the table. "So. Y'all haven't told me how the investigation went today."

"It went very well. I really think it won't take us long to wrap up." Adrian's father set his fork and knife on his plate and lifted his wineglass. "We haven't gotten around to the pertinent portion of the video yet, but unless I'm very much mistaken, we finally got footage today of the little boy your friend Theo spoke about seeing in the wings."

"Oh, that's fantastic!" Greg grinned. "He'll be thrilled."

"The footage of the flapper in the audience from yesterday did come out pretty clearly, by the way," Cecile added. "And it was accompanied by a female voice on EVP. We weren't able to make out exactly what she was saying, but it was definitely a female voice, and it wasn't me, so that's some good, solid evidence."

"Cool. Everybody's always asking me what y'all've found. I know they're gonna be anxious to hear the final verdict." Greg scooped up the last bite of his eggplant parmigiana, popped it into his mouth and chewed.

"I think we've pretty much come to the conclusion that what you have at the theater is at least two separate residual hauntings. Three, if the male figure we picked up turns out to be Professor Koch. We'll have to cross reference as best we can with whatever photos you and Dean are able to find." Sam tossed back the last swallow of the local microbrew he'd ordered and set the bottle on the table. "Nothing we've found so far indicates any kind of intelligent haunting. There's been no purposeful interaction. So, yeah. Looks like residual hauntings."

Adrian nodded. "That could be really great for business, though, don't you think, Greg? I mean, visitors might be drawn to the possibility of seeing a real ghost that they know can't touch or hurt them."

"Yeah, you have a point there. I know if it was me, I'd want to see it." Grinning, Greg bumped Adrian's shoulder with his. "I can't wait to start telling everybody."

Adrian laughed along with everyone else at the table, but he knew how Greg felt. He looked forward to spreading the word about the haunting too. Keeping the PlayMakers Repertory Company strong benefited the town and campus of Chapel Hill, so he would've supported creating increased business regardless. Being in love with an actor in the repertory just gave him one more incentive.

After dinner, Adrian and Greg took Dean up on his offer to drive them back to their apartment, mostly because they wanted to talk to Sam about accompanying Adrian to DogOpolis the next day. They explained the situation to Sam and Adrian's dad in the back of the SUV while Dean and Cecile laughed and sang along to Cecile's pod music mix in the front seat.

"Here's the thing," Greg said, resting his forearms on the back of the seat separating him and Adrian in the rear from Sam and Bo. "There's been weird things going on at DogO lately." His brow furrowed for a second in a way that pinged Adrian's worry radar, though he wasn't sure why. "I've been seeing shadows. Hearing things. Feeling things touch me."

"He had a burn on the back of his neck when he got home yesterday," Adrian added because he felt it was important. "He said he felt something cold touch him there, and when I looked at it I saw a burn about an inch long. Not a bad one, but the skin there was red and blistered."

Adrian's father frowned. "Seeing and hearing things, even feeling things touch you, could be easily explained in non-paranormal ways. But the burn is concerning."

"I agree." Sam looked from Adrian to Greg and back again, studying each of them in turn. "I'm guessing you've already been to check out the place yourself."

Adrian nodded. "I didn't feel anything out of the ordinary. But that was before yesterday. The burn worries me. It worries both of us. I *must* have missed something, Sam. It's the only explanation. Do you think you can come with me tomorrow and see if you can pick up something I didn't?"

"Of course. I'd be glad to." Sam aimed a knowing smile at Greg. "I'm guessing you'd like for us to keep this visit under the radar, am I right?"

"Yeah." Greg rubbed the back of his neck, his smile sheepish. "Sorry. It's just nobody else seems to have noticed anything going on, so I don't really want anyone to know what's been happening to me." He darted a swift glance at Adrian.

For reasons he couldn't quite pin down, the expression in Greg's eyes bothered Adrian. It seemed veiled. Secretive. As if he was hiding something.

Again.

Christ.

"I can completely understand that." Sam exchanged a look with Adrian. Neither of them had to say anything. They'd both been where Greg was right now—experiencing things they couldn't explain and wanting to keep what they'd seen and heard and felt to themselves for fear of being labeled crazy.

A faint crease dug between Sam's eyes. He held Adrian's gaze for a moment, and Adrian heard the unspoken question behind that stare—*What's wrong?* He gave a faint shake of his head. There was no way he could explain to Sam, especially here and now. But the fact that his stepfather noticed his troubled state of mind made him feel loved.

Smiling, Sam reached back to brush Adrian's arm with a comforting touch. "Don't worry. We'll find a reason to come by without it seeming out of the ordinary."

"Thank you," Adrian said, knowing Sam would recognize the double meaning.

Sam squeezed his arm, and Adrian felt better.

"You know, all of us have been saying ever since we arrived that we want to try the food at DogOpolis." Adrian's father rested his elbow on the back of his seat and met Greg's gaze. "Greg, what if we were to call in an order for tomorrow's lunch, and Sam and Adrian went to pick it up? Adrian doesn't have assistant teaching duties tomorrow, so he'll be with us at the theater."

Greg nodded, his brow puckered in thought. "I think it's a good idea. We do deliver, though, so when you call in they're gonna ask you about that."

"I'll just tell them I want to come see my stepson's boyfriend." Sam grinned. "Or that I need a break. Investigating can get pretty intense."

Greg laughed. "Okay, that would work. I know I'm being a little paranoid about it. There's no reason anyone ought to think anything about it if you want to pick up instead of have it delivered."

"Maybe we could all just come in and eat. That way we'd get Cecile's perspective as well. She has the most psychic experience, as well as the most targeted and precise gift." Bo glanced at Sam, eyebrows raised. "What do you think, Sam? Could we spare the time?"

Sam shrugged. "I think we could, yeah. If it's okay with Greg."

"Yeah, I'd be okay with that. It would totally work out, since everybody's been wanting to meet the BCPI gang." Greg looked from Bo to Sam with an excited gleam in his eyes. "So. Tomorrow, huh?"

"Tomorrow." Sam grinned. "I do love a good wiener." He waggled his eyebrows at Adrian's dad, who laughed and smacked him on the arm.

"Oh, my God." Groaning, Adrian leaned back in his seat. "You guys are supposed to be the mature ones."

Greg snickered. "Um. You've known them, like, forever. You should know better."

"Point."

As Adrian's dads faced forward and put their heads together, smiling at one another, Greg took Adrian's hand and laced their fingers, holding on hard. Adrian felt the fear in Greg's iron grip, though nothing showed on his face.

Scooting closer, Adrian pressed his shoulder to Greg's and leaned his forehead against Greg's soft curls. He sent a soothing wave of energy through the indefinable connection between them. Greg didn't say a word, but Adrian sensed some of the anxiety tainting Greg's energy bleed away.

Now if only he could convince Greg to divulge his secret, maybe Adrian could relax. But not before. He had a feeling that whatever Greg wasn't saying, it had the potential to hurt them somehow.

Then why do you want to know so badly?

Why, indeed?

The answer was obvious—because he couldn't allow anything to come between them. Not after everything they'd been through to stay together.

Holding Greg close in the back of the SUV while his family laughed and talked up front, Adrian vowed to himself that whatever was happening to Greg right now, whatever was going on in his heart and mind, he wouldn't have to endure it alone. Adrian would be right there beside him.

Even if he had to fight Greg every step of the way to do it.

Greg spent the three and a half hours between the time he clocked in at work the next day and the arrival of the BCPI team jumpy as a mouse in a room full of hungry cats.

Knowing three powerful psychics were on their way at his request to secretly poke into the place's metaphysical corners would've been enough to put him on edge all by itself. But whatever the hell had been happening at DogO lately decided to kick into overdrive that morning—shadows moving in corners, fingers grasping at the back of his uniform when no one was within touching distance. Low whispers in his ear.

That was a new one. Even his normally oblivious coworkers seemed to take notice of the morning's goings-on, judging by their occasional quick turns and frowns, though no one said anything.

By the time the Bay City Paranormal crew walked in just as the lunch rush was winding down, Greg felt ready to jump out of his skin. He dumped the fresh chips from the fry basket into the warmer and hurried to greet the group without even putting the new basket of sliced potatoes into the oil.

He threw his arms around Adrian's neck and planted a hard kiss on his lips, ignoring the bemused looks from customers and fellow employees alike. "Oh my fucking *God*, I'm glad you're here," he murmured against Adrian's cheek, hugging him close. "Things are *crazy* today."

"I'm guessing you're not talking about the workload." One arm firm around Greg's waist, Adrian laid a hand on his cheek and forced him back enough to gaze into his eyes. "Tell me what's happened."

Before Greg could say a word, Cecile sidled up to them, brown eyes wide. "Guys, I'm picking up some serious energy in here."

"Me too." Sam's gaze cut this way and that, his expression blank. "Adrian? Do you feel it?"

"Yeah." Adrian licked his lips. His face had gone an unhealthy shade of gray beneath his normal golden-brown skin tone. He studied Greg with concern. "Greg? What's been happening?"

Greg glanced toward the counter. Denise was watching him with a scowl. Crystal and Dex took orders without paying him any attention. Behind Denise, he could just make out Malachi's curly head at the hot dog assembly station. Len was out of sight at the drive-up window.

They'd seen at least some of what he had this morning, he felt sure, but none of them had been *plagued* with it the way he had all day. Hell, all *week*. He fought back a wave of helpless frustration.

"I keep seeing things moving where they shouldn't," he said, low enough that no one but the BCPI group could hear. "Something's touched me several times today. And I've heard voices too. That's never happened before. I think even Denise noticed, and she never notices anything." He drew out of

Adrian's embrace, trying to make the movement seem casual. "What the hell, Adrian? What's going on?"

Adrian, Cecile and Sam shared a look Greg couldn't begin to interpret. He put on a happy, greeting-the-boyfriend smile and caressed Adrian's arm. "Okay, y'all are scaring me here. What the fuck?"

Dean flashed a dazzling grin. "I'll just go put in our order, huh? Cecile, tofu dog, right?" He didn't wait for her to answer, but approached the counter, casting a sympathetic glance at Greg on the way.

"Let's go sit down." Bo gestured toward a large empty booth at the window. "Greg, can you join us for a moment?"

"I really can't. I'm sorry. I'm supposed to be at the fryer right now." Greg sucked his bottom lip into his mouth and did his best not to fidget. "Can't we—?"

"Hey, Greg!"

Startled, Greg turned toward Dean, who stood at the counter with all of Greg's coworkers huddled in front of him. Even Len had left the drive-through to talk to him. Greg couldn't help smiling for real at the sight. He'd never met anyone who could wrap a roomful of people around his finger as quickly and easily as Dean.

He walked over to the group, dragging Adrian with him by the hand. Sam, Cecile and Bo trailed behind them. "So, Dean. I guess you've already met everybody."

"Of course." Dean grasped Greg's shoulder. "Hey, the lovely Elena here says you may as well go on and take your lunch break now, since your dads and Adrian are here. What about it?"

"That'd be awesome." Relieved, Greg beamed at his boss. "Thanks, Len."

"No problem. You have to take a break at some point anyway." She gave him a tired smile. "Adrian, good to see you."

"You too, Len. It's been too long." Adrian laid his free hand on his father's shoulder. "Everybody, this is my dad, Dr. Bo Broussard, and my stepdad, Sam Raintree." He pointed at Sam then nodded toward Cecile. "This is Cecile Langlois. You've already met Dean. They're with Bay City Paranormal Investigations in Mobile. They're here investigating the PlayMakers Theater."

"Oh, yeah, I heard about that." Len went to the hot dog assembly station and started putting together their order. "How's it going so far?"

"Very well. We're about ready to wrap up, but we couldn't leave town without coming by DogOpolis." Cecile smiled. "I'm vegan. It's difficult to find tofu dogs in a fast-food place."

"Well, these are awesome." Malachi winked at her.

That did it for Greg's patience. "Okay, sorry, guys, but I'm taking my boyfriend and his family and we're gonna go sit before my lunch break's over. Everybody say, *nice to meet you.*"

The DogOpolis group obediently echoed Greg's words. Mal added, "Except for Greg who is a bossy-boots." Greg threw a relish packet at him before following Adrian to the booth in the corner.

He squeezed into the booth between Adrian and Cecile. "All right, somebody tell me what the hell you psychic types are feeling around here."

That *look* passed between Sam, Cecile and Adrian again— the *what do we say* look.

Greg did not find it encouraging. He dug his fingers into the dark red upholstery and told himself yelling would be counterproductive.

Finally, Sam rested his elbows on the table and pinned Greg with a frighteningly serious stare. "I don't know what it is, exactly. I don't think any of us do." He glanced at Adrian and Cecile, who each shook their heads. "But I think we can all agree on the *type* of energy we're feeling."

Greg swallowed, nervous. "And that is?"

A muscle in Sam's jaw flexed. His gaze darted toward the counter, as if making sure no one was listening in, then fixed on Greg again. "Whatever's here, its energy is strongly negative. And I think it could be dangerous."

Chapter Six

Greg bitched a lot about working at a fast-food place. Everyone who knew him, though, realized the complaining was all on the surface. He liked DogOpolis. The people there were fun to be around and the work itself wasn't bad. He'd done worse things for a paycheck before. Most days, he actually looked forward to work.

Not this afternoon. Not after Sam explained why he thought the negative energy here might pose a physical risk to him.

"Anyone here could potentially be in danger," Sam had said, just as cool as if he wasn't saying the place Greg worked might harbor potentially homicidal spirits. "But from what you've told us, Greg, it seems as though you might be a particular target."

Which had not made Greg eager to return to work after his lunch break. Adrian had been, if possible, even less eager. Only Greg's lingering fear of the *crazy* label—and its power to get him fired—had kept Adrian from finding Len and forcing her to let Greg take the rest of the day off.

So here he was, two long, tense hours later, finally at the end of his shift and ready to get the hell out before whatever the fuck had possessed this place decided to go after him with a paring knife.

He elbowed Mal in the ribs. "Hey. It's time to go, brother. Let's get the fuck out of here."

"Man, you said it." Mal finished cutting his bell pepper, stripped off his gloves, tossed them in the trash and followed

Greg toward the break room. "I like this job, but hell, not today. It's fucking evil today."

Something about Mal's voice made Greg look at him. *Really* look at him. Mal's usual easy slouch was gone, replaced by a tense, jerky stride completely unlike him. His deep brown eyes cut this way and that, as if looking for something he knew was there but couldn't quite see.

Greg spoke before he could second-guess himself. "Hey, Mal? Have you been…well, seeing weird shit around here lately?"

"Kind of. Especially today. I never really paid much attention to it, though. I mean, your eyes can play tricks on you, right?" Mal pulled the elastic band from his hair and shook out the shoulder-length curls. He shot Greg a narrow-eyed look. "You know something."

Greg shrugged. He trusted Mal, but he still didn't feel comfortable spilling all the beans. "Not really. I've been seeing a lot of weird shit myself lately. I had the feeling you had too, that's all."

"Oh." Mal dialed the combination on his locker, opened it and took out his wallet and sunglasses. "Well, shit. I don't know whether to be glad I'm not imagining things or not."

Laughing, Greg opened his own locker and started stripping. "At least you're not insane."

Mal shook his head. "Sometimes it's better to be crazy, dude." He slid his shades on. "See you at rehearsal."

"Yeah, see you."

Greg watched Mal go and wondered how awful it was to be relieved that he wasn't alone anymore.

The whole BCPI crew was waiting at Greg and Adrian's apartment when Greg got home. He wasn't sure how to feel about that, particularly considering the serious expressions on everyone's faces and the way Adrian met him at the door and kissed him like they'd been apart for ten years instead of a couple of hours and change.

"Hey, sexy." Greg nuzzled behind Adrian's ear, turned on and worried at the same time by the unusual level of attention from his man. He lowered his voice to a barely audible whisper. "Get rid of the old people and let's fuck on the floor, what about it?"

Adrian let out a soft laugh, which was a good sign. "I guess you're okay, or you wouldn't be joking around."

"Who says I'm joking?" Greg flashed his very best evil grin. "I don't have to be at rehearsal until six tonight. It wouldn't even have to be a quickie."

Adrian rolled his eyes, but his relief showed through clear as daylight. Which didn't do a damn thing to dispel the nerves that had needled Greg all afternoon.

Greg frowned. "Okay, what's going on? You were obviously scared something was going to eat me alive today, Adrian, and everybody's hanging out here for a reason. Now spill."

Adrian's cheeks flushed. "I didn't think you were going to get *eaten*."

"He kind of did." Dean wandered in from the kitchen with a half-finished brown ale in one hand and a fresh glass of wine in the other. He handed the wine to Greg. "Here. Come sit. We have a proposition for you."

A completely insane vision of himself and Adrian naked in a hot tub with Dean and Sommer flashed into Greg's mind before reason reasserted itself. Nodding, he took Adrian's hand and followed him to the sofa. They squeezed themselves next to Bo and Sam.

Sam turned sideways to look Greg in the eye. "I'll get right to the point, Greg. You know that Adrian, Cecile and I all felt some very negative energy at DogOpolis today, and that I believe it could be dangerous to you in particular, since it's already harmed you once."

Greg rolled his shoulders. The scabbed-over burn on his neck pulled enough to remind him of its presence. "I see your point."

Sam glanced at Adrian, who tightened his hold on Greg's hand. "We've been talking about this issue, and we all agree that we'd like to stay on here in Chapel Hill for a little while and do a formal investigation of DogOpolis. But since you were reluctant to have anyone know what you'd experienced there, we didn't want to do anything without talking to you first."

Whatever he'd expected to hear, that wasn't it. Greg felt Adrian's arm go around his chest. He leaned gratefully into Adrian's embrace and studied Sam's face. Sam held his gaze with a strength and determination Greg figured he really should've expected.

Finally, Greg sighed and looked away. "Yeah, okay. It's probably a good idea anyhow. I'm not the only one seeing things there. I asked Mal today, and he said he's been seeing stuff too. He just didn't really believe it."

"I had a feeling about that boy." Bo leaned forward to peer around Sam's shoulder. "Has Malachi or anyone else experienced anything like the burn you had on your neck?"

"Not that I know of." Greg pulled Adrian's arm tighter around him, for no reason other than it made him feel safe. "But up until today, I didn't think anyone but me even *had* any experiences like I had. And now I find out Mal's seen things like the shadows I've been seeing, only I didn't know it until today. So who knows?"

The room fell silent. Sam glanced back at Bo. Bo covered Sam's hand with his, their fingers winding together. It made Greg nervous because the two of them rarely engaged in such outward displays of affection.

"We'll talk to your boss tomorrow," Bo said after a couple of tense, quiet moments. "Elena Sims, right?"

"Yeah. Len." Greg scrunched as deep as he could into Adrian's arms. "Could y'all maybe not mention that I told you about any of this stuff?"

"We can just say we felt negative energy there." Adrian kissed Greg's temple. "There's no need to involve you at all if you don't want."

Cecile was shaking her head before Adrian finished his sentence. "There's no need to involve you either, Adrian. I know your psychokinesis isn't really a secret, but I also know you prefer not to make a show of it. Sam and I are well known for our powers, however, and all of Greg's coworkers saw us there. It's not a problem for us to base our investigation on Sam and me having felt a negative paranormal energy there."

"I agree." Sam reached across Greg to touch Adrian's arm. "It makes perfect sense that we, as a professional paranormal investigations team, would want to investigate a place where we suspect the presence of a possibly malevolent entity. I don't see any need to bring either one of you into it as a reason for our interest in the place."

Greg didn't need to see Adrian's face to feel his indecision, or to understand it. He gave Adrian's wrist a squeeze. "If BCPI investigates DogO, they'll be in there when it's closed, right? So even if you're in on the investigation, no one has to know if you use your mojo."

"Oh. Right." Adrian's laugh sounded embarrassed. "Wow, I feel stupid."

"Don't." Sam gave him a sympathetic smile. "When you can do the things we can, it's only natural to worry about other people noticing and thinking worse of you for it. Logic has very little to do with that."

"I suppose you're right." Adrian hugged Greg close for a moment, then let him go and rose to his feet. "Okay, I should think about dinner now. Y'all are staying, aren't you?"

"We'd love to. Don't cook for all of us, though, son. Let's order takeout." Bo stood and pulled his wallet from his pocket. "I'll pay."

"Picnic!" Greg suggested before Adrian could do more than shake his head. Bo raised his eyebrows in obvious question, and Greg blushed. "Um. The Picnic Hut. Everything from steaks to vegan wraps, and great prices." Jumping to his feet, he took his pod out of his shorts pocket and pulled up the Picnic Hut webpage. "Here. We can order online."

Everyone crowded around, studying the menu and talking over each other. In the midst of it all, Adrian caught Greg's hand in his and held on tight.

Greg leaned against Adrian's shoulder. Whatever lay ahead in the next few days, he had Adrian to help him through it. That knowledge made him feel like he could face anything. Even a haunted hot dog place.

Adrian wanted to go with his father and Sam to ask about permission to investigate DogOpolis Friday morning, but between his scheduled lab time, the Physics 101 class he taught and the papers he needed to grade, he had a full day ahead.

At least Greg didn't have to work. After what he'd felt at DogO yesterday, Adrian would never have been able to concentrate on work for worrying about Greg's safety.

The memory of the strange, dark energy thumping through his head sent a hard chill up Adrian's spine. He'd never felt anything quite like it before—thick, hot, angry, and weirdest of all, *alive* in a way the ghosts of the dead ought not to feel.

What the hell was it? What was it doing in a *fast-food* place? And why had it targeted Greg?

None of it made any sense. Adrian rested his elbows on the ancient wooden desk in the corner of the lab and rubbed his eyes.

He jumped when his pod started playing the theme from the old TV show *The X-Files*. Scowling, he fished it out of his back pocket. He never should've bought Greg the complete set of Anita Blake books. That's where he'd gotten the idea to keep reprogramming Adrian's ringtones, dammit.

Adrian checked the display on his pod, thumbed it on and held it to his ear. "Hi, Dad."

"Hi, Adrian. Sorry to bother you during your lab time, but I thought you'd like to know we got permission to run a formal investigation at DogOpolis."

"Oh, good." Adrian hadn't seriously doubted they'd be allowed to do it, but still, relief melted away a great deal of the tension he'd been carrying all morning. "When do we start?"

"Sam, Dean, Cecile and I will start tonight. I'm not sure you should be there with us, though."

"What?" Adrian leaned over his desk, stunned. "Dad, I *need* to be there. Greg—"

"Yes, Greg. That's exactly why I question the wisdom of your accompanying us." Adrian's father let out a soft sigh. "I understand why you feel so strongly about this. You love Greg.

You want to protect him. Sam explained to me what he felt in DogOpolis yesterday, and since you felt the same thing, I can certainly see why you're afraid for Greg's safety. But that's the reason I feel you shouldn't be there. We need everyone to be absolutely objective, or the investigation will be compromised."

"I'm *always* objective. You should know that." Adrian didn't like the irritation in his voice, but he couldn't help it. How many times had he worked a challenging case side by side with his father and remained as impartial as anyone else in the BCPI group?

If his reaction bothered his dad, it didn't come through over the phone. "You always have been, that's true. And I know you want to be in this case as well. But, Adrian, I know from experience how incredibly difficult it is to be truly impartial on a case where a person you love is at its center." His voice dropped low. "No matter how hard you try, sometimes it's just impossible. All you can think about is saving that person. Nothing else seems the least bit important."

Adrian's throat tightened with a sudden surge of sympathy. He'd never had to try to put aside his personal feelings in order to work a case until now, but he knew his father and Sam had had to do so more than once. Particularly when they'd had to save Adrian and his brother from the otherdimensional creatures let loose by eleven-year-old Adrian's uncontrolled psychokinesis.

He slumped in his chair and stared up at the ceiling. "I'm sorry, Dad."

As usual, his father seemed to understand what he meant. "There's nothing to be sorry for, son. There never was." He drew a breath. Let it out. "Well. We're going to get some sleep now, since we'll have to do the investigation after midnight. We'll stop by your place before we go to DogOpolis and go over our plans with you, so you can give us any suggestions you might have.

We definitely want your input. We've already spoken with Greg, since he was home and he'll be at rehearsal tonight." He hesitated for a moment. "I know this is difficult for you. I'm sorry."

Adrian smiled at the bar of sunlight gleaming on the wall opposite his desk. "It's okay. Like you told me, there's nothing to be sorry for. I'll see you tonight. Love you, Dad."

"I love you too, Adrian. Goodbye."

The connection cut off. Adrian set his pod on his desk and rubbed his thumbs together, thinking hard.

His dad was right. Remaining objective was going to be extremely difficult. But there was no way in hell he was staying out of this investigation. Which meant he had about eight to ten hours to come up with a compelling case for why he should be allowed to participate.

He dropped his head onto his folded arms with a groan.

The one thing Adrian didn't predict was having Sam on his side in this argument.

Well, actually, he hadn't predicted an argument at all. His dads hadn't quarreled over him in *ages*. As far as he knew, at least. Yet here they were, nose to nose in a thankfully quiet but still heated fight over whether or not Adrian should go with them on the DogOpolis investigation.

Dean and Cecile sat huddled at the table in stunned silence, obviously not wanting to take sides. Even Adrian didn't dare say anything else after presenting his initial reasons why he believed his presence on the investigation to be essential.

"He's the only one of us who can specifically communicate with the dead," Sam said for about the fourth time, sounding as if he'd like to accompany each word with a smack to Bo's head. "What if that skill is what makes the difference?"

"And what if his emotions put him in *danger*, Sam?" Bo glared at his husband in crystal-clear frustration. "No. We are absolutely *not* endangering him just because he wants to protect his boyfriend."

Stung, Adrian opened his mouth to protest his father's overprotective—and, in Adrian's opinion, overbearing—tone. Dean's hand on his wrist stopped him. He frowned at Dean.

A tiny smile turned up the corners of Dean's mouth. "Don't," he murmured. "It's been a long time since they got like this, at least in front of company, but when they do, you don't want to get in the middle of it. Believe me."

"I believe you." Adrian glanced toward the ongoing battle.

"Goddammit, Bo, Adrian is a grown man. You need to start treating him like it."

The room went dead quiet at Sam's sudden shout. Adrian's father blinked. "What?"

Sam blushed, something he rarely did. He rubbed the back of his neck, a sure sign of nerves. "Okay, look. I know why you're worried about Adrian going. I understand that. I'm worried too." He glanced at Adrian with an apology in his eyes, then turned back to Bo. "The thing is, I think Adrian's right about why he needs to come with us. Cecile and I are very strong psychics, but Adrian has skills we don't have, and we might need those skills."

Watching his father, Adrian saw the telltale twitch of a jaw muscle and the tightening at the corners of his eyes. "Yesterday, all of you seemed certain that what you felt wasn't any typical type of haunting. I'm not sure how Adrian's particular ability can help us in that case."

"I don't know *what* I felt, Bo, that's the point!" Sam grabbed his husband by the shoulders and stared hard into his eyes. "Listen to me. I have never. *Ever*. Felt *anything* like that in my life. I don't know what it is. But if it's any form of the dead, anything we can communicate with, Adrian could be the key. And Greg's safety could be at stake here. Can you really expect him to ignore that?" He touched Bo's cheek. "You wouldn't ignore it if it was me, and you know I wouldn't if it was you. And it's for damn sure neither of us would ignore it if it was Adrian or Sean."

No one moved or spoke. Adrian watched the drama, silently pleading in his head for his dad to just please agree with Sam.

Finally, Adrian's father shut his eyes and rested his head on Sam's shoulder. He slipped both arms around Sam's waist. "You're right. Christ."

Adrian grinned. "So you'll let me come along?"

"Tonight, yes. As long as you promise to sleep tomorrow. And you can't come with us in the future unless it will not interfere with your research or your work, and you'll have time to sleep." Adrian's dad lifted his head and pinned Adrian with a solemn look. "Please be careful tonight, son. Promise me."

"Don't worry. I won't put myself or anyone else in any danger, I swear." Adrian jumped up. "Let me get my stuff together and message Greg that I'm going with you."

He found his pod on the kitchen counter. While he was sending Greg a message, he saw his dads kissing out of the corner of his eye.

He wrinkled his nose. "Good grief, do they have to do that?"

Cecile laughed. "You don't have much room to talk, you know." Pushing to her feet, she wandered into the kitchen, took a glass from the cabinet and filled it with water.

"Hell, this is nothing. You should've seen them back in the old days." Dean joined them in the kitchen, since Adrian's dads didn't seem inclined to stop making up. "Good thing Greg's not here. He thinks Sam and Bo are hot, you know." He winked at Adrian.

Adrian smacked him.

"It's not here."

Adrian's father turned to Sam, who'd stopped cold in the employee entrance at the back of DogOpolis. "What's not here?"

"What we felt before. The energy, the entity, whatever it was." Sam walked inside, his eyes wide open but unfocused.

Adrian knew the look—concentration. Feeling for something you *knew* ought to be there but couldn't quite grasp. He glanced at Cecile. Without a word, she took his hand and the two of them followed Sam into the darkness.

Sam was right. The thing Adrian had sensed here on Wednesday was gone. "Wow."

"How does something that strong just vanish?" Switching on her flashlight, Cecile let go of Adrian's hand and wandered into the kitchen. She swung the beam this way and that, her brow creased in thought. "Dean? What's the EMF level?"

Lights popped up all over the room as the rest of the team turned on their flashlights. "Oh point five," Dean answered after a tense moment. He walked in a slow circle, watching the meter. "It's not fluctuating. I'll check the rest of the place. Maybe we've got a hot spot someplace."

"Good thinking. I don't believe it would cause false psychic readings for our group, but I suppose it's possible that one area with a very high EMF could cause intermittent manifestations. If so, we'd want to pay close attention to that area." Adrian's dad went to Sam, who stood silent and unmoving in front of the fryer, and studied his face with obvious concern. "Sam? Are you all right?"

Sam nodded, blinked and smiled at his husband. "I'm fine. I thought I felt a trace of something, that's all. But I couldn't quite get a hold of it."

A memory sparked in Adrian's mind—holding Greg and sensing something different, a vague residue almost like the faint scent of hot dogs and frying oil that sometimes clung to his hair after work.

"I think I've felt it before. Hang on…" Moving to Sam's side, Adrian shut his eyes and opened his psychic shields. The aggressive force he'd felt here the other day didn't hit him like he'd been half afraid it would. But the almost-scent was there, a charged current in the room's atmosphere. He focused on it as best he could and opened his eyes. "It's there. I feel it. Sam? Cecile?"

Sam's expression went blank. After a few seconds, his eyes widened. "There. I have it."

"It's like the energy the other day, but…not." Cecile's voice emerged soft and measured, the way it always did when she was focusing her psychic powers particularly hard. She began pacing the perimeter of the kitchen, dragging her fingertips over the polished surfaces of the appliances. "It feels almost like an aftertaste, doesn't it?"

"Yes. Exactly." Sam licked his lips, as if trying to catch the essence of the elusive thing they were all trying to mentally nail down. "Adrian. You've felt this before?"

Adrian nodded. "I've sensed it a couple of times in the last few days. On Greg."

On the other side of the service counter, Dean let out a humorless laugh. "The plot thickens."

"Indeed." Adrian's father set the heavy equipment bag he carried on the floor. "Do you have any thoughts about this..." he circled a hand in the air as though trying to conjure the right word, "...this residual energy, let's say? Any thoughts about what it might be, or even any general impressions?"

Adrian frowned, digging as deep into his memories as he could. "It didn't feel like what we sensed here the other day. I certainly never would've connected it with any kind of haunting or entity. I mean, having experienced both things now, I can tell that the energy I felt here and the energy I felt lingering around Greg are related. But at the same time, what I sensed on Greg—which is definitely the same thing I'm sensing now—wasn't even in the same league as what we all felt the other day. It's like comparing a tiny baby squid that can sit on your finger to a fully grown male colossal squid a hundred feet long."

His father's eyebrows went up. "Do they get that big?"

"Does it matter? You see my point." Adrian turned to Sam for support. "*You* know what I'm saying, right?"

"Yeah, I do. So does your father, but you know how he is." Ignoring Bo's eye-roll-and-head-shake combination, Sam watched Adrian with a thoughtful expression. "What I'm having trouble explaining is *why* we would be feeling a residual energy at all. The only other time I've ever felt any such thing was on the interdimensional portal cases, after the portals were closed. And I think we can all agree that this is *nothing* like those cases."

"Agreed. And thank God for that." Cecile rubbed her arm with her free hand. "I also wonder why we can all sense such a strong psychic energy, but only intermittently."

"Or maybe even only that once," Dean interjected from the dining area. "I haven't found any EMF hot spots, by the way, but the whole place is a little on the high side. Not dangerously so, but it's up some. About oh-point-five all over, just like at the door."

Adrian's heart lurched. Dean was right when he said the EMF level wasn't dangerous. It bothered Adrian anyway, though. Elevated EMF enabled paranormal phenomena. And the EMF might be higher during business hours, with all the appliances, lights, etcetera turned on.

It did nothing to alleviate his concerns for Greg's safety.

"Hmm." Adrian's father picked up his bag again and headed for the dining area. "Let's start setting up the cameras and microphones. Adrian, if you're willing, I'd like for you to keep track of the EMF while we have the lights on and are setting up equipment. I'd also like for you to flip on a few of the simpler machines and see if that makes any difference in the electromagnetic field. Dean, did you already check closely around the refrigerator and freezer?"

"Yup. Nothing any different. It's still around oh-point-five."

"All right, Adrian, you can skip those." Bo set his bag on one of the tables. "Keep your psychic senses open, but be careful. Drop your shields and let me know immediately if you start sensing any change in the energy here, all right?" He pointed at Sam and Cecile in turn. "That goes for the two of you as well. I don't want anyone getting complacent and ending up hurt because of it."

"Yes, boss." Sam saluted.

Bo shot him a dark look, but the corners of his mouth turned up enough to keep Adrian from worrying about another fight. "Remind me why I married you, again?"

"Because you need someone to keep you in line." Sending his husband a grin Adrian preferred not to think too hard about, Sam gestured to Dean. "C'mon, Dean, give Adrian the EMF and let's go get the rest of the equipment out of the van."

"'Kay." Dean jogged over, his flashlight beam bouncing against the gleaming metal of the fryer and the giant freezer. He handed Adrian the EMF detector. "Here. You know how to use this new one that automatically records the readings, right?"

"Yeah. Dad showed me last time I was home." He smiled at Dean. "Thanks."

Dean gave his arm a squeeze. "Hope you're caffeinated, kiddo. Looks like it's gonna be a loooong night."

Starting a sweep of the kitchen as Cecile switched on the lights, Adrian couldn't decide whether to be glad for the promise of a quiet night, or disappointed that he wouldn't be able to learn more about whatever had been haunting Greg—literally—during the past week or so.

As he passed the office, he caught the faint thread of that strange leftover energy once again. He couldn't keep track of it unless he stood motionless with his eyes shut and concentrated on nothing else, and he lost it as he moved around the kitchen. Faint and transient as it was, however, it still tasted like a thin shade of the buzzing, furious, overwhelming presence he'd sensed here on Wednesday.

This felt like a watercolor hologram of something that could tear a person into bloody ribbons if it wanted.

Adrian swallowed. Yeah, he wished whatever it was would show itself tonight. Greg was strong—much stronger than his wisecracking public face would lead a casual observer to believe—but he didn't have the right sort of skills to fight whatever this thing was.

Adrian did. And he had no intention of letting some evil entity hurt the man he loved.

Chapter Seven

Five hours and change after Adrian got home—at the ungodly hour of five thirty a.m.—Greg sat slouched in one of the plush new seats in the PlayMakers Theater and hoped like hell the whole DogO investigation wouldn't be this rough. Who knew he would've lost the ability to go to sleep by himself?

Of course, if Jon could learn to concentrate on his damn job, Greg would be up there onstage rehearsing one of the group numbers instead of sitting out here in the audience trying to keep his eyelids open.

Jon chose that moment to glance at him. *Fuck.* Greg glared. John looked away with a guilty start when Noemi spoke sharply to him.

Behind Greg, Malachi chuckled. "What'd you do to your boyfriend?"

Greg frowned. "Huh? What do you mean? Adrian's at home asleep. I barely even talked to him when he got home."

"He's talking about Jon, genius." Myah elbowed him, grinning. "Better watch it, Greg. Jon might make a move on you, and then Adrian'll be jealous."

"Oh, my God." Covering his face with both hands, Greg planted his feet on the back of the seat in front of him and sank as far into his chair as he could. "Don't make me start thinking of that right now. Who the hell knows when I'll catch Adrian alone again."

Myah frowned. "Wait, why—?"

"Myah. Honey. Think about it." Greg laid a hand on her arm. "When Adrian's jealous, he gets all possessive. When he gets all possessive, he likes to, shall we say, show me how much he loves me." He met her light-bulb-moment look with a wide smile. "Get it now?"

She rolled her eyes. "Yeah, yeah. You and Adrian fuck all the time. I think everybody knows that already, thanks anyway."

Mal snickered behind them. "Come on, you set yourself up for that, Myah."

"Shut up, Mal," she told him without turning around.

"Aw, don't be mad. If you ever get tired of that dude you live with, give me a call." Leaning over the back of her chair, he kissed her cheek and jumped back out of the way before she could smack him.

Myah twisted around in her seat, lunged at Mal and pinched his arm. He covered his mouth with his hand to stifle a yelp. Greg laughed.

Noemi turned and aimed a warning look at them. "Children! If you don't mind."

Greg clamped his mouth shut. Beside him, Myah sat up straight and clasped her hands in her lap. Mal's snickering continued behind them, quietly now.

Since they'd gotten themselves on Noemi's radar, the three of them settled down. With nothing to do except listen to the leads and the couple of other actors onstage play through the same scene over and over again, Greg tuned out and turned his mind to the DogO investigation instead.

The news that the whatever-it-was had apparently made itself scarce last night bothered him. Not because he missed it. Hell, he'd throw a damn party if he thought for a minute it was gone for good. But his gut told him it wasn't. In fact, he thought he could spot a pattern here if he squinted—now you feel it, now you don't. That scared him even more than the thing's presence in the first place, mostly because he didn't understand it. How could something show up strong enough and different enough to impress a group like the BCPI gang one day, and vanish without a trace the next? And more importantly, *why?*

The obvious answer to question number one was it hadn't vanished at all. Whether the entity—ghost, demon, space alien, whatever—had skipped off someplace else for the night or it simply had the power to hide itself from psychics, Greg had no idea. But it hadn't really gone anywhere. He'd never felt more sure of anything.

As to the why of it... Well. That was the *real* puzzler. He couldn't pretend to understand how paranormal beings usually operated—if they even had a usual—but he was pretty sure this hide-and-seek business didn't qualify. So what made this thing different? Was it one of a kind, or were there others out there? How did it do the things it did?

An image of his mother popped into his head, telling him with an amused quirk of her lips and a twinkle in her eye to *Go look it up, little question monster.* He smiled to himself. He'd always been a curious child, pestering his parents with endless questions about this or that aspect of everything from the nature of the farthest stars to how the TV worked. His mom's answer had often been for him to go research and find out, once he got old enough to read and use the computer.

Good advice was still good advice. And between college and Dean, he'd learned a lot about how to research.

He was thinking about whether he ought to ask Mal and Myah to help him out when an icy touch brushed against his left cheek. At the same time, a low whisper hissed in his ear.

It took everything he had to remain silent and seated. He clamped his hands hard around the armrests and reminded himself that he was unharmed, and dammit, the theater was *haunted*. What kind of a ghost hunter would he be if he couldn't handle an up-close-and-personal encounter?

He glanced sideways at Myah, who was staring into space with an expression suggesting she was thinking of anything at all other than what was going on onstage. "Hey. Myah."

She blinked, turned her head and focused on him. "Yeah?"

Ignoring his tendency to feel stupid, Greg licked his lips and forced himself to ask. "Are, um. Are there any...you know. Ghosts? Nearby?"

She eyed him with more caution than he would've thought necessary. "Why?"

You're not crazy. She doesn't think you're crazy. Nobody does.

He wasn't sure he believed himself, but he plunged onward anyhow. "Something cold touched my face just now. And I heard a voice. I couldn't understand what it said, but I heard it."

Myah's face lit up. "Oh my God, it was the flapper lady! She touched me once and whispered in my ear. She does that sometimes."

Relieved, Greg smiled. "So she was here?"

"Well, I didn't see her, but it must've been her, since she's done the same thing to me before." Myah frowned. "Did I tell Bo that? I'm positive I did."

Greg patted her hand. "I'll check with Adrian and make sure."

From the stage, Noemi shot them a glare. They shut up.

As Greg settled back into his seat, he noticed Jon staring at him. *Staring*. Blatantly. With an intensity that made Greg's skin prickle.

For the first time, Greg wondered about the true roots of his recent experiences.

Rehearsal ran long. Not much, but enough to make Greg antsy. He called Adrian as soon as Noemi released them to the dressing room.

"Hi, Greg." Adrian sounded awake and upbeat. He must've gotten more sleep than Greg had. "How'd rehearsal go?"

"It was okay." Plopping onto one of the benches, Greg toed off his dance shoes. "Listen, I'm heading over to the library to do some research, but I ought to be home before you and the team leave for DogO."

"Okay. Research on what?"

Adrian's curiosity was thick in his voice. Greg smiled. "It's kind of hard to explain over the phone. I'll tell you all about it when I get home."

Adrian laughed. "Oh, I see. You're in the dressing room and you don't want everybody to know your business."

"This is funny to you?" Greg stood and shoved his dance shorts off with one hand.

"No. Believe me, I totally get it." The sound of the kitchen cabinet closing floated down the airwaves. "All right. I can't wait to hear about it. I love you."

"Love you too. Bye."

He broke the connection and stuck his pod in his dance bag. He tried to ignore the feeling of being stared at. After he'd finished changing, he grabbed his bag, slipped on his flip-flops and hurried out of the dressing room without looking in Jon's direction.

Mal was on the way out at the same time. He fell into step with Greg as he passed. "You look thoroughly perturbed. Everything all right?"

"Yeah, it's nothing. Let's get out of here." Greg started toward the lobby at a brisk pace, anxious to escape the feel of Jon's gaze on the back of his neck.

Mal trotted to catch up. "What's the hurry?" He glanced over his shoulder at the sound of voices behind them. "Oh. Your stalker's getting extra creepy, huh?"

"Yes." Greg thought about it and decided there was no point in being more dramatic than absolutely necessary. "Well, no, not really. It's just annoying, that's all."

"I feel your pain, man. Denise is not nearly as subtle as she thinks she is."

"This is *so* true." Pushing open the lobby doors, Greg gestured Mal through ahead of him. Mal pretended to swoon, so Greg popped him on the butt. They both laughed as they crossed the lobby to the exit. "Did you hear she broke up with her boyfriend?"

Mal's eyebrows rose. "Well. Good. She can do better." He pointed a stern finger at Greg before he could do more than open his mouth. "Not a word, G. Not a word."

Greg lifted both hands in surrender. They walked out into a muggy, overcast evening that smelled like oncoming rain. Greg wrinkled his nose. Normally he didn't mind riding the bus home, but he felt restless today. He'd been looking forward to the walk. He didn't want to get soaked, though, so walking was out. Dammit.

As if reading his mind, Mal lifted his face to the threatening sky and scowled. "Aw, man. Fucking rain." He glanced at Greg. "I gotta book if I want to catch the bus. See you later."

"Yeah, see you." Greg waved at Mal and they each jogged off in opposite directions.

Greg hadn't expected the research to be easy. His best search term was poorly defined, and he wasn't sure whether Paranormal Studies or News Archives would be the better place to look, so he decided to dig through both sections. It narrowed down the field considerably compared to the entire library, thus saving him a lot of time he would've otherwise spent weeding out results from Davis's huge fiction collection, but he still ended up with hundreds of results. Greg got as far as the forty-third dead end before he admitted to himself that this whole thing was even harder than he'd thought it would be.

"Man, this is crazy," he muttered to himself after a couple of hours' worth of skimming various scientific periodicals he'd never heard of.

He raked both hands through his hair in sheer frustration. So far he hadn't found much. He'd dug up an article in a paranormal journal about poltergeists, but the BCPI team would've already thought of that. Adrian and his family had lived through their own personal poltergeist hell when his psychokinesis first manifested in spectacular fashion at age eleven. If anyone would recognize such activity right off the bat, it would be them. He'd also found an article about different kinds of malevolent spirits. It seemed to hit closer to the mark, so he'd sent the link to his personal account. The only thing that didn't match up was that such spirits apparently couldn't cause physical damage to people, at least as far as the authors of the article knew. Still, it was close enough to what he'd experienced to give Greg the creeps.

It was the third article, though, that sent waves of gooseflesh up his arms and made him look over his shoulder just in case.

It was linked from article number two, stating that people who thought they had malevolent spirits might actually have a demon. The text contained a surprising number of mathematical equations and other scientific stuff Greg didn't get, but toward the end came the part he *did* understand.

According to the authors, a demon could not only attach itself to an inanimate object, it could also attach itself to a human being, either through that object or through direct contact. And once it became attached to that person, it would actively work to harm him or her.

Greg leaned back in his chair, both hands over his mouth. His heart raced and his stomach churned.

I've got a demon attached to me. Fuck, fuck, fuck. How such a thing had happened, he had no clue, but there seemed to be no doubt. Somehow, he'd gotten a demon stuck to him.

But what about Adrian? Adrian, with his wonderful, spectacular mojo. Adrian, who could sniff out paranormal energy like a hound smells blood. He'd pick up demon energy in a hot minute.

Right?

Maybe not. Maybe that's why he didn't sense it before, at DogO. Maybe demon energy isn't something he can sense, because it's not like ghost energy. It isn't human. It was never alive.

It wasn't something that had ever occurred to Greg before. The thought terrified him.

But if that was the case, what in the nine hells had Adrian, Sam and Cecile sensed at DogO before?

He didn't know, but the whole thing was giving him a headache.

Closing his eyes, he forced himself to take slow, deep breaths, in and out, until the confusion and anxiety receded and he felt calmer. Whatever was going on, whether it had to do with him or DogO or fucking sunspots, Adrian and the BCPI team would help him figure it out. Getting all upset about it wouldn't help.

Footsteps shuffled behind Greg. His eyes popped open. He dug his fingers into the edge of his chair and refused to turn around. Just because he didn't see anyone walking away meant nothing. It was a library. People walked through here all the time. He was letting his imagination get the better of him.

A loud *bang* echoed off the walls. This time, he jumped several inches, but he clamped his mouth shut to keep himself from yelping. The source of the noise wasn't hard to spot. A group of boys not far from Greg stood shaking with stifled laughter while one of their friends picked up the stack of heavy books he'd dropped onto the tile floor.

Deciding his frazzled nerves couldn't take any more, Greg messaged the demon article to both his own account and Adrian's, signed off the terminal and got out of the library as fast as he could.

Outside, clouds covered the sky and a fine drizzle shrouded the campus. He considered walking home in spite of the rain. But the thought of being alone right now made his skin crawl. Hunching his shoulders against the sensation of something unfriendly watching him, he clutched his bag close and jogged to the bus stop.

Adrian stared across the room at Greg. "Are you serious?"

"Yes. Look, did you read the article?"

"I did, but—"

"But nothing. It fits." Greg wandered in from the kitchen with a glass of wine in one hand and a blue plastic UNC cup in the other. He settled onto the sofa beside Adrian and handed him the cup. "Here's your water."

"Thanks." Adrian took a long swallow. It helped relieve the sudden attack of dry mouth he'd gotten when Greg outlined his theory about the origin and nature of the paranormal presence at DogOpolis. Or attached to Greg himself, if you bought that theory, which Adrian wasn't so sure he did. "You really think it could be demonic?"

"Yeah. Believe me, I wish I didn't. I'd sleep better tonight." With a deep sigh, Greg curled his feet beneath him and leaned against Adrian's side. "But the more I thought about it, the more sense it made."

"I guess it does fit the facts of the situation." Just admitting to the possibility scared Adrian. He put an arm around Greg and pulled him close. "I don't like it. What are we supposed to *do* about it, if this is really some sort of demonic...?" He searched his mind for the right word and realized he didn't know it. "Hell, what do we even call this?"

He didn't say the word *possession*. But it lurked at the edges of his mind, and he knew Greg thought the same.

Greg pinned him with an unusually somber stare. "I know this is a lot to swallow, and I know you probably never believed in demons and stuff. Neither did I. But then again, I never believed in ghosts before you came along."

"A fair point." Setting his cup on the table beside him, Adrian wrapped both arms tight around Greg and nuzzled his neck. "I'm glad you have all-day rehearsal again tomorrow. I don't like the thought of you being at DogOpolis with a demon."

"Can't say I'm crazy about the idea either." Greg rubbed his cheek against Adrian's hair. "But what if it's not DogO, Adrian? What if it's me?"

Adrian felt as if a huge hand took hold of his chest and squeezed. He tightened his arms around Greg. "It's not you. It's that *place*." He stroked Greg's hair, breathing in his scent and wishing he could protect him from everything that might hurt him. "Don't go back there."

"I have to, babe. It's my job. It may not pay a lot, but it pays more than the Repertory Company, and we need the money." Greg wriggled his arm free and pushed Adrian back enough to peer into his eyes. "Adrian. Listen to me. Maybe it *is* DogO. But what if it's not? What if it's me?"

Adrian was shaking his head before Greg finished speaking, which he knew Greg hated, but he couldn't help it. Greg couldn't have a demon attached to him. He just couldn't. Not so much because it wasn't possible as because Adrian didn't think he could handle it. His mind would not see beyond the idea of Greg saddled with a demon to the practicalities of how to deal with it. And if Adrian couldn't see it, couldn't handle it, couldn't *fix* it, then it absolutely, positively could not be the truth.

"I don't sense anything on you. I'd sense it." Adrian was sure of it. After all, he'd sensed the blast of negative energy at DogOpolis before, right?

When Greg was there, you did. Not when he wasn't there.

But he also hadn't felt anything the first time Greg asked him to come check out DogO, and Greg had been there then. And he sensed nothing now, with Greg right here in his arms.

Nothing?

The memory of that faint aftertaste of energy lingering on Greg—almost like a faded perfume—prodded at Adrian's mind.

He leaned in and breathed deep. And caught a metaphysical whiff of the same thing.

He sat back in his chair, feeling like he'd been punched. What did it mean? Did it mean anything?

Greg watched him with wide, blank eyes. "You can feel it, can't you?"

Wanting to comfort him, Adrian raked his fingers through Greg's curls, which were still damp from his shower. "Not really. All I feel is the same residual energy I felt before. It could be leftover energy from whatever's haunting DogOpolis. It might not mean anything at all." *Or it might mean you're right and you have a demon attached to you. I have no idea and that terrifies me.* "But either way, I can't pretend I'm not scared for you. I've never dealt with any kind of demon anywhere, if that's what this thing is. I don't really know anything about it. Even if it's haunting DogO instead of you—which I still think is the case, by the way—it still scares me, because you work there. What if something happens and I can't help you? What if you get hurt? I don't know what I'd do, Greg. I really don't."

"Oh, I've thought of that. And honestly? I don't blame you for being scared for me. I'm scared shitless myself." Greg set his untouched wine on the coffee table and took both of Adrian's hands in his. "But I can't run away from this. I know you understand that." A humorless smile curled his lips. "Seriously, if I have a demon attached to me, I can't run away from it no matter how much I want to. I'm kind of stuck with it, so I might as well figure out what to do about it."

Adrian's heart lurched. He'd give anything to have this not be true, but if it was, he would by God do everything in his power to rid Greg of the thing riding him.

Pushing Greg backward onto the cushions, Adrian leaned over and kissed him, a long, slow, deep kiss that soon had Greg arching upward in search of full-body contact. Adrian gave it to him, pressing himself between Greg's open thighs while the kiss went on and on and on.

It felt familiar. Comfortable. Wonderfully domestic. At the same time, every stroke of Greg's tongue, every soft moan, every slide of Greg's thigh against Adrian's hip, brought the same electric rush of excitement as the first.

Adrian loved that after all this time his psychokinesis still reacted to Greg's touch as strongly as it had the first time they were together. Thank God he'd learned to relax and enjoy it, or the intensity of it might've destroyed his mind ages ago.

After several glorious minutes, Greg broke the kiss. He rested his forehead against Adrian's, one hand fisted in Adrian's hair and the other clamped in a death grip on his ass. His breath panted warm and quick against Adrian's lips. "How much time do we have before the gang gets here?"

Grinning, Adrian reached out with his mind to undo the zipper on Greg's shorts. "Enough."

Adrian hoped his dad and the rest of the BCPI team would spot a flaw in Greg's demon idea and dismiss it. It would've been a relief to have that particular weight off his mind. Unfortunately, all four of them thought Greg's theory was plausible, if not all that likely.

They didn't share Adrian's level of fear for Greg's safety, though, which both irritated him and made him feel better.

His own contradictory feelings told him he needed to take an emotional step back before his father said as much.

"It's easy to get too close to a case," his dad said as the group entered the darkened restaurant just after one a.m. He switched on the kitchen lights. "We've all been there, believe me. You need to find a way to deliberately distance yourself. It's the only way to solve this case and, in the end, ensure Greg's safety." He gave Adrian a comforting smile. "Think about it, son. Greg's only had one experience that's at all worrisome, and that was here. Correct?"

Adrian nodded. "Yes."

"Exactly so. And everything we've found at the theater so far backs up multiple residual hauntings, which would easily explain anything that's happened to him there." Adrian's father eyed him with concern. "We certainly don't want to brush off anything that might be worrisome, though. Is there something we ought to know? Something you haven't told us?"

In his head, Adrian rifled through every detail of what Greg had told him—the noises and shadows in the theater, in the library, here at DogOpolis. Truthfully, a lot of it seemed to be the product of a fertile imagination pumped up by too much stress and an inherent desire to experience the paranormal.

But not all of it. Too much, in fact, for Adrian's comfort.

Then there was the burn still healing on Greg's neck.

"I've told you everything," he said at last, when everyone had stopped what they were doing to listen because he'd taken so long to answer. He hunched his shoulders. "But, Dad, it bugs me, because I keep catching that weird trace of energy on him. And I don't know what to make of it. I mean, I always thought I'd be able to sense any kind of paranormal energy, and of course I sensed the negative energy here that day just like Sam and Cecile did, but..." He shook his head, unsure of his precise point, just knowing that *something* about this whole thing was tying his gut into knots and he couldn't lay his finger on it. "I don't know. I don't *know*, Dad. Something's wrong, and I can't figure out what it is."

"EMF level at the theater is near zero."

Adrian swiveled along with everyone else to stare at Dean, who'd set his bag on the checkout counter and started unpacking. "What?"

Dean raised his head and met the collective gaze of his coworkers with eyebrows hiked up to his hairline. "C'mon, guys, don't do that. You're freaking me out."

Adrian's father took his hand and pressed it to silence him. He clamped his mouth shut and let his dad speak. "Dean. Could you please explain your point about the EMF?"

"Sure." Dean dug an EMF meter out of the bag and tapped the screen. "When we were investigating the theater, the EMF reading was close to zero the whole time. About oh-point-oh-three or lower. Here it's higher." He cast a meaningful look around the room. "I'm just saying, if someone had a demonic being attached to them, maybe the higher EMF might make it easier to sense. I don't *know* that, obviously, it's just a thought. We'd have to look into it and see if it's true or not."

Adrian felt the room spin around him. He clutched his dad's hand for support. Good God, he hadn't even thought of that possibility. It felt like his last hope was being ripped away.

"Adrian. Stop." Dropping his hand, his father moved in front of him and took him firmly by both shoulders. "It's a theory. Nothing more. At this moment, Greg is fine. He hasn't been harmed, not really. You have to stay calm, for Greg's sake. You have to be the scientist I know you are and get to the bottom of this. Okay?"

Holding his dad's gaze like a lifeline, Adrian nodded. "Yes. You're right." Adrian looked from one to the other of the people he'd grown up with. People he trusted with his life, and Greg's. "Do you think Greg's in any danger? Tell me the truth."

Sam came to him and squeezed his hand. "No one can predict that for certain. Documented cases of demonic entities are rare, and there's not much agreement on exactly what they

117

are or what they're capable of." He and Bo exchanged a glance loaded with meaning Adrian couldn't quite decipher. "If you want my opinion, I think we ought to wait and watch, but keep a close eye on Greg. Just in case."

That didn't make Adrian feel the least bit better, but he had a feeling it wasn't supposed to. He drew a deep breath, blew it out and nodded, trying not to look as scared as he felt. "All right. Yes. Good idea." He gave his dads a sheepish smile. "Sorry for freaking out. I'm okay."

Chuckling, Sam pressed his fingers once more, then let go. "That hardly qualified as a freak-out. You should've been around for some of your dad's meltdowns back in the day."

"What, he's stopped?" Dean blinked in fake surprise. "Since when?"

Cecile laughed as she went to help Dean get the equipment set up. Adrian grinned in spite of himself.

His dad shook his head. "You see what I have to put up with. Is it any wonder I lose my temper sometimes?" He dropped his hands from Adrian's shoulders without breaking his gaze. "In all seriousness, though, son, Sam is absolutely correct that you hardly freaked out. There's nothing to be sorry for. I think we all realize how difficult this is for you, and we want to know you're all right."

Adrian nodded, warmed as always by his parents' love for him. "I'm fine. It just kind of hit me hard for a second there, you know?"

Sam and Bo exchanged one of those looks again, the kind that held worlds of shared experience too complex for words. A faint, melancholy smile turned up the corners of Bo's mouth. "Yes. I think we know exactly what you mean."

Not for the first time, Adrian felt a wave of gratitude for the fact that both his dads were still here, alive and in one piece.

"Do you think there's any way we can find out for certain whether or not this entity is actually attached to Greg?" He turned to glance at Cecile and Dean in turn, including them in the question.

"I don't think any of us knows enough about the subject of demons to know how to proceed without doing a little research first." Cecile carried her bag toward the dining area, set it on a table and started pulling out equipment. "I'll be glad to do some digging around and see what I can find out."

"I'll help you," Dean offered. He wandered toward Cecile, the EMF detector in his hand. "Although I feel like I have to point out that none of us knows for sure that this thing is actually a demon."

"You're absolutely right about that." Adrian's father paced toward the counter where Dean had spread out the cameras, picked one up and fiddled with the controls. "I suppose the best way to approach this is with simple scientific methodology. We'll need to observe Greg in and out of DogOpolis, and we'll need to observe DogOpolis—open, not closed like now—with and without Greg here."

Sam groaned. "Greg isn't going to like that last bit, is he?"

"No. Not much." Adrian followed his dad and Sam to the pile of equipment so he could find something to do with his restless hands. "But I think he'll be okay with it if it helps us figure out what's going on. He's scared."

No one answered, but Adrian knew they were all thinking the same thing as him—that Greg had good reason to be afraid.

"Wait, so, you're saying the EMF level at DogO might be making this demon thing stronger?"

"Or at least easier to sense, yes." Adrian chewed his lower lip. "It's just a theory."

Greg stared at Adrian with his pulse thudding in his ears. Normally, Adrian's nervous lip-biting gave Greg an almost irresistible urge to pounce. Now? Not even a twinge. All he wanted to do was hide under the bed.

He'd do it, if he thought it would help any.

With a deep sigh, Greg flopped onto the sofa next to Adrian. "Great. What the hell am I supposed to do about *that*?"

"You don't need to do anything." Adrian wound an arm around Greg's shoulders and pulled him close. "I'm keeping a metaphysical eye on you, in and out of DogOpolis, watching for any change in your energy. Anything that might indicate that the entity is actually attached to you."

"Oh joy," Greg muttered, wrinkling his nose.

Adrian aimed a reproachful look at him but otherwise ignored him. "And we want to observe DogOpolis both with and without you there, to see if the energy is any different."

The plan made perfect sense. Still, Greg hated the idea of the BCPI group going there without him. All his coworkers would know something was up. They wouldn't likely guess that the Bay City gang was investigating the possibility of Greg having a demon attached to him, but that didn't make Greg like the attention it would draw any better. Besides, who knew how the demon would react?

"You don't have to go today, do you?" he asked when Adrian started to fidget at his side.

"Well." Adrian twisted his fingers together and stared at his lap. "You're off today, so it would be the perfect time."

Adrian had a point. Not that practicality had as much chance of moving Greg as the humble curve of Adrian's neck and the way he glanced sideways at Greg with his brown eyes all wide and pleading. This time, though, Greg wasn't even tempted to cave.

He crossed his arms. "I'd really rather you didn't."

"Fine." Adrian pushed to his feet. "When are you off next?"

"Thursday afternoon." Greg pointed at Adrian before he could say anything. "Don't, okay? You guys can always go there after I leave work on some other day."

"Yeah, maybe." Adrian wandered into the kitchen and returned a moment later with a can of iced tea. He popped it open and took a long swallow. "I don't understand why you don't want us to go today, though. What's the difference?"

What *was* the difference? Greg wasn't sure he understood it himself.

He slouched farther into the cushions and tried to find a way to explain. "It seems so soon, is all. I want to have time to prepare, you know?"

"Prepare for *what*?" Adrian sat beside Greg again, looking annoyed. "I'm sorry, Greg, but I don't see what the big deal is with us going in to feel the place out when you aren't there." He laid a hand on Greg's arm, stopping his automatic protest. "I know you think everyone's going to assume we're there for some reason like..."

"Like what you're actually going there for," Greg jumped in when Adrian trailed off. "Yeah, wonder why I might not want that to happen? Hmm." He rubbed his chin in exaggerated thoughtfulness.

Adrian rolled his eyes. "Come on."

"What, you don't think the people I work with are smart enough to come to that conclusion?"

"I didn't say that."

"Well, it's what you're implying." Feeling exhausted all of a sudden, Greg leaned forward until his head rested on Adrian's shoulder. "I don't want to fight about it, Adrian. Just humor me, okay? Please? Don't go there today. Wait until Monday or some other day." He kissed Adrian's throat. "I can leave something there when I leave work and you can go get it for me, since I'll be at rehearsal. Sam can go with you since you'll be hanging out with him."

Adrian laughed. The sound vibrated through his collarbone. "Okay, okay. You talked me into it." Lifting Greg's chin, Adrian pressed a soft kiss to his lips. "But I'm coming to DogO during lunch on Monday to check on you. No arguments about that, because it's happening."

Smiling, Greg swiped Adrian's iced tea and drank deeply before handing it back. "Deal."

The second Adrian walked into DogOpolis at lunchtime on Monday, the thing's energy slammed into his mind like a runaway truck.

The demon—he no longer doubted the truth of it— hammered at his psychic shields with such strength his knees wanted to give under the pressure. He kept his eyes open and his feet moving forward by sheer willpower. It seemed incredible to him that no one else noticed the malignant force so thick in the air Adrian found it hard to breathe. When a thing became this powerful, he couldn't help thinking that even non-psychics ought to sense it.

Thankfully, the place was less crowded than usual for lunchtime on a Monday. The cold front bringing the weekend rain had moved to the east, meaning every Chapel Hill resident not stuck inside working was spending their afternoon outdoors. Adrian made his way to the counter on shaky legs and tried to lean against it without looking like that's what he was doing.

Apparently he didn't succeed very well, considering the frown on Denise's face when she approached him. "Hi. Adrian, right? Are you okay?"

"Um. Yeah. Just a little tired, is all. Didn't get much sleep last night." It was true, even though his dads had both banned him from the investigation the previous night since he had lab time and a class to teach today. Not that he'd missed anything, apparently. His dad said the third night had been just as quiet as the first two, the only sign of the entity being the faint residual Sam and Cecile were still able to pick up if they concentrated. He forced a smile and hoped it didn't look as pained as he feared. "Uh. Can I get a couple of salsa verde dogs and some O chips, please? And a Dr. Pepper. Oh, and if Greg's not too busy, I'd like to see him for a minute."

"Sure." She studied him with transparent alarm for a moment, then strode off toward the back, presumably to put in his order and fetch Greg. Hopefully without saying anything about how Adrian was acting weird.

A couple of minutes later, Greg came out to the front with a tray of hot dogs, chips and two drinks. His expression told Adrian he was in trouble. Greg skirted the counter and leaned close. "Can you get to the table by yourself?"

"Yes." Adrian peered at Greg's blank face and wide, frightened gray eyes and knew he wasn't about to hear anything encouraging. His heart lurched. "Greg—"

"In a minute. Come on."

Greg headed toward a table in the corner, as far away from everyone else as he could get. Adrian trailed behind, feeling cold inside.

They sat beside one another, as they often did. No one would think anything of it, and it made talking easier. Adrian slipped an arm around Greg's waist, pulled him close and kissed him. "Are you all right?"

"Yeah. I'm fine." He peered at Adrian with concern. "Are *you?*"

"Well..." Adrian shook his head when Greg's eyes went wide. "I'm okay. Tell me what's going on here. You look stressed."

Greg sighed, sat back and crunched on an O chip. His gaze darted around the restaurant like he expected the demon to show itself any moment. "I think this thing's gotten worse. It's completely insane today."

Adrian tightened his arm around Greg, as if he could protect him that way. "What's happened?"

"The usual, only *more*, you know? Like I hear growling noises instead of just whispers, and I keep seeing a solid figure at the corner of my eye instead of just shadows. And I swear I felt something push me one time." Greg shook his head. "I don't know. Maybe I'm only imagining things are worse." He dropped his voice to a whisper. "I'm not imagining anything, am I?"

God, Adrian wished he could tell Greg everything was in his head. It wouldn't necessarily make him feel any better to think his grip on reality might be slipping, but at least he wouldn't have to fear for his physical safety. They'd promised to be truthful with one another no matter what, though, and downplaying what was happening here wouldn't help Greg anyway.

Especially if Greg was at the center of it all.

Adrian didn't want to think about that.

He leaned his head on Greg's. "You're not imagining things. The energy here is definitely stronger today. I can barely hold it back."

"Shit." Greg turned to stare at him with alarm plain on his face. "You shouldn't be here. What if it gets past your shields?"

"It won't." Adrian sounded more confident than he felt, but he still believed his words to be true. He wouldn't knowingly risk his mind unless Greg's life was at stake, and if he was honest with himself, he didn't think things had come to that point. "But I know I can't stay for a long time."

"No kidding." Greg picked up one of the chili cheese dogs he'd made for himself and bit off a good third of it. He chewed for a few seconds, took a sip of whatever soda he'd filled his thirty-two-ounce cup with and swallowed. "What did they find last night?"

"Same as before. Nothing." Adrian popped a chip into his mouth. "They're not going tonight. Sam and I will come over here to check out the place after you leave like we talked about yesterday, then we're going to get together and review the evidence. We'll see if anything shows up."

"But it's here now. Stronger than ever." Greg tore off another bite of his dog. He ate silently for a few seconds, an unhappy crease digging into his forehead. "It's coming from me. It *has* to be."

A one-two punch of empathy and demon power squeezed Adrian's chest. He shook it off and did his best to answer without sounding breathless. "We don't know that." He leaned closer before Greg's suspicious look could develop into recognition of exactly how difficult a time Adrian was having keeping the entity at bay right now. "I don't sense it any stronger here next to you than I did when I first walked in."

"Then why do you look like you're about to pass out right now?" Greg drew back and pinned him with a half-sad, half-terrified gaze. "Let's face it, Adrian. I have a fucking demon attached to me. I don't know how I got it or where it came from, but there it is." Stuffing the last of his hot dog in his mouth, he chomped on it with an anger Adrian figured was directed more at the demon than the food. When he finished, he gulped some of his drink, planted both elbows on the table and covered his face with his hands. "Shit. What the hell do we do?"

Feeling helpless in the face of Greg's distress, Adrian pressed a kiss to the side of his head. "I know you're afraid. But I really think assuming that this entity's attached to you is premature, no matter how obvious it might seem to you." He answered Greg's glower with the best smile he could muster. "Whatever the case, we'll get to the bottom of it. And you know I'll do everything in my power to protect you. I'd rather die than let anything happen to you."

Greg's expression softened into the sweet smile that always did funny things to Adrian's insides. "I know. But you better not let anything happen to yourself either. I'd be pretty pissed off at you if you died trying to keep me from getting hurt."

Adrian laughed. "I'll do my best."

"Good." Tilting his head, Greg kissed Adrian's lips. The contact, brief though it was, quieted the buzz of energy in Adrian's head a little. Greg leaned back in his seat and pointed at Adrian's still-untouched dogs. "I'm leaving my wallet here, in my locker. You and Sam can come over and pick it up for me, and bring it to the theater if you don't mind. And you can tell me what you find out, because I won't be able to wait until I get home to hear it."

"I know." Adrian crunched a chip. "I really feel like whatever this thing is, it'll still be here after you leave. I don't think it's you, Greg."

"We'll see, I guess." Greg didn't seem convinced, but he smiled anyway. "Now eat your lunch and get out of here. Or do you need it to go?"

To go would probably be a good idea, but Adrian didn't want to leave. Not yet. Not with fear still pulling at the skin around Greg's eyes in spite of his smile.

"No, I'm fine. I'll stay here with you and eat." He picked up one of his salsa verde dogs and tried to take as big a bite as Greg. He fell short by a couple of inches.

Greg shook his head. "Some guys just can't swallow as much wiener as others."

"Hmm." Adrian finished chewing his mouthful, then leaned close to Greg's ear. "Depends on the wiener."

Greg snickered. Smiling, Adrian took another bite.

Greg's happy glow lasted for nearly half an hour after Adrian left. Then the growls and whispers, the cold fingers that weren't really there, and especially the black figure hovering at the edge of his vision, dragged his spirit back down into the depths again. He resumed his place at the hot dog assembly station next to Malachi and tried to resist the urge to look over his shoulder every few seconds.

"They got *nothing* last night. Not a damn thing." Greg took several packs of thawed dogs of several varieties out of the fridge, carried them over to the oven and started loading it from the back. He figured it said something profound about his mood at this point that he didn't even consider cracking a joke about wieners up the rear. "I mean, they still have to review the evidence, but Adrian says when they don't see or hear *anything* and don't pick up any psychic vibes, then they usually don't get any hits on evidence either."

At the counter beside him, Mal let out what Greg chose to interpret as a sympathetic noise. "Well, maybe that's good. Right?" He darted Greg a cautious sidelong glance while he loaded the paper hot dog trays into their holder. "I mean, maybe the you-know-what's moved on."

Greg resisted the urge to roll his eyes, but it was a near thing. He didn't exactly *regret* having told Mal what he found out about the possibility of a demon hanging around here. He'd started to think maybe it hadn't been his best idea ever, though. Mal had been jumpy as a kangaroo ever since he'd mentioned it.

Good thing he hadn't said anything about his theory that the demon was attached to him. Mal might run away screaming.

"Seriously? C'mon, Mal." Greg dropped a tofu dog on the floor. "Fucking shit on a stick."

Mal laughed. "Don't say that too loud, someone'll want to sell it."

"You are a gross and disgusting person." Squatting on the floor, Greg picked up the wiener, dropped it in the trash, rose and changed his gloves. "Anyhow, you know as well as I do that it's not gone. You feel it too."

"Okay, yeah. You're right." An order popped up on the terminal screen in front of them. Mal glanced up at it. "Beef wiener on a wheat roll."

Greg fetched the requisite wiener and roll from the ovens, put them together in a paper holder and handed the hot dog to Mal. He topped it with mustard and onions, then set it on the order shelf. "Order up!"

As Crystal fetched the order and went back to the front, the ominous shape darted at the edge of Greg's vision. He clutched the counter and ordered himself not to turn around, even though he felt the cold at his back. At least the goddamn thing didn't growl at him this time.

Mal stared at Greg. His eyes were wide with transparent anxiety. "Does it feel cold to you?"

"Yeah." Icy breath touched the side of Greg's neck. He jumped. A low voice hissed in his ear before moving away. He sagged, shaking all over. "Fuck. It's getting really bad, Mal."

"I noticed." Another order appeared on the screen—two chipotle dogs and a plain one with just ketchup. Mal bumped Greg's shoulder with his. "Go take a break. I got this one."

The suggestion put Mal up a few notches in Greg's estimation, since Mal would be alone with the demon if Greg took a break right now. Well, if said demon were not attached to Greg, which of course Mal didn't know about, so it was still a damn brave thing for him to say. God, Greg would love to get away from all the weirdness for a few minutes. But it wouldn't do any good. He'd just take it with him, since the thing was riding him like a fucking horse. Even if it wasn't, he couldn't run off and take a break while all his friends were still here with an honest-to-Pete demon. If he left and something horrible happened to his friends while he was gone, he'd never forgive himself.

While he stood there lost in indecision, Len emerged from the office, looking tired and pasty with exhaustion. She gave Greg a wan smile on her way to the drink machine.

Greg watched her pour herself a soda, speak to Denise, then head back to the office. She didn't look strong enough to defend herself against a harsh word, never mind a demon attack. Which sort of made up Greg's mind for him. "If you're sure it's okay, Mal, I think I'll go talk to Len. I need to ask her about my schedule."

Mal gave him a pitying look. "That's not exactly what I meant by taking a break, but sure. Go on."

"Thanks." Greg stripped off his gloves, tossed them in the trash and crossed the kitchen to Len's office.

"I'm busy," she called when he knocked.

Greg cursed under his breath. Crap. Whenever she said that, it meant she was in a bad mood, which meant he probably wouldn't get what he wanted. Oh well, nothing ventured, nothing gained and all that. "I have something important to ask you. It won't take but a minute."

Her aggravated sigh came right through the thin door. "All right. Come on in. But make it fast."

He walked into the room, wracking his brain for the best way to ask what he needed to ask. He flashed his best smile. "Hi. That's a really nice necklace. Is it new?" He gestured at the cameo hanging around her neck. He'd only seen her wear it in the last couple of weeks.

"It is, yes. Thanks." She raised her eyebrows at him. "So? What'd you want to know?"

He studied her face. She tapped her fingernails on the desk, radiating impatience. Deciding he might as well just spit it out and hope for the best, Greg squared his shoulders. "I need to take some time off."

"So fill out the vacation form like everybody else." She frowned. "What the hell, Greg? You know how this works."

He kept going before he could lose his nerve. "Now. I need time off now."

She blinked. "Now? Like *now*?"

"Yeah." He twisted his fingers together. "In fact, I really think I ought to leave right away."

The irritation on her face morphed into concern. "Oh my God, Greg, you're not sick, are you?"

"No." The minute he said it, Greg wished he'd lied instead. Len would never let him off without a compelling reason, and he could hardly tell her the *real* reason he had to stay away from here. "I mean, not like *that*. But—"

She held up a hand. He shut up. She stared straight into his eyes. "Greg. Are you dying?"

"No."

"Having major surgery?"

"Well, no, but—"

"What about Adrian? Is he sick? Dying? Having surgery?"

Greg thought about saying yes, but he knew he'd never get away with it. He sighed. "No, he's not. His dads aren't either. Nobody I know or love is dying or having surgery."

"Then why are you asking me to give you an unspecified amount of time off, starting right now this minute?"

Greg peered into her tired, annoyed face and had no idea what to say. But what could he do? Every second he spent here put Len and everyone else in danger.

Frustrated and afraid, he rubbed his hands over his face. "Look, I can't explain what it's all about. I'm sorry. But I have to have some time away from here. It's not just important for me, it's important for everyone. I know that sounds crazy, but it's true." He leaned both palms on the desk and aimed his best pleading look at Len. "Please, Len. *Please*. I'm begging."

She watched him for a long, thoughtful moment. "I don't know what's going on with you. But okay. I can give you a week of paid time off, then you can take some unpaid time after that if you can come up with an acceptable reason according to the company rulebook."

Greg's knees sagged in relief. "Thank you."

"Sure thing." She reached over to touch his hand. "I can't let you go today, though. We're already one short with Jolissa out sick and you know Monday afternoons have been busy lately with the campus crowd."

"Oh." Swallowing his disappointment, he forced a smile. After all, she'd given him more than he'd expected. "Okay, that's fair." He grasped her hand in both of his and squeezed it, then let go and backed out of the office. "Thanks again."

He shut the door on her startled expression and strode past his coworkers without looking at them.

When Greg returned to the assembly station, Mal stopped dicing tomatoes to stare at him. "What's wrong?"

Dammit. Kicking himself into actor mode, Greg wrinkled his nose. "Boss-lady is *not* in the mood for a chat about time off right now." Greg took a fresh pair of food-prep gloves from the box on the counter and pulled them on. "But I got some of what I asked for, and I found out she has a new necklace. So it wasn't a total waste."

Mal laughed. "Awesome."

"Yeah." Something shuffled behind Greg. He stiffened in knee-jerk alarm until he heard Dex call to Eden, then relaxed. The front door opened, admitting at least a dozen middle-aged men and women. A group of college kids entered right behind them. "And the after-lunch rush begins. Hope you're ready to put together some dogs."

"Better hope you can keep up with me, man." Setting his knife aside, Mal scooped the tomatoes into their designated bin. He bumped Greg's arm with his. "Hang in there, G."

The fact that Mal didn't actually know what Greg was going through made his support mean even more. Greg shot his friend a grateful smile. "Thanks."

He set his hands on autopilot and turned his brain to the problem of the demon. Not that he expected to figure out a way to rid himself of it while assembling hot dogs, but trying had to be better than standing here and taking it.

An hour and a half later, he still hadn't budged from his spot except to fetch more wieners and buns once. Customers had been trickling in ever since those first two large groups arrived, and now the place was packed with what seemed like every freshman on the UNC campus.

Greg didn't mind. The good thing about being super busy—other than getting through the day faster—was that he no longer had much time to notice the black figure lingering in his peripheral vision, or the low, sinister whispers in his ear. At least the thing no longer seemed interested in touching him.

"I'm going to get more relish." Mal took off his gloves and tossed them in the trash can. "Anything else we need from the fridge area?"

Greg glanced into the warming ovens. "We're good for wieners. Might need more buns soon."

"Okay. I'll go ahead and grab your buns." Mal grabbed a double handful of Greg's butt and squeezed, then headed for the other side of the kitchen, laughing.

Greg shook his head. "You're just disappointed you didn't get to grab my wieners, pervert."

"Plural. You and Adrian must have an interesting sex life."

The mental picture made Greg laugh. "I am *so* telling Adrian this story."

Mal snickered, which was par for the course, but he was looking out front, which was strange. He answered Greg's question before he could ask it. "Your other boyfriend's here."

133

"Fantastic." Greg looked. Jon's gaze locked with his. Jon smiled and waved. Unable to make himself act like a total ass, Greg waved back and even managed an anemic smile. He ducked as far out of sight as possible the second Denise distracted Jon by taking his order. "Why the hell can't he go eat someplace else?"

"C'mon, everyone knows if you want dogs you gotta go to DogO." Grinning, Mal slapped Greg on the back. "Don't worry, I won't let him molest you."

Greg's smartass reply was cut off by a sharp exclamation from Len, who'd pulled Dex off fryer duty and taken it over herself when he'd fallen behind in the after-lunch rush. Setting his half-built chili-cheese dog on the counter, Greg hurried to where Len stood rubbing the back of one shoulder. Mal followed, looking worried.

"Len?" Greg started to touch her and pulled his hand away when she jumped. He frowned. "You okay?"

"Yeah. Fine. Just got a twinge in my arm." She stared up at Greg with wide eyes, her chest rising and falling with breaths coming way too fast. "My neck's been hurting a lot lately. The doctor said I probably have a pinched nerve."

Greg studied her face. She looked as if she hadn't slept in about a week, and she was twitchy enough that he questioned the wisdom of her working with hot oil. She was stubborn and contrary as hell when she felt like her abilities were being called into question, but he had to try. "You want me to do the fryer? Hot dog assembly would probably be easier on your neck and arm."

She glared at him. Glanced at the fryer, then at Mal, who gave her a shrug-and-nod combination that Greg assumed meant he agreed with Greg's assessment of the situation. She sighed. "Yeah, okay, we'll switch." Behind her, the fryer beeped. She started, though she had to have been expecting it. "Just let me get this load of chips out, and you can put the next one in, okay?"

Len turned back to the fryer and took hold of the basket handle to remove it from the oil. Greg felt an icy hand at his neck and heard a growl he wished didn't sound so damn familiar. The air between him and Len dimmed with a black fog.

Beside him, he heard Mal as if from far away, wondering what the hell was going on. Greg lunged for Len, to keep whatever was about to happen from happening.

Too late. His hand closed over Len's wrist as the oil in the vat bubbled up and over and hit them both in a scalding wave.

Chapter Eight

Agony like nothing Greg had ever felt before paralyzed him, stole his breath and held him silent while Len screamed, the sound raw with pain and terror. Mal yanked them both away from the bubbling vat and pulled them toward the break room, shouting for someone, anyone, to call 911 and get some cold water.

In the break room, Mal shoved Len into a chair and started unbuttoning her shirt. "Stop it," he ordered when she shoved at his hands, sobbing. "You're burned, Len. We need to get this off you, if we can. The paramedics are on the way, Denise is calling them."

She moaned, her face contorted. "Oh my God. Hurts."

"I know, hon. I know." Mal opened Len's uniform shirt and let out a hiss. The skin on her stomach and over the swell of her breasts hung in ragged strips from dark crimson splotches. "Jesus."

Greg staggered over on shaking legs and dropped into one of the other chairs. "Mal. Her hand."

Mal looked and went pale. Len's right hand and her arm nearly up to the elbow were burned a deep, angry crimson and covered with raw blisters. The fingers had begun to swell. Mal swallowed. "Okay. Hopefully somebody's gonna be bringing me some cold water to flush these wounds until the ambulance gets here." He glanced down at Greg's hand. "You're burned pretty bad too, Greg. That's going to need cold water. Can you do it, or do you need somebody to help you?"

Greg didn't want to look at his left hand, but he did it anyway. The burn was smaller than it felt—an irregular blotch about six inches long and three inches wide at its widest point, stretching from the web between his thumb and forefinger along the back of his wrist and up his forearm. It was ugly, though, every bit as red, weepy and swollen as Len's.

His stomach tried to climb out his throat. He forced it back in place through sheer willpower and nodded. "I can do it. Take care of Len. She's burned really bad."

"Yeah." Mal eyed Greg with obvious concern. "Don't try to be a hero, G. Let someone help you, if you need it."

"I'll be fine. Honest."

He was saved from Mal's disbelief with the arrival of Denise with a long hose in hand. To his surprise, Jon trailed behind her. Denise started talking before he had a chance to ask what the hell Jon was doing back here. "Okay, Jon here attached the hose to the kitchen faucet for me. Dex! Turn it on!" She held the hose over Len's chest. If the sight of the burns bothered her, Greg couldn't tell. "Okay, Len, this is going to be cold. It's probably going to hurt at first. Just bear with me, okay? Hopefully it'll help. And we'll do your hand next."

Len's eyelids fluttered, but she didn't answer. Her face was white, her forehead beaded with sweat. Then the water hit her. Her eyes popped open and she let out a cry.

Greg wanted to stay and make sure she was okay, partly because she seemed about to slip into shock any second and partly because in spite of what he'd told Mal, he wasn't sure he could stand up. But Jon was walking toward him looking scared and determined, and Greg thought he knew what was coming next.

Sure enough, Jon bent to gently take Greg's good arm. "Come on. I'll help you get that burn flushed out with cold water."

The part of Greg that had been semi-stalked by Jon for weeks didn't want to go. But the pain in his hand had gone from merely excruciating to unbearable. The more he considered it, the more it made sense that a nice stream of icy water might douse the fire sizzling inside his skin. Besides, he couldn't deny Jon was being nice, even if he was acting a little bit...guilty, almost?

All the times Jon had stared at Greg during rehearsal flashed through his mind, along with the weird things he'd almost-seen from the tail of his eye at the theater. Nothing quite hooked up in his head, but he couldn't dismiss the link he thought he could see if he squinted.

The throbbing in his hand insisted he leave the detective work for later. He glanced up at Jon. "Okay. Thanks."

Pushing to his feet with Jon's help, he let Jon slip an arm around him and lead him to the bathroom at the rear of the break room. Inside, Jon turned on the cold water and Greg held his hand under the faucet.

The paramedics arrived a couple of minutes later. They looked at Len first and promptly got a stretcher in there to take her to the hospital. Greg was a little surprised when they wanted to take him in too.

"It's just that one spot," he argued, holding up his hand to prove his point. "Can't you just wrap it up and let me go home?"

The middle-aged man who'd examined Greg shook his head and manhandled Greg's hand back into position for treatment. "This is a second-degree burn. The ED doc'll most likely treat you and release you to home, but they'll probably want to debride this wound first."

Greg frowned. "That sounds unpleasant."

"It basically means cleaning it out, taking out any dead tissue and foreign material—stuff that doesn't belong there and might cause an infection, that is. Then they'd give you a dose or two of IV antibiotics, possibly a prescription for antibiotic pills to take for a while, depending on if they think you need it or not, and send you on your way." The man smiled, reminding Greg of Sam for a second. "They'll give you a prescription for pain pills regardless. I *know* you're going to need that. So you might want to stop trying to talk us out of taking you in."

"Not that you can," said the man's partner, a woman of very few words indeed. "We're ready to role, Charlie. Malachi here says no one else was injured."

"Okay." Charlie secured the damp gauze around Greg's hand and wrist, then stood. "Greg, if you want to call anyone to meet you at the hospital, you can do it now while we're taking you out to the ambulance."

Greg kept his humiliation at being strapped onto a damn gurney to himself. At least they were letting him call Adrian. He pulled his pod out of his pocket. Seeing Mal watching him, he held out his good hand. "Mal. Thanks, man."

A smile curved Mal's lips. He took Greg's hand and bent for a hug. "Sure. Be good, G. Let me know how it goes."

"I will. Bye." He watched Mal turn and walk out of the break room, then twisted around enough to look at Jon, who stood silently out of the way. "Thanks, Jon. I appreciate it."

Jon flushed pink. He shrugged, his gaze not quite meeting Greg's. "No problem. We actors should always help each other out."

Greg's sense of something off about Jon intensified, but he was out of time to think about it, even if he felt like mulling it over right then, which he didn't. He hit Adrian's speed-dial number on his pod while Charlie and the silent woman raised his gurney and wheeled him toward the employee entrance.

God, he hoped Adrian hadn't noticed Greg had been messing with his pod again. This was one time Greg really needed the damn thing to ring.

The key to Adrian's difficulties with his quantum level equations came to him in a burst of inspiration during his afternoon lab time. He was so swept up in the excitement of seeing the waveforms correct themselves before his eyes on the giant touchscreen workboard that he ignored the Ice Cream Truck music coming from his pocket when he first heard it.

It took him a moment to remember that was the ringtone Greg kept setting for himself every time he got into Adrian's pod.

Dropping the stylus in its tray, Adrian snatched his pod out of his jeans pocket and hit the answer button in one movement. "Greg? What's wrong? Do I need to come back there?"

"No, not here. I don't have but a minute to talk, just...shit..."

Adrian heard a rustling noise, then Greg's muffled voice saying something Adrian couldn't make out. In the background, he heard a woman crying. He sat on the chair he kept beside the equation board for thinking purposes, his pulse racing. "Greg? Are you there? What's happened?"

"I'm here. Crystal was upset, I needed to talk to her for a sec."

"Why's she upset? What's going on?"

"There was an accident with the fryer. Len was burned pretty badly, and I got a bad-enough burn on my hand that they're taking me to the hospital to get it checked out."

Adrian's heart slammed into his throat. "Oh my God." He jumped to his feet, spun around and saved his equations, then shut down the workboard. "Where are they taking you? The university hospital ER?"

"Yeah. They're loading me in the ambulance now. We should be there in a few minutes."

Greg's voice was tight with pain, and Adrian wanted nothing more than to teleport to his side and make everything better, somehow. Unfortunately, he was only human, which meant he had to do it the hard way. "I'll meet you there. Should I go home and get the car? Will they send you home from the ER, do you think?"

"Probably. Sorry you have to walk home."

"Stop that. You know I don't mind."

"Yeah. I know." Greg let out a soft sound that made Adrian move faster, the better to get to Greg's side sooner. "Ugh. Damn. I'll see you soon. Love you."

"Love you too. Hang in there."

The connection died. Adrian stuck his pod back in his pocket, grabbed his keys off the desk and ran out the door.

The last thing he expected when he arrived at the emergency room was the pulse of furious energy slamming against his psychic shields. He stumbled to a chair and collapsed into it, his vision blurred and his breath coming short. What the hell? Why was he feeling the strange negative energy from DogOpolis *here*?

Maybe because Greg was right. Maybe because it's been him all along.

Which didn't explain the whole thing, and he knew it. But neither did it discount it. If Dean's theory about higher EMF levels making it easier to sense the entity was true, this could happen whenever Greg went somewhere with even a mildly elevated EMF. It stood to reason that a place with as much equipment as an emergency room might have a raised EMF level.

Closing his eyes, Adrian forced himself to take slow, deep breaths. He visualized his shields as a solid steel wall, tall as the sky and as wide as the world. When he could sense the energy without being overwhelmed by it, he opened his eyes again.

The woman at the triage desk had finished with the person she'd been talking to when he walked in and was watching him with a frown. Pushing to his feet, he strode over to her and asked the question foremost on his mind before she could say a word. "Can you tell me where Greg Woodhall is, please? I'm his partner, Adrian Broussard. He was injured at work, and he called to tell me the ambulance was bringing him here."

She gave him an assessing look. "Hang on." She entered what Adrian assumed was Greg's name into the computer interface. "Yes, they brought him in a few minutes ago. They told me to send you right back when you got here." She arched an eyebrow at him. "Apparently your guy was very vocal about wanting you there with him for whatever they have to do, or he was leaving."

Adrian managed to resist covering his face with his hand, but just barely. "Yeah, that sounds like him."

Smiling, she handed him a clip-on badge with *visitor* printed on it in bold letters. "Here. Put this on your shirt and keep it on. I'll get somebody to take you back." She pushed her rolling chair away from the desk to an open door behind her and leaned around the doorframe. "Hey, Clive? Can you take Mr. Broussard back to room 27, please? He's here for Greg Woodhall."

A smiling older man in a Carolina-blue Volunteer vest emerged from the room and gestured to Adrian. "Come on with me, sir."

Adrian followed the man—Clive—through a set of double doors, through the large, bustling emergency department to a door in the back corner. All the while, the weird energy sizzled at the edge of his mind. It frightened him, because keeping his shields up against it took far more deliberate concentration than it should have. He hadn't had to work this hard at fighting off a paranormal presence since he'd helped Sam push back the otherdimensional beings and close the portal between their two worlds when he was eleven.

Clive rapped on the door, pushed it open and peered inside. "Mr. Woodhall? Your partner's here." He held open the door for Adrian.

"Thank you." Adrian managed a smile as he went inside the tiny room. Clive nodded and walked off.

Greg lay on a narrow stretcher, his face pale and pinched, his left hand bandaged to a few inches above the wrist and an IV running into the bend of his right arm. His lips curved into an anemic version of his usual sunny grin. "Hey, Adrian."

"Greg. Oh, my God." Hurrying to his side, Adrian bent over the bed and planted a gentle kiss on Greg's mouth. "Are you okay? Are you in a lot of pain?"

"Yeah to both. It's not that big of a burn, but man, it hurts like a bitch." Greg let out a deep sigh as Adrian settled himself on the edge of the stretcher and took Greg's uninjured hand. "Len was burned pretty bad, though. It got her right arm almost to the elbow, plus part of her chest and stomach. I don't know much about that sort of stuff, but her arm and hand looked really bad. I'm seriously worried about her."

"God. Poor Len." Inside Adrian's head, the energy beat against his mind like metaphysical fists. He clung to Greg's

143

hand and blinked until the fog cleared from his vision. "What...what happened, exactly?"

Greg fixed him with a narrow-eyed stare. "You're feeling something right now."

Shit. "Listen—"

"Don't bullshit me. I know that look." Greg struggled to sit up, cursed at his bandages, the IV tubing, heart monitor and oxygen tubing crisscrossing his torso, found the bed controls and pushed the button to raise the head. "What're you feeling, Adrian? And don't even try to tell me nothing because I know better."

Adrian studied Greg's determined expression and decided he might as well come clean now and avoid the whole song and dance. With a glance over his shoulder at the half-open door to make sure no one was listening in, he leaned closer and dropped his voice. "It's the same energy from DogOpolis."

Greg's eyes saucered. "You're sure?"

"Positive." The pressure in the air thickened, pulsed, hammered against Adrian's mental walls until he feared they might collapse. He pictured the earth rising up, molten rock pouring over the vast metal barrier that represented his psychic shields and hardening into an impenetrable obsidian. Instantly, the throb in his head eased and he could think again. He met Greg's worried gaze and squeezed his hand. "It's stronger than before. *Much* stronger. Even stronger than it was earlier today. I don't know how or why, but it is. I'm having trouble holding my psychic shields against it."

"Fuck." Greg stared at Adrian with wide, frightened eyes. "It's me. I knew it."

"We don't know that." Greg gave him a *don't be stupid* look, and Adrian sighed. "Look, I know you're convinced it's you, and I'll admit it looks bad, but the evidence is all circumstantial."

Greg sank back against the pillows, his expression thoughtful. "Okay, this is gonna sound dumb, but do you think there's any way one person can, like, give a demon to another person?"

Adrian wondered how much pain medicine Greg had taken already. "What?"

"See, here's the thing." Greg glanced around as though he expected someone to be hiding in the corner eavesdropping. His voice fell to a whisper. "Jon was there today. He was *staring* at me when this happened. And then he came back into the break room to help take care of me and Len, and he acted *guilty*." He raised his eyebrows in clear expectation.

Adrian didn't quite know what to say. *You've taken paranoia to a whole new level* didn't seem like something Greg would react to well, even under the influence of narcotics.

The demon saved him from answering by crashing into his shields with the force of a wrecking ball. He staggered and fell into the recliner beside the stretcher.

"Adrian?" Greg leaned over the gurney railing, fear and worry stamped into every line of his face. "Shit, are you all right?"

Adrian nodded, even though his head ached with the effort of holding back the power trying to get in. "Yeah, I'm okay."

The look in Greg's eyes said he saw right through Adrian's lie. "You have to get out of here."

"What? No!" Adrian shook his head. "I didn't want to leave you earlier, no way am I leaving you now."

"But if it's weakening your shields—"

"I'm having trouble. But I can hold it." Adrian wished he were as certain as he sounded, but he wasn't about to tell Greg that. "I am absolutely *not* leaving you here with this thing when you're injured and not as able to look after yourself as usual."

He almost mentioned Len, who was extremely vulnerable in her current weakened state, but thought better of it. Since Greg believed the demon was attached to him, he'd no doubt believe himself responsible for her injuries. Adrian would rather not put the idea in Greg's head if it wasn't already there.

Greg darted a nervous glance around the room, as if he could see whatever it was Adrian felt. "You think it caused the accident, right? I do."

Instinct told Adrian it had, but the scientist in him reminded him not to jump to conclusions. "I don't know. What happened, exactly?"

"I'm not sure. It all happened really fast. Len was on fryer duty, and I offered to switch with her because her arm and neck were bothering her. She went to take the basket out of the fryer when it was done, and I..." Greg shook his head, his brow scrunched in thought. "I felt something touch me. Something cold. And I thought I heard a voice in my ear. Everything went kind of dark and foggy, and I got this *feeling* like something really bad was going to happen. So I went to grab Len to get her away from the fryer, and the oil in the vat just"—he made a mushrooming gesture with both hands—"boiled over. Not even like regularly boiling, it was like it *jumped* out of the vat like a wave. It hit both of us, but it got Len *way* worse than it got me."

Fear dried Adrian's mouth and kicked his heartbeat into a nauseating gallop. If this entity, whatever it was, could manipulate matter with an intent to harm, then Greg was in serious danger here. Adrian wanted to scoop Greg into his arms and run. Get him away from the raging energy still tearing doggedly at Adrian's shields.

The problem was, if this entity had truly attached itself to Greg, they couldn't get away from it that way. Also, if Dean's EMF theory was correct, Adrian couldn't even count on his abilities to sense the thing.

There was also the small matter of Greg's burn, which not only still had to be treated, but might leave Greg more open to attack by weakening his natural defenses. So Adrian kept his butt firmly parked at Greg's side and his attention fixed on the thing in his head.

"This isn't exactly a scientific conclusion, but it does sound to me as if this energy might have had something to do with what happened. At least, it's a possibility we can't dismiss." Adrian scooted forward in the chair and took Greg's good hand before his stricken expression could become verbal self-blame. "Listen to me. I'm still not entirely convinced this entity is attached to you. But even if it is, and even if it caused the fryer accident—which is still a big *if*, you know—no one in their right mind could possibly consider what happened to Len your fault. It would be the *demon's* fault, no matter how you look at it. Okay?"

Greg didn't seem entirely convinced, but he nodded. He lay back, gray eyes full of sadness.

Keeping hold of Greg's hand, Adrian fished his pod out of his jeans pocket. "I'm going to call my dad and Sam. I think they should know about this, and I'd really like Sam's opinion about the energy here in the ER."

He'd barely finished his sentence when a man and a woman in scrubs walked into the room. The woman, a tall, keen-eyed person with neat cornrows and a rumpled white jacket, gave them a friendly smile. "Hello, gentlemen. I'm Dr. Wright, the trauma surgeon. Greg, I believe you've already met your nurse, Miguel."

The young man behind Dr. Wright grinned as he moved to the shelf beside Greg's bed and began taking down supplies. "Dr. Wright's going to have a look at your hand now, Greg. I brought some morphine for you. I'm gonna give you that first, if that's okay. It'll help keep the pain under control."

Greg shot a decidedly unenthusiastic look in Adrian's direction. "I don't know."

"I think you should." Adrian pressed Greg's fingers and tried to convey his true meaning with his expression. "This is likely to be painful otherwise, and I really don't think the pain medicine can hurt you. Okay?"

Greg peered at him for a long moment but finally nodded. "Okay."

Adrian smiled, a genuine one this time. Whether Greg was the entity's true focus or not, instinct told Adrian that calmness and quiet would help keep Greg safe.

Dr. Wright gave him a sharp look. "You must be Greg's partner."

"Um. Yeah." Rising to his feet, he held out his hand, hoping his nervousness didn't show too badly. "Adrian Broussard. I hope it's all right that I came on back. Greg needs me here."

Smiling, she grasped his hand in a firm grip and shook. "It's fine. It's good for our patients to have their loved ones at their side." She let his hand drop, her expression turning sober. "That said, I'm afraid we'll need for you to step out of the room while we examine Greg's hand." She turned her attention to Greg. "From what the paramedics told me, I expect we'll need to debride the wound—that is, clean out the dead tissue and any foreign material—and wash it out extensively. We may be able to do that here at the bedside, depending on how severe the burn is. If it's bad enough that I think you'll need surgery, we'll redress your hand and let you talk over your decision with Adrian and anyone else you wish to discuss it with first. All right?"

Greg nodded, gray eyes wide and face white. "Okay." He looked at Adrian with an expression full of barely hidden fear. "So. I guess I'll see you in a little bit."

Ignoring the other two people in the room, Adrian bent to kiss Greg, a slow, lingering kiss meant to communicate the depth of Adrian's love and reassure Greg that Adrian would be right outside the door the whole time.

"I love you," Adrian whispered when he drew back. He touched Greg's cheek. "I'll see you soon."

Greg smiled. "I love you too."

Walking out of that room was hard, but Adrian made himself do it. Three people guiding a stretcher nearly ran over him. He hopped out of the way, his pod still in hand, and almost tripped over a young woman pushing an elderly man in a wheelchair.

"Oh God. Sorry." He backed out of the way—glancing over his shoulder first to make sure he didn't run into anyone else— found a niche in the wall between two rooms, shoved himself into it and hit his dad's speed-dial number.

It rang five times before his father picked up. They must've been reviewing evidence or something. "Adrian? What's wrong?"

"Sorry to interrupt you, but there was an accident at Greg's work. He and Len were both burned. I'm at the hospital with Greg now."

"Oh God, Adrian. How bad is it? Is Greg going to be all right?" In the background, Adrian heard Sam's voice asking what was wrong, and Bo telling him Greg had been injured. "Are *you* all right, son? You sound...very stressed."

Adrian fought the completely inappropriate urge to laugh. "Yeah. Greg's burn is on his hand. He says it's not that bad, but I haven't seen it. The doctor's in there now looking at it and seeing if they can debride it there at the bedside or if they need to take him to surgery. He said Len's injuries were much worse."

"Poor Len. I'm glad Greg wasn't injured too badly, though." In the background, Cecile said something Adrian couldn't make out, then Dean. Sam's voice came through again, nearly obscured by shuffling noises. "Yes, I'll tell him. Adrian, Sam and I are coming over there. I hope you don't mind, but I think you should have your family with you right now."

A sudden swell of emotion cut through the constant pounding of dark energy in Adrian's head. Tears stung his eyes. He hung his head and blinked, embarrassed. "Thanks, Dad. I...I wanted you to come."

"I know, son." The connection went quiet for a second. "Something's wrong, isn't it? Besides what happened to Greg."

A man and a woman emerged from the room closest to Adrian. The woman was crying. The man gave him an unfriendly look. He walked away, moving along the row of rooms. "The energy Sam, Cecile and I felt at DogO? It's here."

Adrian's father didn't question him about it. Adrian was grateful for that. He knew his dad's thoughts were following the same path his own had a little while ago.

The energy kept getting stronger. Adrian focused all his concentration on his dad's voice coming over the pod. "Do you have any idea where it's coming from?"

He didn't ask out loud if Greg might be the source, but Adrian heard the question all the same.

"I can't tell for sure. I—"

A ragged female scream tore from the room just ahead of Adrian. At the same time, the energy battering Adrian's psychic shields exploded in his head like an invisible bomb. He clenched his teeth, locked his knees and remained grimly upright, his free hand on the wall and his eyes blinded by a gray fog. If Greg hadn't told him about having heard voices, Adrian would've sworn the growls and whispers in his ears were his imagination. But they weren't, any more than the surge of cold raising the hairs on his arms.

"Adrian? Adrian! What's happening? Are you all right? Please talk to me!"

His father's voice sounded frantic, and his pod felt as if he'd pressed it to his ear hard enough to break the skin. Adrian gave himself a mental shake. "I'm fine." He didn't sound fine at all. He sounded weak and terrified, but there was no help for it. At least he could talk now.

"What happened? I heard a woman scream, then you didn't say anything, and..." Bo drew a deep, shaking breath. "Tell me what's going on. We're on our way out of the hotel now. We should be there soon. You're at the university ER, right?"

"That's right. I felt a really strong pulse of the energy just now, when the woman in the room next to me screamed." Two nurses rushed past Adrian toward the room in question. Adrian plastered himself to the nurse's desk to get out of their way. The door opened. He caught a glimpse of the woman in the bed, and suddenly everything made sense. "Oh, my God."

"Adrian? What?"

The woman's gaze caught his as the door shut, and the naked terror there sent a hard chill up his spine. "It's Len, Dad. It's all coming from Len."

Chapter Nine

Adrian's dads arrived not ten minutes later, both wearing white visitor badges clipped to their shirts. Relieved, Adrian went straight to his father and hugged him hard. "Dad. Thanks for coming over."

"Of course. You know we're here for you and Greg, any time." Bo rubbed Adrian's back, grasped his shoulders and pushed him back enough to look into his eyes. "Are you all right, son? You're shaking."

"Oh." Adrian stared at his own trembling hand in surprise. "Yeah, I'm okay. It's just hard keeping my shields up against this thing."

"I can see why." Sam walked up, his gait slower than usual and an expression of deep concentration on his face. "I feel it. Its power's increased exponentially since the other day, but it's definitely the same thing." He laid a hand on Adrian's shoulder. "Where is Len? Do you think they'll let us see her?"

"She's in that room up there. Number 32." Adrian nodded toward the room, which was quiet now that they'd presumably given Len something to ease her pain and fear. "But I don't know if they'll let us go in. We're not family or anything."

"Hmm." Adrian's father scratched his chin. "Well, if we can't, we can't. I would've liked to speak with her before we see Greg, but—"

The door to Len's room opened. Adrian and his dads all fell silent. Two nurses rolled a stretcher out of the room. Len lay curled in the midst of the tangled sheets, her right arm bandaged to the elbow and more white gauze peeking out from the neck of a blue gown so big it made her look like a child. One large and two small IV bags dripped into her left arm through clear tubing. Her eyes were closed, her face grayish beneath her tan. She twitched and whimpered as if suffering a nightmare.

Judging by the tide of malignant energy that threatened to overwhelm him when she rolled by on her stretcher, Adrian thought *nightmare* might not be strong enough of a word.

Sam's hand tightened on Adrian's shoulder. "You're right," Sam whispered after the nurses rolled Len through the double doors and out of sight. "Whatever this thing is, it's attached to her."

Adrian's father glanced toward the hallway where they'd taken Len. "Any idea how? Or why?"

Sam shook his head. "There's no way to know for sure without speaking to her."

He and Bo both looked at Adrian. He leaned against the desk, fighting a wash of dizziness as the sense of the entity's presence seeped out of his head. "I'll ask Greg when he's able to talk to me. He might know something helpful. If not, he can help us get in to talk to her."

Not far away, the door to Greg's room swung open and Dr. Wright emerged. Sam glanced toward her. "We'll deal with it in a little while. Right now it looks like you need to go talk to the doctor."

Nodding, Adrian headed toward his lover's room with his dads beside him.

For Greg, the hours between the first shot of morphine in the ER and Adrian practically carrying him up the steps to their apartment passed in a haze. By the time Adrian got him settled on their sofa with a glass of iced tea in his hand, his head had begun to clear and he remembered some of the things that had happened well enough to wonder about them.

Greg waited until Adrian curled on the couch at his feet and Sam and Bo settled into the two chairs on the other side of the room before asking the question he'd been thinking about since they got home. "Okay, what's the deal with Len? I heard y'all talking about her in the ER. You think it's her, don't you? You think she's the one with the demon, not me?"

Adrian and his dads glanced at one another as if trying to decide what to say. Finally, Adrian rested a hand on Greg's knee and looked him in the eye. "When I left your room to call Dad, I went down the hall a bit because I was getting in people's way. I ended up going past Len's room, and I felt the energy stronger than ever then. I could tell it was coming from her somehow."

"Adrian was on the phone with Bo at the time," Sam explained. "He told Bo he thought the energy was coming from Len. When we got over there, I felt it also. It was extremely strong. The nurses took Len out of the ER room and wheeled her upstairs while we were there. They rolled her right past us." Leaning forward, Sam propped his elbows on his knees and peered at Greg with unnerving seriousness. "Greg, from the feel of the energy, I believe Adrian's right. Whatever this entity is, it's attached itself to Len."

Greg's chest tightened with a guilty mix of relief and dismay. "Crap. I'm glad it's not me, but I didn't want it to be somebody else instead. What's it doing to her?"

"It's hard to say without knowing exactly what it is." Sam's gaze slid sideways to Bo for a second before returning to Greg. "But I'm fairly certain that it's probably demonic, like you thought. Benign entities don't attach themselves to humans."

"Maybe it's a poltergeist." It wasn't and Greg knew it, but right now he really, really wanted to be wrong about this thing being a demon.

Sam shook his head. "I wish it were. If Len had undetected abilities causing poltergeist activity, helping her would be relatively easy. But we've been involved in many poltergeist cases, and I've never felt an energy like this before. It's definitely nonhuman."

"And it's not a ghost." Adrian rubbed his thumb in circles over Greg's kneecap, his face thoughtful. "Well, I should say it's not any form of human dead. Which is not to say it isn't some other type of spirit, I suppose."

"Well, you have those links I sent you on malevolent spirits. But the latest research I found said they can't cause physical harm, and this thing sure as fuck did. If it caused the fryer to boil over, and I really think it did." Greg reached for Adrian's hand and laced their fingers together. Fear for his friend formed a hard knot in his stomach.

"Unfortunately, Greg, you're correct about that. It does look as though we're dealing with something demonic." Kicking off his shoes, Bo curled his legs beneath him in his chair. "We'll need to talk to Len as soon as she's able."

Greg nodded. "I'll go see her tomorrow."

Adrian's hand tightened around his. "Greg, I don't know—"

"Babe, I love you, but I remember the nurse telling you I could go back to my regular activities as long as I keep my wound clean and the dressing dry and don't drive under the influence of pain meds. So don't tell me I can't go visit Len in the hospital." Greg raised his eyebrows at Adrian, who subsided with a smile. "As I was saying. I'll go talk to her tomorrow. What kind of stuff am I trying to find out?"

"Again, it's hard to say exactly." Bo rubbed his chin. "Has she been anywhere different? Met anyone new? Acquired anything new to her, especially something old or with a history? Has she done anything unusual lately, such as participate in a séance? No detail is too small. Not much is known about demonic entities, so we need to find out everything we can in order to figure out how this thing became attached to her."

The mental picture of him asking Len those questions wasn't pleasant. Greg groaned. "It's gonna be interesting thinking up a way to ask that without sounding like a nutcase."

Sam gave him a grim smile. "Welcome to the wonderful world of paranormal investigation."

Greg laughed. It sounded as weak and scared as he felt, but some of his tension dissipated along with it and he felt better. He lifted his bandaged hand in a clumsy salute. "About damn time."

Greg didn't think Adrian felt the weird energy when the two of them walked into the hospital lobby the next day. Unless he was hiding it really well. Adrian was certainly capable of faking if he felt like it. When they walked out of the elevator onto the floor where Len had been admitted the previous day, though, Greg saw the change in Adrian right away.

He took Adrian's hand in his unbandaged one. "Are you all right?"

Adrian nodded, though he sure as hell didn't look all right. "I'm fine. Which room's Len in?"

"Five-fifteen. Which you'd remember if you didn't have some freaky-ass demon thing sitting in your brain right now. The lady at the desk told us not two minutes ago." He pushed the down button on the elevator bank.

"I know, I know. I can handle it, though." Adrian frowned when the elevator opened. "Wait, what are you doing?"

"You're going down to the lobby while I talk to Len." Letting go of Adrian's hand, Greg gave him a push. "Go get a coffee. I'll meet you down there in a little bit."

Adrian caught himself with a hand on the elevator door. It started closing, hit his palm, opened again and beeped in protest. Adrian ignored it. "I don't want to leave you alone up here with that thing."

"Len's been living with it for..." Greg waved his good hand through the air in frustration. "I don't know how long. You can't be in there, Adrian. It's too much for you. I can't even feel it. That means I'm going in alone. Now stop arguing with me and go downstairs."

The elevator door started closing again. This time, Adrian got out of its way. Unfortunately—to Greg's mind—he stepped out of the elevator instead of into it, letting the door slide shut behind him. At least the obnoxious beeping stopped.

"I'll stay out here in the waiting room," Adrian said before Greg could do anything more than glare at him. "But I'm *not* going back down to the lobby and leaving you up here with that thing. And save the lectures about how Len's been living with it. I know that. We're here to try to fix that particular problem. That does not mean I'm willing to leave you here without any way of monitoring the situation."

A nurse walked by, casting them a curious glance. Greg led Adrian to the thankfully empty waiting room nearby. "I don't like it. It's pretty obvious you have a hard time shielding against this energy."

"I told you, I can handle it. Don't worry." Adrian's lips curled into the half-sweet, half-evil smile he knew damn well would make Greg do anything he wanted. "Go on and talk to

Len. I promise I'll go down to the lobby if it gets to be too much."

"Fuck." Hooking his uninjured hand around Adrian's neck, Greg pulled him close and kissed him. "Fine. If you need to leave, go downstairs then message me. I'll meet you there."

"Okay." Adrian touched his cheek. "Be careful. If things start getting weird, come get me, okay? Promise?"

Greg stared into Adrian's deadly serious brown eyes and nodded. "I will." He ran his fingers through Adrian's hair, just because he liked the silky feel of it, then let his hand drop. "Okay. See you in a few minutes."

Adrian didn't say anything, but Greg felt the weight of his gaze all the way to the turn of the hallway.

Len's room was the third one after he turned the corner. A sign on the closed door read "Contact Isolation" and warned him not to touch Len's wounds without wearing the special gown and gloves provided in dispensers on the wall. He didn't want to *look* at her burns again, never mind touch them, so he skipped the protective gear. He washed his hands with the antibacterial liquid provided, gathered his courage and knocked on the door.

"Come in."

Len sounded more or less normal. Tired and subdued, but Greg supposed he could hardly expect anything else. He pulled the door open, slipped inside and shut it behind him before he turned toward his friend.

She looked awful—pasty and clearly exhausted, black circles bruising the skin under her eyes. The bulky gauze bandages on her arm had been replaced by a thin gel-like covering. He figured the burns on her chest and abdomen were dressed with the same stuff.

He swallowed. "Hi, Len. How're you feeling?"

She gave him a wan smile. "Like crap. How about you?"

"I've decided burns hurt worse than anything else there is." Feeling slightly braver, Greg walked closer. He nodded toward the machine on the other side of the bed hooked to Len's good arm by a clear tubing. "Tell me that's pain medicine."

"Yeah. The big bag is fluid and the syringe in the machine is Dilaudid. It's a narcotic. It helps. The bandage helps too, actually. The doctor said it's got some kind of pain-relief thing in the gel as well as stuff to heal the burns." She held up her arm, studying it as if it was the most fascinating thing she'd ever seen. "It's pretty new. Just approved by the FDA. Apparently they've had really good results with this in healing second- and third-degree burns, as long as the third-degree burns aren't too extensive, and mine aren't, thank God. If it works, I won't have to have any skin grafts. It might not even scar too badly."

"Wow. That's amazing." Greg pulled the single straight-backed chair to the side of the bed so he could sit facing Len and parked himself on the edge of the seat. He still hadn't thought of a good way to broach the subject of the whatever-it-was haunting her. Which meant more small talk. He could do that. "So, how long are you gonna have to stay here? Did they give you any idea?"

"Doctor Irani said I'll probably be in about a week. By then, they'll know whether or not the gel's working and I can go home with home health, or if I'll need skin grafts."

"Oh." Moved by a surge of empathy, Greg leaned forward and took Len's uninjured hand in his. "I'm really sorry, Len. I wish I could've stopped it. I tried, I really did, but I was too late. I'm so, so sorry."

Her fingers curled hard around his. "I know you tried to save me. And you ended up getting hurt too." She took a deep breath. "And that's *my* fault, because whatever's been going on, it's because of me."

Greg's heart hammered at the base of his throat. "You've noticed the weird things happening at DogO?"

She laughed, a sound as sharp as broken glass. "Don't play dumb. I know you know all about it. The shadows, the voices, the things that touch you and throw stuff at you in the middle of the night." Before Greg could get over his shock enough to answer that last bit, Len's grip shifted from his fingers to his wrist. She stared at him, desperation stamped all over her face. "It's not just DogO, Greg. It's happening at home too. I haven't had a whole night's sleep in *weeks*. It's even happening here." Tears welled in her eyes. "I don't know what to do. How do I make it stop?"

"I don't know, hon." Greg lifted his hand, with Len's fingers still wrapped tight around his wrist, and gently brushed the tears from her cheek. "But we're going to figure it out."

"She's had weird things happen at home as well as at work. In fact, she said she's had problems at home even *longer* than at work." Greg took the glass of orange juice Cecile handed him with a smile. "Thanks. It's kept her from sleeping and her grades are dropping. You guys know it's gotten even stronger at the hospital, and I'm afraid it's gonna cause problems with her recovery. She looks like hell."

Adrian sat on the sofa beside Greg and took his hand. He'd heard the whole thing on the way home from the hospital. He couldn't help being relieved that Greg wasn't the one saddled with the demon, but his heart went out to Len. "I sat out in the waiting room, since Greg wouldn't let me go in the room with him." He smiled in response to Greg's arched eyebrow. "The entity is still very strong, though it seems to have settled some since yesterday."

"Hmm." Cecile curled into one of the armchairs, her forehead furrowed in concentration. "Did anything happen in the hospital today?"

Greg shook his head. "It felt kind of tense, you know, like something might happen any minute. But nothing did."

"Has the activity she's experienced been threatening before yesterday?" Adrian's father asked from the kitchen, where he was cooking a late lunch for the group.

"Yeah." Greg's grip on Adrian's hand tightened. "She said she's had things thrown at her in the middle of the night at home, had dishes break, even woken up with bruises she didn't know how she got."

Cecile made a soft sound. "Poor girl."

"I know. I feel awful for her." Greg slumped against the cushions behind him, his glass of juice balanced on the arm of the couch. "She said the stuff going on at work has been pretty mild compared to home, up until yesterday. The thing with the fryer's the worst that's happened to her yet. She's really scared."

"I don't blame her." Sam, who'd been pacing the living room ever since Greg and Adrian returned, stopped and pinned Greg with a thoughtful look. "I'm glad she was willing to talk to you and let us help her. Were the two of you able to reach any conclusions as to what might've changed in her life recently to bring about this...?"

"Stalking?" Dean suggested, walking out of the kitchen with a stack of plates in his hands. He set them on the table, picked up the pile of forks on top and set them aside. "I'd call it a possession, but that's not exactly right."

"No, I think 'stalking' is pretty accurate." Sam shot a smile at Dean, who winked at him and headed back into the kitchen. "Did anything stand out to either of you as being a possible cause of this paranormal stalking?"

Greg shook his head. "She went to Myrtle Beach with some of her friends before school started, and she went to an estate sale a couple of weeks before all this stuff started happening, but that's it."

Sam rubbed his chin. "Did anything unusual happen on either of those trips?"

"No séances or anything, if that's what you mean. She and her friends went out to eat and went to bars and stuff at the beach, and she bought a few things at the estate sale." Greg shrugged. "I don't know. Do you think this thing could've attached itself to her without her knowing it just from her going someplace?"

Adrian had no idea what to say. Nothing Greg had said sounded anything but innocuous to him. Feeling helpless, he caught Greg's eye and tried to convey with a look his desire to fix the whole mess, and how sorry he was that he couldn't. In return, Greg gave him a sweet, crooked smile that meant he understood and Adrian needn't worry. Adrian squeezed Greg's hand.

"We'll have to go to her home."

Adrian blinked at Cecile. She had a strange expression on her face. "What're you thinking of, Cecile?"

"Demonic entities can become attached to humans through objects, right? They're attached to the objects, the person brings the objects into their home, and the demon then attaches itself to the person." Cecile glanced at Sam, who stood nearby. "I think we need to take a good hard look at the things she bought at the estate sale. They're likely to be objects with a history, which makes them more likely to have a demonic entity attached."

Sam nodded, his expression thoughtful. "That's a very good point. Greg, what all did she buy?"

"A cameo necklace, an antique fan—she collects those—a couple of teacups, three books, and a doll for her niece. The doll's still at her apartment, so no need to track it down." Greg took a swallow of his tea. "I asked her if we could go to her place if we needed to. She said yes."

Adrian's father came in from the kitchen with a huge bowl in his hands and a wide smile on his face. "Very forward thinking of you, Greg. Good job."

Greg blushed to the roots of his hair, something he only ever seemed to do around Adrian's dads. Adrian found it unbearably cute. "Thanks."

The sparkle in his father's eyes told Adrian he found Greg's uncharacteristic shyness amusing, but thankfully he kept that to himself. He set the bowl on the table. "Lunch is ready. Come get it." He pointed at Greg. "You stay put. We'll set up trays for you and Adrian so you don't have to get up. Adrian, is it time for his pain pill?"

"I believe it is." Adrian leaned over and kissed away Greg's glare. "You know it's been hurting you. Just take the damn pill."

"Fine." Greg let go of Adrian's hand so he could get up. "What'd you cook, Bo? It smells fantastic."

"Nothing fancy. Just some Cajun-spiced vegetable stir-fry over rice." He started spooning the fragrant mixture onto the plates. "Sam and I are meeting with Noemi about the theater investigation results tomorrow morning. I'd love to be able to start looking into Len's case as soon as possible. Tonight, if we can. Do you boys think there's any way we can manage that?"

Adrian and Greg glanced at each other. "All the stuff Len had at work with her when she was burned is still in her locker at DogO," Greg said. "She already told me I could go get her keys and we could go in her apartment whenever we need to. So I guess we could do that tonight, if y'all want."

All the BCPI team members shared a meaningful look, and Adrian knew what was coming. He hurried to the kitchen counter, grabbed the bottle of pain pills and strode up to his dad. "Don't say it," he murmured, a hand on his father's arm. "He is *not* going to take this well."

The familiar we're-doing-this-my-way-like-it-or-not expression settled over Bo's face. "I'm aware. But he's already been injured once by this thing. Do you really want him in harm's way again?"

Adrian had no answer for that, of course. Sighing, he took one of the full plates and a fork, trudged back to the sofa and set the food on the TV tray Dean had dragged out of the closet for him. "Listen, Greg—"

"No. No way am I staying out of this."

Adrian took one look at the stubborn set of Greg's jaw and mentally girded himself for battle. "Look, you've already been hurt—"

"I know, you keep on reminding me." Greg held up his good hand. To Adrian's surprise, everyone who'd been about to argue shut up. "I know everybody's worried about me. Thank you. Seriously. I appreciate the concern. But just think about it for a minute. If this demon's attached to Len and still bugging her at the hospital, how can it be in her apartment too?"

Adrian looked at his dads, who knew way more about these sorts of things than he did. Sam shook his head. "It might not be. On the other hand, as I've said before, no one really knows enough about demonic entities to be able to say for certain what they can or can't do. I don't want to dismiss the possibility that

164

it can split its energy, or move back and forth between places without Len being there."

"Plus, you've already proven to be a sort of secondary target," Adrian's father added. He brought a plate to Adrian but kept his gaze trained on Greg. "Demonic or not, this thing is dangerous, and you're more likely than any of us to be hurt by it. I know you don't want to be left behind, and I think we all understand your reasons. But you could be in real danger if you go with us. I don't want you to get hurt again. None of us do."

Greg's expression softened. For a moment, Adrian thought Greg might actually give in and do as he was asked for a change.

"I know. Believe me, I don't want me to get hurt again either." Greg squared his shoulders. His grip on Adrian's hand went from tight to painful, and Adrian let out a defeated sigh. Greg shot him a look that promised bad things later if he didn't keep quiet now. "But you need me on this investigation, especially if Len's not around. Y'all don't know her. I do. I've been over to her apartment before. I remember what it's supposed to look like. I can tell you if something's out of place, and I can find the stuff she bought at the estate sale, if that's gonna be a focus of the investigation."

He had a point. Dammit. Adrian turned to his dad with a silent plea.

"He's right," Sam said, looking every bit as unhappy about it as Adrian felt. "Bo?"

Adrian's father sighed. "If we let you come along, you'll have to promise to stick with Adrian the whole time. All right?"

Greg's face lit up. "I will. I promise."

Bo wasn't done yet. "And *both* of you *will* leave if Sam tells you to. I'm putting him in charge of safety. This is not negotiable. Is that understood?"

Greg nodded, beaming. Adrian groaned. "Dad, come on."

His father crossed his arms. "No arguments, Adrian. Either you agree or neither of you are coming with us."

Greg glared at Adrian. He slumped in his seat. "Fine. Sam's in charge. We'll leave if he tells us to."

"Good." His dad smiled. "Now eat your lunch before it gets cold." He turned back to the bowl of stir-fry with an air of finality.

Adrian hunched over his plate, defeated. Then Greg leaned against him and nuzzled his neck, and the realization of time slipping away hit Adrian like a brick to the head.

He wound an arm around Greg, pulled him close and kissed his temple. In a few hours they'd be heading to Len's place to try to find the source of the thing that had been tormenting her. He had only a short time not only to prepare himself for whatever waited for them there, but to come up with a plan to protect Greg if the entity attacked.

He just hoped he could keep Greg safe if things went to hell.

The minute Adrian followed his father into Len's apartment that night, he knew the demon wasn't there.

Well, not entirely. He felt the spark and snap of its energy, but it was like listening to a stereo playing at top volume on the other side of the house—you couldn't ignore it, but it didn't paralyze your senses the way it did if you shared a room with it.

"I can feel it," Sam said, stepping in behind him. "It's not all here, is it?"

"I was thinking the same thing." Adrian paced down the short hallway toward the living room. A strip of light shining through a gap in the curtains provided the only illumination. Something else, a not-quite-light, pulsed just beyond the range of his vision. "It's weird, though. I can almost see it."

"Greg, leave the lights off for a minute, if you don't mind." Cecile walked past Adrian and turned in a slow circle. "I know what you mean, Adrian. The energy does seem almost visible. Which is odd, because it isn't as strong as it was at DogOpolis."

"Or at the hospital." Sam went to an open door that must lead to Len's bedroom and stood peering inside. "Cecile? Is it okay if we turn on the lights now?"

She nodded. "Go ahead."

"This place doesn't have overhead lights in the living room. Hang on." Greg turned on the kitchen light, then brushed past Adrian and switched on the lamps on either side of the sofa. He looked around. "I think I can find the rest of the stuff she bought at the estate sale. Do y'all want me to gather 'em all together? What's easiest for you guys?"

Adrian glanced at Sam and Cecile. He felt sure he'd be able to help pinpoint the source of the demonic energy if it was here, but he had no idea whether having them all in one place would help or hinder the effort. They'd picked up the cameo necklace at DogOpolis—Len had apparently been wearing it when she was injured and one of her coworkers had taken it off and put it in her locker—but Adrian hadn't been able to sense anything from it on the ride over.

"I think we should try sensing them where they are to start with, then bring them all together in here. What do you think, Cecile?" Sam wandered around the periphery of the room, his expression vague the way it usually was when he tuned in to

167

his psychic perception. "For what it's worth, I'm not picking up anything that's drawing me strongly in one direction or another. Including toward the necklace."

"Agreed. On both how to proceed, and on not feeling a strong draw to anything in particular." Crossing to where Greg had settled on the couch, Cecile sat beside him. "May I see Len's cameo, Greg?"

"Sure." He pulled the necklace out of the plastic bag in which he'd put all Len's things from the restaurant and handed it to Cecile. He watched her with clear curiosity as she turned it between her fingers, her forehead furrowed and her eyes blank. "What—?"

"Sometimes you can pick up something more specific through touch," Adrian explained, not wanting Greg to interrupt Cecile when she was concentrating. "Like when we found Lyndon Groome's body, I touched a piece of his clothing and got a flash of his memories."

Greg nodded, still watching Cecile. "Okay, yeah. That makes sense."

Cecile opened her eyes. "I'm still not getting anything from this. Why don't we leave this here on the coffee table for now, then once we're finished we can put it with the rest of her jewelry? Provided we decide it isn't the culprit, that is."

"I doubt it is, if you're not getting anything." Dean rose from the floor where he'd been silently digging through the equipment bag and crossed to stand in front of Greg and Cecile. He carried the touch-screen tablet Bo had eventually bought to replace notepads and pens on investigations. "Greg, tell me what all I'm looking for and I'll help you find the goods."

"I think Bo and I should set up video cameras and do a general investigation of the apartment, especially if I'm going to monitor the situation with the entity for safety purposes." Sam halted his circumnavigation of the room beside the window and turned to face the group. "Bo, you can keep an EMF running. I'll do audio. Cecile, you can go with Dean and psychically feel out the objects he finds while they're in place, if you don't mind."

She nodded. "That sounds like a good plan to me."

"Sam, I'll take audio and EMF both," Adrian's father added. "I'd really rather you were free to concentrate completely on monitoring the entity."

Sam chuckled. "I had a feeling you'd say that."

Smiling, Bo crossed to the equipment bag, knelt beside it and started pulling out the things they needed. "Thanks, Sam."

Adrian perched on the arm of the sofa beside Greg and put an arm around his shoulders. "Greg? How does this all sound to you? Are you sure you feel up to it all?"

Greg tilted his head back and smiled up at Adrian. "Yeah, I'm fine. Especially since Dean's gonna help me find all the stuff." He saluted Dean with his bandaged hand. "Thanks, man."

"No problem." Dean plopped onto the sofa beside Cecile. "Okay, tell me which things you want me and Cecile to check out and we'll get started."

After a few minutes of conversation, they settled on a split while Adrian's dads set up the video cameras. Dean and Cecile headed into Len's bedroom to look for the books and the doll Greg figured would be in there while Adrian followed Greg into the L of the living area, looking for the fan and the teacups.

Greg found both teacups in a hutch next to Len's small dining table. Adrian stopped him before he could take them out. "No. Don't touch them."

Greg gave him a curious look but backed off. "Why?"

"No reason, probably. I just don't want to take any chances." Adrian opened the glass doors of the hutch and put his hands on the shelves without touching the cups. The vague, angry buzz in his head didn't change at all. Digging his teeth into his lower lip, he stroked a finger over the rim of the paper-thin cup with the hand-painted dragon on it. Nothing happened. He curled his palm around it, then the one with the stylized flowers. Still nothing. He turned to Greg. "I'm not feeling anything from either of these."

"Okay. Let's put 'em on the table and move on."

The two of them moved the cups and saucers to the dining table, where Sam had already put the cameo necklace. That done, Greg continued the hunt for the antique fan.

It wasn't as easy as Adrian would've thought. After several minutes of fruitless searching, Greg let out a frustrated huff. "Dammit. This place is *not* that big. Where the hell could she have hidden a fucking fan?"

Adrian shook his head. "Maybe she put it in storage or something? You said she collected antique fans. If this one's valuable—"

"Guys?" Sam leaned around the doorway of the laundry room, which he'd just entered. "I think I found it."

Adrian followed Greg to the cramped little room beside the front door. Sam stepped out to make room for them. A white washer and dryer stood along the wall to the left. An ironing board and a tiny round table took up the right-hand wall. Directly in front of them was a box marked *Recycling*. The fan sat on the lowest of two shelves on the wall above the recycling box.

It didn't look particularly impressive—squat, the metal gone blackish-green with age and neglect, the cage around the blades a strange octagonal shape. A large purple rubber band held the frayed cord in a neat coil at its side. Adrian wondered how old it was.

Greg wrinkled his nose. "If anything's got a demon, it's that. Ew."

"Actually, I think you may be right." Slipping into the room beside Adrian, Sam edged nearer the fan. He held out his hand, close but not quite touching. "It's stronger here. Adrian, can you feel it?"

Adrian moved to stand beside Sam. A bit of concentration made the fan flare in his mind like a metaphysical torch. He swallowed hard. "I feel it, yes."

"Shit." Greg clamped a hand onto the back of Adrian's shirt. "What now?"

"We make sure." Adrian stretched out a hand to touch the fan. The force of the entity crackled across his skin from inches away, but the scientist in him wouldn't let him say for certain they'd found their demon-haunted object until he'd confirmed it as best he knew how.

Sam grabbed his wrist before he could lay his palm on the object in question. "Let me do it, Adrian. This could be dangerous, and if that's the case, then I should be the one running the risk. I have a lot more experience dealing with these things than you do."

"With *demons*? No you don't." Adrian's father pushed his way into the already crowded room. "You haven't ever faced a demon any more than Adrian has."

Adrian pressed his lips together. Agreeing with his dad out loud at this point wasn't going to help.

Sam met his husband's stormy expression with determined calm. "I know you're not saying Adrian ought to do it."

The "mad muscle", as Greg had dubbed it ages ago, twitched in Bo's jaw. "What I'm saying is that there must be a way to determine if the entity is attached to this particular fan without putting *anyone* at risk."

"I don't think there is, really." Everyone turned to look at Greg, who hunched his shoulders under the scrutiny. "I mean, I know I'm not an expert or anything, but I've done a little reading, and it looks to me like any kind of test to see if an object's possessed or whatever involves at least *some* danger to the people doing the testing." Greg moved close to Adrian and leaned against his side. "But I'm still with Bo. I'd rather find some other way."

One corner of Sam's mouth turned up in a wan half-smile. "I understand that. I think we all do. But I'm an extremely strong psychic, and I have excellent control of my psychokinesis, if I do say so myself. I think the danger to me is less than the danger to anyone else." He rested a hand on Adrian's shoulder. "Before you say anything, I know you're at least as powerful as I am, and you also have excellent control. But experience does make a difference. I hope you understand."

Adrian did, though it still stung a bit. He nodded. "Yeah. I'm staying nearby, though, in case you need me."

"Good. Don't do anything unless you have to, but I'm glad to know you're ready if need be." Sam clapped Adrian on the shoulder then peered out the door. "Dean? Cecile? Are y'all there?"

"Here." Cecile peeked around the edge of the laundry room door. "I've got my senses open too."

"And I'm ready to call 911 if we need an ambulance." Dean held up his pod. "I have a first-aid kit, of course, but as usual with this crowd if we have any emergency, it's not likely to be one I can treat with an Ace wrap or an EpiPen."

Greg laughed, sounding anxious. "Stand by, Dean. I might have a heart attack from nerves."

Adrian put an arm around Greg. "You should go wait in the living room."

"No way. I'm staying here." Greg pulled away, looking pale and scared but determined.

Adrian gave him an encouraging smile. Greg smiled back, and Adrian felt a tiny bit better.

Sam stepped closer to the fan. "All right. Here goes." Squaring his shoulders, he reached out and curled both hands around the octagonal cage.

Instantly, the steady sizzle of energy in Adrian's head erupted into a white-hot wall of flame. He cried out, blinded by the flare of light. An ominous hissing drowned out the voices around him. He caught the faint, faraway stench of burned flesh.

All of which lasted no more than a heartbeat. When he blinked away the spots floating before his eyes, Adrian's heart jumped into his throat.

Sam lay curled in a heap on the floor, unresponsive, eyes rolled back to show the whites, the fan clutched to his chest in white-knuckled fingers.

Chapter Ten

As soon as Sam went down, Greg knew what Adrian would do. He flung both arms around Adrian's waist to stop him. "No. Adrian. No. It'll kill you."

"It's got Sam, dammit! He can't fight it off alone. I have to help him." Adrian wrenched himself free and fell to his knees beside his stepfather.

Bo lunged for Adrian at the same time as Greg did. But neither of them were fast enough. Adrian threw himself sideways out of reach and clenched one hand around Sam's wrist and the other onto the fan.

He jerked once and collapsed just as suddenly and shockingly as Sam had. Fine tremors shook his body from head to toe. In the stillness, Greg heard a rattling noise he identified after a moment as Adrian's teeth clacking together.

Overcome by an overwhelming need to get Adrian *away* from that fucking haunted fan, Greg knelt and reached for him. A hand at his shoulder stopped him. He shook it off. More hands took hold of him, pulling him to his feet and away from Adrian.

Frustrated, he tried to fight off Bo and Dean, who were dragging him out of the laundry room and into the hall. "What're you doing? We have to help them!" He struggled but couldn't break their combined grip on him.

"Greg. Listen to me." Bo took Greg by the shoulders and turned him so that he had no choice but to look Bo in the eye. His expression was stern, but the slight quaver in his voice gave away his fear for his son and husband. "I know exactly what you're feeling right now. You're scared for Adrian. You want to bring him back, and Sam too." His gaze cut sideways to the two men curled around that horrible fan, Sam still as death and Adrian twitching like he was being hit with electric shocks. For a second, Bo's mask dropped and a jumble of terror, anger and frustration flowed across his features before he got himself under control. He stared at Greg again. "But we don't know enough about this to interfere. If we touch either of them—or that fan—right now, we could make things much, much worse. We might put their lives in danger."

Greg hadn't thought about it like that. Hell, he hadn't thought about it at all. He'd seen Adrian collapse and simply followed the urge to save him. He looked at Adrian. His face was pale, his lips moving as if he was talking to someone Greg couldn't see. His fingers gripped the fan's cage so hard they shook. The other hand dug into Sam's wrist with enough force that Greg wondered if Sam would have bruises later.

If the two of them *had* a later.

To Greg's shame, tears stung his eyelids. He sagged in Bo's grasp. "I just want to *do* something, Bo. I feel totally helpless just standing here."

"I know, son. Believe me, I know." Bo relaxed his hold on Greg's shoulders and took both his hands in a strong, comforting grip. "All we can do right now is be here, be ready to help them when they need it, and trust their strength in the meantime." He smiled, though it looked as sad and afraid as Greg felt. "The two of them have fought things that could give any demon a run for its money. And Adrian did it when he was only eleven. I'd say they stand a good chance of beating this entity, especially working together."

"Bo's right. Sam and Adrian both have a really strong psychokinesis, and they know how to control it. In any case, we don't have any choice but to trust them now." Dean glanced up from where he'd knelt beside Adrian and Sam, carefully not touching them. "As far as I can tell, they both seem to be fine physically speaking. Keeping in mind that I can't get all the information I need without touching them, and of course they're both unresponsive, so I have no way of knowing if their brains are affected."

A fresh wave of dread sent Greg's stomach into a slow, sickening roll. He sucked his bottom lip into his mouth, fighting back the urge to scream. Or throw up. Or both.

Bo shut his eyes. His fingers tightened around Greg's, then let go. When he opened his eyes again, his gaze locked with Greg's. Only for a split second, but it was enough. Beneath his veneer of control, Bo was clearly just as desperate with worry as Greg.

Sam let out a harsh grunt. His eyelids fluttered, then drifted shut. As if in response, Adrian's body shook harder. A low sound emerged from his lips—whispered words Greg couldn't understand.

"My God." Bo sank to his knees, one hand hovering between Sam and Adrian in an obvious desire to touch one or both of them. "What's happening?"

No one answered. They all knew he wasn't asking them, anyway. Greg stared at Adrian, wishing as hard as he could for Adrian and Sam to win whatever battle they were fighting right now.

Something touched his hand. He jumped, startled, before he realized it was Cecile. She didn't say a word, just slipped an arm around him and rested her head on his shoulder. He pulled her close to his side, grateful for her silent comfort.

Sam's head snapped backward, hitting the recycling box with a solid *thunk*. Harsh, panting breaths hissed from between his clenched teeth. Beside him, Adrian shouted a string of half-formed words. His legs thrashed as though he were trying to run from something.

"Fuck, fuck fuck fuck." Greg leaned against Cecile to keep himself upright. "Jesus, what the hell's happening to them?"

"I wish I knew." Dean scrambled out of the way to keep from being kicked by Adrian. "Shit."

"Wait." Bo, who'd managed to wedge himself in the narrow space behind Sam's back, held up a hand to silence the group. "I think he's coming around." He leaned low over Sam's face. "Sam? Can you hear me? It's Bo. Please talk to me. Please let us know you and Adrian are all right."

Sam groaned, stirred and opened his eyes. He blinked at Bo. "What...?"

Relief lit up Bo's face. "I don't know, Sam. You collapsed as soon as you touched that fan." His eyes clouded again. "And Adrian—"

"Oh my God. Adrian." Twisting his wrist free of Adrian's grip, Sam took hold of his shoulder and shook him. "Adrian. Come back. It's over. You need to come back to our reality now." He stroked Adrian's hair away from his face. "Come on, kiddo. Follow my voice. Follow my energy. You can do it."

Greg clung to Cecile and waited. It felt like a nightmarish millennium before Adrian finally stilled, quieted and opened his eyes. He peered at Sam and Bo with confusion stamped all over his face. "Dad? S-Sam? Is this real?"

"Of course it is, son." Bo cast a worried glance at Sam.

Sam smiled, though he looked exhausted and older than he had only a few minutes ago. "It's real, Adrian. We beat that thing. We're back in our world." He let go of the fan, scrunching up his face as if he'd held onto it for so long it hurt to move that hand, then pried Adrian's fingers loose as well. "Come on. Let's get away from that thing so we can talk. We need to explain to everyone what happened."

"Yeah." Adrian's gaze lit on Greg and held. He smiled. "Greg. You don't know how happy I am to see your face."

For some reason, Adrian's words broke Greg's tenuous control to pieces. Launching himself forward, he fell to the floor beside Adrian, flung both arms around him and held him as tight as he could. Since the tears would not be stopped this time, apparently, he buried his face in Adrian's hair and let them come. He'd gone way past the point of embarrassment by now anyway.

Adrian shifted enough to sit up and hug Greg close. He stroked Greg's back, buried a hand in Greg's hair, pressed a cheek to the side of his head. "It's okay," Adrian murmured. "I'm all right. I'm so sorry I scared you. But Sam needed me. He might've ended up with that demon riding him if I hadn't helped."

"I know. I really do, I promise. You did the right thing." Greg sniffed hard, blinked and wiped his eyes, trying to get himself together. He sat back to look Adrian in the eye. "But I swear to God, if you *ever* do that to me again, I'll haunt you so bad you'll *wish* you had a demon."

Adrian laughed. Not that Greg blamed him. It was a toothless threat, not the least because it made no sense. Right now, though, Greg couldn't bring himself to care. Adrian and Sam were both alive, safe and sane. Nothing else mattered.

He got an arm around Adrian's rib cage. "Come on. I'll help you up."

Cecile came to his aid. The two of them got Adrian to his feet, while Bo and Dean helped Sam up, then all of them went into Len's living room to talk.

"So what happened in there?" Bo lowered Sam carefully into a large, comfy-looking chair, then perched on the arm of it. "It sounded as if the two of you were *literally* fighting off the demon."

Sam's expression grew thoughtful. He took Bo's hand and laced their fingers together. "We were. As soon as I touched the fan, it felt as if that energy, that negative energy, just sucked me in. It was like falling into a whirlpool. I couldn't get out."

Cecile sat cross-legged on the floor, frowning. "That's very odd. How on earth did anyone ever buy or sell it, if it can't be touched?"

"I don't know for sure, but my hunch is that only a person with a strong psychokinesis such as Adrian and I have would get sucked in like that. Anyone else wouldn't, because it's not physical, it's *meta*physical. If that makes sense. Though I do think people without strong psychic abilities would run a high risk of ending up with a demon attached to them, like Len did." Sam shrugged. "That's purely speculation on my part. I'm pretty sure I'm right, but I certainly don't want to test that theory here and now."

"I'm sure you're right too. I felt the same way when I touched it." Adrian's hand clutched Greg's tight. His thigh pressed against Greg's where they sat side by side on the sofa. He looked from his dad to Dean to Cecile and sideways to Greg. "I could sense Sam in the whirlpool—that's a good way to describe it—but I couldn't *see* him, exactly. It was like the demonic entity was trying to trap us there, or something. But it wasn't working, so it wanted to take over one of us instead. It seemed to be going for Sam."

Dean's eyes went wide. "Oh hell. It wanted to bind someone—or something, I dunno—else to the fan in its place, but it can't bind a human. So it tried to possess you instead, because it's a demon and they're evil like that."

Sam rubbed his chin, his expression grim. "That's certainly plausible. In any case, with our combined strength, Adrian and I managed to fight off the entity's attempts to possess me. And I think we managed to get it away from Len and bind it back to the fan."

"Seriously?" Greg stared in awe from Adrian to Sam and back again. "How?"

"Truthfully? I have no idea." Sam let out a tired laugh. "I wish I knew more about demonology. I'm not sure precisely what we did. But it felt a lot like sending the things from the other dimension back through the portals."

Goose bumps rose along Greg's arms and scalp. The thought of the interdimensional portals the BCPI group had dealt with all those years ago—never mind the intelligent but vicious creatures living on the other side—gave him the creeps. He'd almost rather deal with demons. At least they were part of *this* reality.

Adrian nodded. "It did. Not exactly, but enough to feel kind of familiar. And I think you're right, I think it's bound back to the fan. There was a sort of *click* in my head, you know?"

"That would be cool." Dean grinned. "Now we'll have to start renting you out as a demon hunter, Sam."

He shook his head, laughing. "Thanks, but no thanks. I'm hoping this'll be the first, last and only time."

"Binding this entity back to the fan is a wonderful first step." Bo squeezed Sam's hand between both of his. "The question is, now what?"

No one had an answer for that.

Being off work sucked.

Actually, it didn't. Greg enjoyed spending a lazy day with Adrian on his days off, strolling around town, watching TV or just lying in bed. But being forced to stay out of work because of an injury sucked. Greg's burn still hurt enough to require pain meds, and finding anything fun to do one-handed—other than the obvious—was surprisingly difficult. With Adrian busy in class and working on his research project, the day after the demon-fan incident—as Greg had dubbed it in his head—seemed to last forever.

Eventually, sick of his own company and feeling restless, Greg got dressed and caught the bus to campus. He messaged Adrian on the way to tell him he was heading to the library to do some research.

Adrian messaged back a moment later. *Sure ur up to it?*

Greg smiled. After all Adrian had been through yesterday, he still worried about Greg. *Cant stand sitting at home alone, gotta do something. Figure ill look into getting demons out of fans.*

Good luck. C U later, love you

Thx. Luv U 2 babe

Greg stuck his pod back in his shorts pocket and slumped in his seat to watch the city go by outside the window. He wished he'd been able to talk Adrian into staying home today. Not that Greg minded doing research. In fact, he'd caught the bug and looked forward to it. Adrian shouldn't be at work this soon, though. The encounter with the demon had taken a lot out of him. He'd picked at his dinner last night and gone to bed early, then woken with a shout at two in the morning, shaking all over and soaked in sweat. He'd eventually gone back to sleep with Greg clutched tight in his arms, but he hadn't rested easy, and Greg was worried about him.

He wasn't the only one, either. Bo and Sam had both taken Greg's side on the issue when Greg brought it up yesterday, for all the good it did. Now Adrian was hard at work on quantum equations or whatever the hell it was he focused that impressive brain on in the physics lab, and Greg was trying to make himself feel useful with research since he couldn't take care of Adrian at home like he wanted.

At least the scenery from the bus window was more interesting than what he had to look at in their apartment. The ride to campus followed by the short but pleasant stroll in the sunny afternoon relaxed him. By the time he reached the library, he felt calmer. Yeah, Adrian probably should've stayed home. But he was smart enough to know when he wasn't performing up to par. If he thought for one second his health or state of mind might negatively affect his research, he'd step away in a heartbeat.

Inside, Greg headed for an interface in the back corner, near the window. He sometimes got distracted by the people passing by when he sat here, but the thought of using an inside interface made him feel claustrophobic right now. After yesterday's encounter with the demon thing, he didn't feel safe unless he could see the sky.

Of course, he didn't feel safe without something solid at his back either, but a guy couldn't have everything. Especially in a library.

Stomping down the thread of panic taking shape inside him, he thumbed on the interface and began his search.

He read for three and a half hours straight. He probably would've stayed longer, devoured article after horrifying, fascinating article, if his pod hadn't started playing the *Doctor Who* theme. Heart hammering with the suddenness of it, he shut down with a touch to the screen and snatched his pod from the desk. "Hi, Adrian." He rose and headed for the door, flashing his brightest smile at all the people staring at him. "What's up? How're you doing? Are you feeling okay?"

"I'm fine. I was calling because it's almost dinner time and I wanted to see if you felt like going out. Dad says Sam's getting stir-crazy. Why're you talking so quietly? You're not still at the library, are you?"

"Well, yeah." He pushed open the door to the airlock with his hip. "Okay, now I'm not. I'm outside." He opened the outside door and stepped into the sunshine.

Adrian laughed. "You must've found something really interesting."

"You could say that." Greg flopped onto a nearby bench. "There weren't a lot of articles about un-demonizing objects. Most of them had more to do with people. But I found a few about objects."

"And what did they say?"

Adrian sounded wary. Greg didn't blame him. He had good reasons, which he was about to find out. "They didn't all agree about *how* to do it, but everything I found said you have to have a priest to do it."

"Shit." Adrian sighed. "How do you go about hiring a priest?"

"I don't know." Greg scuffed his sneaker against the uneven spot in the sidewalk. "Hell, will a priest even agree to help us? The Catholic church still thinks gays are evil."

"Maybe we get can Cecile to make the call." Another sigh, deeper and full of frustration. "Crap. We'll talk about it at dinner. Dean and Cecile were going to do some researching of their own while Dad and Sam went to present the findings of the theater investigation to Noemi. Maybe they turned up something."

"That would be cool. So should I meet y'all at the hotel, or d'you want to come by the library and we can walk together?"

"We'll meet you at the usual spot on Franklin. I don't much feel like walking, so I asked Dad if they'd pick me up."

Greg frowned. "I told you you shouldn't've gone in today."

"No, I'm fine, honest. Just tired." Adrian's workboard chimed in the background, signaling that he'd saved his work and shut down. "You probably shouldn't be out yourself, you know. Those pain pills make you loopy."

"Yeah, well, I haven't taken any since this morning."

"I know you get restless, but I hate to think of you in pain just because you wanted to get out of the apartment."

The note of reproach in Adrian's voice made Greg smile. "It's not too bad. I took some ibuprofen and it helped."

"Well, good. Still, I think I'll ask Dad if we can stop by our place before dinner so you can take one of your prescription pills."

"If you insist." Greg wiggled the fingers on his burned hand. The healing skin pulled painfully. "Okay, since they're coming to pick you up, I'll walk over and meet you at your lab."

"All right. I'll see you in a few minutes. Love you."

"Love you too. Bye."

Greg cut the connection, stuck his pod back in his pocket and rose to his feet. It wasn't a long walk to Adrian's lab, but he'd just as soon get going. Now that Adrian had brought it up, Greg sort of wished he'd taken his pain pill before he came over here, no matter how drunk it made him. His hand hurt like fuck. Besides, he was hungry. It was his own fault for skipping lunch, but still. He started down the sidewalk, wondering where they were going for dinner.

"Hey, Greg. Wait."

He almost pretended he didn't hear. The last thing he wanted to do right now was talk to Jon, in spite of how Jon had helped him when he'd been injured. In fact, his guilt over his former suspicion toward Jon—even though Jon didn't know about it—made him even less eager to talk to the man. But Jon called out again, and since ignoring him apparently wasn't possible, Greg stopped and turned to face him. "What, Jon? What do you want?"

Jon looked so taken aback that Greg felt bad for snapping. He didn't get a chance to say so, though, because Jon spoke first. "I'm sorry. I just...I couldn't help but overhear you back there, and—"

"*What?* What the fuck do you mean, you *couldn't help but overhear?*" Greg stepped closer and glared up at the taller man, all traces of his previous guilty feelings evaporating in a blast of fury. The staring and eighth-grade-style pigtail-pulling were annoying enough. Eavesdropping, though? That crossed the line. "Okay, look. I know you helped me at DogO, and I appreciate that. But I'm about tired of how you act toward me. You ignore me or insult me all the time, but you won't stop staring at me like you're a kid with a crush. And whenever anyone mentions Adrian, you act like you're a fucking spurned girlfriend or something, which is just..." he waved both hands in the air, looking for the right words and not finding them, "...just *stupid*. And now you're sneaking around, listening in on my private conversations? What the actual *fuck*, Jon?"

Jon's eyes cut sideways. He looked nervous. Greg thought he damn well ought to. "I...I didn't mean—"

"Shut up," Greg ordered. Jon's teeth snapped together with an audible *clack*. Greg resisted the urge to gloat. "Right now, you remind me of my ex. He fucking *stalked* me after I left him. He would not leave me alone. When he crossed the line with me, I had him arrested. You, my friend, are about to cross the *fucking* line."

Jon's face went dead white. "Greg, no, you don't—"

Greg stepped closer, his pulse racing and his whole body trembling with adrenaline. "Give me one fucking reason why I shouldn't call the cops right now."

"Shit." Shutting his eyes, Jon rubbed both hands over his face. "I'm really sorry. I didn't mean to listen in, I just...I was..."

"You were following me!" Greg's shout rang out across the campus. Heads turned his way, people stared. Greg ground his teeth together and told himself to get it together before someone called the cops on *him*. "Goddammit. Look, I don't want for things to be like this, especially after you helped me out at DogO. But I can't pretend that things between us are normal either. All I want is for you to admit you were following me, all right?"

"Okay, I *have* been sometimes. Occasionally. I have." Jon dropped his hands and met Greg's gaze. His eyes were red-rimmed, making the blue stand out brighter than ever. "Look. I *do* have a crush on you, okay? You're not stupid. You know that. I just..." His shoulders sagged. "I don't deal well with these kinds of things."

"I'll say." Greg crossed his arms, still not ready to forgive but willing to listen. "You do realize that the way you've been acting isn't the way to get someone you like to like you back, right?"

"I know." Jon hung his head. "It's not like I'd have a chance with you even if you *weren't* with Adrian, though."

Greg rolled his eyes. He gave himself full credit, however, for not telling Jon to grow a pair and stop being so damn dramatic. "All right, so you said you've followed me 'sometimes'. Why were you following me today? Because you still haven't told me why I shouldn't call the cops, and I'm sort of in a hurry. Adrian's waiting for me."

A soul-deep sadness filled Jon's face for a second before that automatic actor's training kicked in and his expression
186

went blank. "I wasn't actually following you this time. I was leaving the library right behind you. You didn't see me because you were talking on your pod." He stared at the concrete at his feet. "Although I've been thinking lately that I ought to talk to you. Clear the air between us. I don't like the tension, I don't like that I've made you dislike me so much, and I especially don't like how trapped I feel. And it's all my own fault, of course." A faint smile curved his mouth. "Didn't mean to dump that on you right *now*. Sorry."

Because Jon seemed sincere—and heartbreakingly lonely— Greg decided to stay and listen. He stuck his hands in his pockets and studied Jon's face. "It's okay. I think you're right, we do need to have an honest talk and clear the air." A thought struck him. "Why did you stop me to tell me you overheard me? Doesn't seem like a very good idea."

Jon let out a soft laugh. "No, in hindsight it really doesn't."

"So, why did you?" Greg was genuinely curious at this point.

"You said you needed a priest."

"Yeah. So?"

"So, my dad's a priest." Jon glanced at him with the kind of shy sweetness Greg had never, ever seen on the other man's face before. "I know he'd be willing to help you with whatever it is you need, and I thought, well... Maybe if I put you in touch with him, it would be a good first step to mending fences between us."

Ah. "Well, that's cool. And I appreciate that you're willing to offer the contact, but are you *sure* he'd be willing to work with us? Catholics don't always want to. No offense or anything." A thought struck Greg, and he frowned. "Wait, I thought Catholic priests had to be celibate."

"Well, not always. It's complicated." Jon rubbed nervously at the back of his neck. "But my dad's not Catholic."

Greg raised his eyebrows. "Okay, I'm confused."

Jon smiled, erasing the sadness from his face and making him look like a different person from his usual sour self. "He's Episcopal."

Greg couldn't help it. He laughed. Adrian and his dads didn't know it yet, but they were about to find help where they least expected it.

He only hoped he wouldn't get in too much trouble for bringing in an outsider, especially without asking first. Bo in particular was pretty firm in his rule about keeping "civilians" out of investigations.

Greg smiled at Jon's puzzled expression. "Jon, I'd really like for you to meet Adrian's dads. Follow me."

A hint of apprehension slid through Jon's eyes. His smile faded a bit, but he trailed behind Greg anyway.

Chapter Eleven

If someone had told Adrian this morning that by the end of the day he'd witness Greg being friendly to Jon Hudson, of all people, he'd have laughed. Greg didn't hate Jon, exactly, but Jon's constant, unwelcome attention annoyed him. Adrian suspected it scared him on one level as well, after the whole thing with his ex-boyfriend the year he and Adrian first got together, even though Jon had never shown any tendency toward violence the way Harrison had.

Crazy as it would've sounded not so long ago, though, here they were—Jon perched on the edge of a chair in Sam and Bo's hotel suite, with the rest of the group sitting on the beds, the small sofa and the other chair. Except for Adrian's father, who'd adopted his usual thinking-things-through mode of pacing the floor.

He'd barely even scolded Greg for bringing Jon in on this without asking. Adrian figured that came down to the fact that Jon had a connection they might need in this case.

The whole thing was only slightly less surreal than the sight of Greg approaching the physics building with Jon in tow in the first place.

Jon's eyes had grown rounder and his face paler as Sam explained the whole problem with the fan and its unwelcome demon attachment. By the time Sam finished talking, Jon looked as though he might bolt any minute. "Jesus. This is bad."

"It is, yes." Adrian's dad stopped pacing and pinned Jon with a solemn stare. "You were very kind to step in and offer to put us in contact with your father, Jon. We do appreciate that. But there's no need for you yourself to be involved in this case. It absolutely has the potential to become quite dangerous. We'd just as soon keep anyone who isn't a professional out of it."

Adrian didn't miss the pointed glance his father cast at him and Greg where they sat side by side on the sofa. He pursed his lips and kept his arguments to himself, for the time being. He knew his dad only considered him a professional when the case was a safe one. The moment things turned truly dangerous, Adrian became a civilian in his father's eyes. Always had. It irritated him, but fighting about it in front of Jon was *not* going to happen. Which his dad most likely knew.

He ought to know he couldn't shunt Adrian aside so easily, though. Where his dads went on this case, Adrian went. Period. He shot his dad a glare to tell him so.

Greg's fingers tightened around his. He didn't have to turn to know Greg was giving him the same look he'd just given his dad. He stifled a sigh.

Jon hunched his shoulders. "I know I'd only be in the way dealing with a demon." He shook his head, a faint smile curving his mouth. "God, I never really believed in any of that. But it's all true, isn't it?"

"Seems to be. Though what exactly a demon *is* sort of depends on who you ask." Uncurling his legs from underneath him, Dean planted his feet on the floor and leaned forward. "This might seem like a stupid question, but is it all right if we tell your dad you gave us his name, or should we leave you out of it?"

Jon's smile widened. "I understand why you'd ask. But it's fine to tell my dad. We had a pretty troubled relationship when I was growing up, but after I came out we had a long talk and settled a few things that had been problems between us for a long time. We actually get along better now than we ever have."

"That's good." Cecile, sitting in the chair next to Jon's, reached over and touched his arm. "Jon, are you sure you won't come to dinner with us? You're welcome to join us, you know."

"No. Thank you, but I have to go to rehearsal. I appreciate the offer, though." With a surprisingly sweet smile for Cecile, Jon rose from his seat. "All right. Well, Dr. Broussard, you have my dad's number. Thanks for taking the time to explain everything to me. It was nice to meet all of you."

"You too, Jon. Thanks very much for your help in this." Adrian's father smiled and held out his hand. "Please, call me Bo."

"Bo. Okay." Jon shook, his cheeks pink and his smile suddenly shy in that way so many people seemed to get around Adrian's dad.

Jon shook hands and said his thank-yous and goodbyes to everyone. His blush deepened when he got to Greg and Adrian, and his gaze didn't quite meet Greg's, but he clasped Greg's hand anyway and mumbled the same words he'd said to everybody else.

After Jon had gone, Adrian turned to Greg. "I sort of feel sorry for him."

Instead of scolding him, Greg nodded. "Me too, now. We've all had those unrequited crushes before. It sucks. And I gotta be honest here, if it was me crushing on some dude who ignored me all the time? I wouldn't go out of my way to help him find a priest."

Adrian laughed. "You have a real way with words."

"So I'm told." Grinning, Greg squeezed Adrian's hand. "We talked a little bit, and we're gonna talk some more later on. It'll be good to get things cleared up between us. It'll help Jon get past his crush, and hopefully we can be friends."

Oh, yay. Adrian faked a smile. "Good. That's good."

Greg raised his eyebrows but didn't say anything, for which Adrian was grateful. Wishing Greg and Jon would stop at nodding acquaintances instead of friends made him look petty. Or maybe it made him *actually* petty. Either way, he'd just as soon not draw Greg's attention to it.

"I know everyone's hungry." Adrian's father furrowed his brow, which was never a good sign. "But I really think we ought to take a few minutes to talk this whole thing over before we go to dinner."

"You mean, like, do we really need to call a priest?" Dean nodded. "I hear you."

Cecile frowned. "I understand your hesitation. We usually use much more scientific methods. But this case is far beyond anything we've dealt with before." She twirled her bangles around her wrist. "Sam? Adrian? What do you think?"

"Well, you know I'm pretty much in step with Bo when it comes to the church. I really don't believe in any of that stuff. At all." Sam rubbed a hand over the back of his neck. "But I have to say, when Adrian and I were fighting that thing, it was *strong*. It was all we could do to bind it to that fan, and it was already halfway attached to it. Honestly? I don't think the two of us together have the strength to force it out."

Bo shot him a skeptical look. "And you think a priest does?"

Sam shrugged. "I have no idea. But I don't know what else to do. We can't simply discard the fan, like a lot of the sources we've found say you can do, because no one can touch it without the risk of possession or at least attachment. I don't think any of us are willing to put anyone in that kind of danger."

"Which means it doesn't follow the normal rules of demon-possessed objects," Adrian added. "Which means maybe you and I *can* banish the entity ourselves." He smiled weakly at Greg, who was staring at him as if he'd sworn he was the tooth fairy. "Come on, Greg, you don't believe in exorcisms and all that any more than I do."

"No, but I believe we all decided this thing must be a demonic entity, whatever that means, and I believe Sam just said he didn't think the two of you together could budge it out of that stupid fan. Which means I think we have to try something else." Greg scratched his chin, thinking hard. "Maybe Jon's dad doesn't have divine powers, but the church trains priests to deal with demons, right? Maybe that'll make a difference."

Adrian's dad nodded. "Greg, you make a very good point."

Predictably, Greg's face turned hot pink. "Thanks."

With a quick smile for Greg, Bo surveyed the group. "So, since we appear to have no other real option, do we have a consensus on calling Jon's father for help?"

"I'm for it," Sam answered. "What've we got to lose?"

"An innocent person's life, if this guy turns out to have no experience with exorcism." Cecile raised both of her hands palms up in a placating gesture when Bo frowned at her. "Relax, Bo. I'm sure you'll ask him about that. And I'll agree, since it really does seem that we don't have any other option."

Dean nodded. "Ditto."

Adrian didn't much like bringing in someone they didn't know to perform a ritual none of them truly believed would work, but he said okay anyway. At the very least, he could keep his psychic shields down and his power trained on the thing during the exorcism. If he could talk Sam into doing the same, maybe they'd be able to cast out the entity when the priest's ceremony inevitably did nothing.

"All right, then. That's settled." Dean skirted the end of the bed and headed for the entryway, where he'd left his sandals. "Anybody mind if we call this preacher guy after dinner? I'm starved."

"Me too." Cecile stood, looping her purse strap over her shoulder. She turned to address Adrian and Greg as they rose to follow her. "I hope you boys don't mind going to Med Deli. Dean told me about it, and I really wanted to try it."

"No, that's cool. We love Med Deli." Once Cecile moved out of earshot, Greg leaned closer to Adrian and lowered his voice to a whisper. "I think we should set Jon up with Omar."

Adrian grinned, amused by Greg's about-face in his attitude toward Jon. "*We?*"

"Fine. Me, then." Greg let out an exaggerated sigh. "You scientists have no sense of romance."

"Oh, that's nice. After I got you flowers and candy for your birthday too." Adrian pressed a hand to his heart.

Greg arched an eyebrow, and Adrian laughed. Sam cast them a curious glance as they all left the hotel room. Adrian pretended not to see. No one—least of all his stepdad—needed to know exactly how creative their sex life got when they combined plants, chocolate and psychokinesis.

Dr. Dale Hudson occupied a small, sunny office tucked into the back of the All Saints Episcopal Church on the south side of town. When Adrian and his dads walked in, Dr. Hudson stood and greeted them with a smile and an outstretched hand. "Hi there." He grasped Bo's hand. "You must be Dr. Broussard. I'm Dale, it's nice to meet you."

"Nice to meet you too, Dale, I'm Bo." Adrian's father smiled and gestured at Sam. "This is my husband and business partner, Sam Raintree, and our son, Adrian Broussard."

"Wonderful to meet all of you. Jon speaks very highly of you." Still smiling ear to ear, Dale shook Sam's hand, then Adrian's. "Please, sit down."

Adrian took a chair beside his father, trying to keep his surprise from showing. Obviously Jon would've told his dad about them, but Adrian wouldn't have believed he'd go out of his way to say good things about them if Dr. Hudson—Dale— hadn't just said so. Priests didn't lie. Adrian believed that, for the most part, even if he didn't believe in much else that went with the job description.

"So." Back behind his desk, pale and dignified in his black robes, he looked much more like a holy man than he had a few minutes ago. "When we spoke earlier, Bo, you said you needed me to help you banish a demon. Can you tell me more about that?"

"How much did Jon tell you?" Sam asked.

"Nothing. Just that you needed a priest, and that you'd rather work with the Episcopal church than the Catholic church for your own reasons." Dale turned his head slightly to look at Sam. The early afternoon sunshine caught his glasses at just the right angle to hide his eyes, giving his smile a sinister edge completely at odds with his personality. "He said he'd rather you explained the situation yourself because he didn't want to speak for you."

Once again, Jon went up a few notches in Adrian's estimation. Maybe he should help Greg fix Jon's love life after all. He seemed lonely, and Greg said Jon and Omar talked all the time at rehearsal already. Greg thought the two of them would be a good match, and Greg was usually right about things like that.

It would have to wait, though. Right now he and his dads had work to do.

The three of them had agreed ahead of time to let Bo do the talking, so Adrian and Sam sat quietly while Adrian's father explained the situation with the demon, including the reasons why they felt it was unsafe to try to throw the fan away. Dr. Hudson took notes on a touchpad and asked questions here and there. He never once acted as if he didn't believe their story, for which Adrian was grateful. He'd gotten used to cautious glances and silent skepticism from nearly everyone who learned about his abilities, but familiarity didn't mean it never hurt.

Once Adrian's dad finished his story, Dale looked up, his expression grim. "I can perform an exorcism on the fan." He rubbed his chin. "I've never done it on an object, but I've assisted with one on a person before, in my days as a missionary overseas. The ritual is essentially the same. I have a text with all the necessary prayers and everything I need at hand."

Some of the tightness melted from between Adrian's shoulder blades. He knew priests did exorcisms, but he'd still worried Dale would say he couldn't do it. The unhesitating *yes* was a relief.

"It'll be dangerous, though." Dale looked between them with a seriousness that made Adrian nervous all over again. "A demon can attach itself to an object, but it always prefers a human soul. When cast out of an object, it will find and possess a human being if it can. The people physically closest are generally in the most danger, but your friend Len will also be in danger. The demon already knows her, so it may seek her out."

A muscle twitched in Bo's jaw, but the growing-short temper Adrian knew he felt didn't show in his face. "Is there any way we can protect her?"

Dale shook his head. "Not that I know of. Demons are unpredictable by nature. All we can really do is pray that it will run back to its master rather than seek a human host."

Relying on prayer didn't sound too promising to Adrian. He kept his doubts to himself, though. Scorning a priest's faith in his own office when you needed him for an exorcism seemed like a bad idea, not to mention unforgivably rude.

Luckily, his father kept the pointed words Adrian knew he wanted to let loose to himself as well.

"I suppose we'll just do the best we can, then." Bo cast a swift glance at Adrian, as if he knew exactly what Adrian was thinking. "We'll need to speak with Len and get her permission to do this, especially if it's going to put her in further danger. I'll call you back and let you know what she says. Assuming she agrees, could we plan on performing the ceremony tomorrow morning?"

"I'm officiating at a wedding tomorrow morning. How about tomorrow afternoon? I should be free by around one."

Bo nodded. "That'll be fine."

Beside him, Sam shifted in his seat. "Where do we do this? Should we make an attempt to bring the fan here to the church? Maybe we could manage without touching it."

Dale's eyes went wide behind his glasses. "Oh no. No, no. Considering your experiences before, I'm inclined to think that would be too risky. The demon might try to attach to any person attempting to move the fan even if you touch it indirectly, using a hook or a net or what have you."

Adrian's stomach did a slow roll. He kept his silence in spite of the tiny voice in his head prodding him to speak up about his ability to move things with his mind. He was good, but he seriously doubted his ability to hang on to anything long enough to take it several miles from Len's apartment to the church—or, hell, to neutral ground somewhere—without losing control of it somewhere along the way.

His father squeezed his knee in a brief but comforting touch before standing. "All right. We'll come pick you up here then and bring you to Len's apartment. Thank you very much for agreeing to work with us, Dale. We'll be in touch soon."

Dale flashed his wide, sunny smile again as he stood and skirted the desk for a round of handshakes. "It's my pleasure, Bo. All part of God's work."

Adrian bit back laughter at the uncomfortable look on his dad's face. Dale wouldn't notice, thankfully, but Adrian had always found it amusing how his father could work with pretty much anyone, yet had never felt at ease dealing with religious sorts. He tended to feel judged for his sexuality, his work, or both, whether that was actually the case or not. Sam said it was a hangover from the times in which he and Bo both grew up. Adrian could see that, even though he himself had grown up in a much more open-minded world.

They all said their goodbyes, shook hands with Dale and left his office. Adrian trailed behind his dads, thinking hard while the two of them talked. It occurred to him that he and Sam might be able to get rid of the demonic entity for good, once Dale cast it out of the fan. If that, in fact, happened. There was no guarantee, of course—as far as Adrian knew, no one had ever tried what he had in mind—but he thought it was worth a try. At the very least, they might be able to keep the thing away from Len. He and Sam stood a decent chance of fighting it off. Len didn't.

When they exited the church into the front parking lot, Sam turned to Adrian with a suspicious gleam in his eyes. "Okay, Adrian. What're you plotting back there?"

A warm glow filled Adrian's chest. Sam knew him so well. He was every bit as much of a father to Adrian as Bo was. Adrian felt lucky to have two dads who loved him, and who he loved equally.

He pushed his way between his dads and slung an arm around each of them. "I have an idea."

His father stopped walking and pinned him with a fierce glare. "No. Absolutely not."

Adrian blinked, taken aback. "But, Dad, you don't even know—"

"The hell I don't. You think you and Sam can use your combined psychokinesis to send the entity into some other dimension, just like you did those things when you were eleven." He stepped closer, eyes blazing with a fury Adrian sort of understood and a trace of mournful resignation he totally didn't. "Tell me I'm wrong."

Adrian sighed. Sometimes he thought his dad was a closet psychic. "No, you're right. But listen, I don't think it's nearly as bad as you're making out. Sam and I together are strong enough to do this."

His father laughed. The bitterness in the sound brought back memories of the tumultuous months during Adrian's parents' separation and divorce. "You really believe that."

"Yes, I do." Angry now in his own right, Adrian met his father's glower with his own. "I know it's risky. And it's untested, which makes it riskier. I'm aware of *all* that. But I really believe we stand a good chance of pulling this off. If I didn't think so, I wouldn't even bring it up. I don't want to put myself at unnecessary risk, and I sure as hell don't want to put Sam at risk."

A charged silence fell. Behind Bo, Sam raised his eyebrows at Adrian but kept quiet.

Finally, Adrian's father sighed. "I know, son. And I'm sorry if I seem a bit overprotective." He grasped Adrian's shoulders and peered into his eyes. "Just know that it's because I love you. You and your brother and Sam. You're my life, the three of you, and I'd do anything to protect you. Anything." One corner of his mouth hitched up in a sad shadow of a smile. "It's hard sometimes, knowing I can't always keep you safe the way I'd like to."

Adrian swallowed around the lump in his throat. "I know, Dad. I love you too." Wrapping both arms around his father, he hugged him hard.

His dad hugged him back, strong arms snug around him in the way that had made him feel safe all his life. When they drew apart and Bo smiled at him, Adrian knew he had permission to at least try his plan, even though his dad would still fret and worry.

Sam touched his arm. "We can do some research on this today, Adrian. See what, if any, precedent there is. At the very least, we can educate ourselves on the process of exorcism involving inanimate objects so we'll know what to expect, if it works. Then we'll come up with a solid plan for how to face down the entity and attempt the interdimensional move. The more prepared we are, the better."

"Good idea." Adrian grasped Sam's hand. "Thanks, Sam."

He smiled. "We're in this together, kiddo. All of us."

They headed to the BCPI van, which they'd all agreed to take since this was an official visit. Bo unlocked the doors and slid behind the wheel. "Adrian, when do you need to pick up Greg?"

Adrian thought it over. They'd dropped Greg at the hand surgeon's office for his check-up before coming over here. "Well, if the doctor's running on time and everything's okay with Greg's wound, it probably won't be too long. Maybe twenty minutes from now?"

"Let's go back to the hotel and get Dean and Cecile," Sam said, buckling into the front passenger seat. "Then you can take the three of us to the library to get started on research while y'all go get Greg."

"I'll call you after I get Greg home and explain what we're doing. I imagine we'll go over to the hospital to talk to Len after that." Adrian thought about it as his dad backed out of the parking place. "It might take me a few minutes to talk him down off the ceiling."

"Yeah, I don't imagine he's going to be any happier than your dad is." Sam glanced over at his husband with an affectionate smile then turned to look at Adrian. "Just treat him gently, okay? It's the hardest thing in the world to watch someone you love put themselves in danger on purpose, especially when you can't do anything to stop it, or to help. Let him know you understand how he feels, and be patient with him."

Adrian knew Sam wasn't only talking about Greg, and he appreciated Sam keeping the reference to his dad veiled. He smiled. "I will. I really do understand, you know?"

"I know." Settling back into his seat, Sam laid a hand on Bo's thigh. "We both do."

"You have got to be fucking kidding me."

"Um. No." Adrian raked a hand through his hair the way he always did when he was nervous, though Greg didn't think he realized he did it. "We want to try it. If it makes you feel any better, Sam's with me on this. He thinks we can do it too."

Adrian's eyes cut down and sideways. Only for a second, but it was enough to tell Greg what Adrian was saying wasn't the whole story. Not that Greg saw that particular tell very often—in fact, Adrian tended more toward painful honesty than hedging on the truth—but he found it especially irritating right now, since what Adrian was talking about here meant a serious threat to his life.

Greg started to cross his arms, remembered he couldn't because it always hurt his hand when he did that, and scowled at his bandages *and* his boyfriend. "Dammit, Adrian. You don't have any idea if y'all can do this or not, and don't try to tell me you do. I mean, come on. Sending a demon into another dimension?" He shook his head. "I'm pretty sure no one's ever done that before."

"Maybe not." Adrian seemed reluctant to admit it, but he couldn't very well deny it. "But look, we're researching it, okay? Sam, Dean and Cecile went to the library as soon as we got done talking to Dale. Dr. Hudson, that is, Jon's father. And Dad went on over after he dropped us off." Adrian took Greg's hand. "We're going into this with as much knowledge as we possibly can. We're reading up on exorcism, on demons, looking for anything we can find on the use of psychokinesis against demonic entities and banishing them to other dimensions." He moved closer, his dark eyes pleading. "We want to be safe. I swear to you, we won't take any unnecessary risks."

"Other than doing it in the first place, you mean." Sighing, Greg leaned against Adrian's chest. Adrian's arms went around him, and he snuggled close, nuzzling Adrian's throat. "I can't talk you out of this, can I?"

"No." Adrian stroked Greg's back. Pressed a soft kiss to the side of his head. "I understand why you're worried, and I understand why you're angry. But I really feel like we need to do this. Dr. Hudson said anyone around could be in danger of being possessed by the demon once it's cast out of the fan. He said it could even reattach itself to Len. I'd never forgive myself if I didn't at least *try* to keep that from happening."

Hearing Adrian talk about demon possession with a straight face was surreal, but Greg couldn't laugh because it was *serious*. It was real—maybe not the way the church portrayed it, but real enough anyway—and the man he loved more than anything was about to put himself in deadly danger by facing that demon and risking possession, whatever that actually meant. All to keep everyone else from having to risk it.

Adrian's tendency to do sweet, noble shit like that both frustrated the crap out of Greg and made him love his one-of-a-kind man even more.

Overcome with conflicting emotions, Greg bit Adrian's neck hard. Adrian hissed but didn't push him away. "Ow. Stop it."

Greg unclenched his teeth. "Sorry."

"It's okay. You always turn into a five-year-old when you can't decide if you're really mad at me or not."

This was news to Greg. Or rather, the fact that Adrian had noticed was news. He snaked his good arm around Adrian's waist and clung so Adrian wouldn't see him blushing. "Yeah, well. It's frustrating when you do stuff that pisses me off but I can't yell at you because you're being all heroic. Biting makes me feel better."

Adrian chuckled, the sound vibrating through his chest where their bodies pressed together. "Okay, first of all, you already yelled at me. Second of all..." He rubbed his cheek against Greg's hair, slipped a hand downward and squeezed Greg's butt. The familiar tingle of Adrian's power raised goose bumps on Greg's arms, and he moaned. Adrian's voice dropped low. "Second of all, there are other physical ways to take out your frustrations, you know."

Adrian's metaphysical touch intensified, wrapping Greg's balls in a cocoon of electric warmth just this side of too much. His knees shook. "Uh. I see your point."

"Thought you might." Adrian shoved both hands—his real ones—down the back of Greg's shorts. "Bed or couch?"

"Bed. More room." Hooking his thumb into the belt loop on Adrian's jeans, Greg slung his other arm around Adrian's neck and tilted his head for a kiss.

Adrian took it, every bit as rough and eager as Greg had hoped. They stumbled toward the bedroom joined at the lips. Greg heard the scrape and bump of shoes, clothes and God knew what else flying out of their path at the command of Adrian's mojo.

The mere *thought* of all that power—and Adrian's complete, utter control over it—sent Greg's excitement shooting up into the ozone layer. He grabbed Adrian's ass and thrust their groins together, nearly sending the both of them tumbling to the floor.

Adrian smiled against his lips. "I love how turned on you get when I use my psychokinesis."

"Yeah?" Greg snaked his hand between Adrian's legs and squeezed his cock through his jeans, partly because he loved Adrian's cock and partly because he couldn't get enough of the way Adrian flushed and moaned when he did that. "I get even *more* turned on when you don't say science shit like 'psychokinesis' in bed."

Adrian's eyebrows went up. "We're not in bed yet." He glanced at the bed about two feet behind Greg.

Greg knew a challenge when he heard one. Grinning, he spun Adrian around, pushed him onto the mattress and jumped on top of him.

Adrian *oof*ed when Greg landed on him. "Good grief, you're crazy." He smiled up at Greg.

"Yeah. Humor the crazy person and fuck me." Greg pulled the meanest scowl he could manage.

Laughing, Adrian reached up and cupped Greg's face between his palms. "I always want to fuck you. Crazy."

Greg's throat tightened the way it always did when Adrian looked at him like that. Unable to speak, he bent and covered Adrian's mouth with his.

The kiss went from needy to ravenous in seconds. By the time they pulled apart, Greg's heart raced so fast he panted like a marathon runner, and Adrian had that look on his face that usually meant Greg had better get undressed fast unless he wanted his clothes to end up in shreds.

Once was enough to brand that experience on a guy's brain forever. Greg cherished the memory, but he really liked what he was wearing. Forcing himself to push away from Adrian, Greg yanked his T-shirt over his head and threw it on the floor. "Shorts. Help."

It didn't make much sense, but he knew Adrian understood him anyway. Adrian always did. Grasping Greg's waist, Adrian flipped him onto his back. Before Greg could properly reorient himself to the position change, his shorts and underwear had joined the T-shirt on the floor and he lay naked on the still-unmade bed.

He grinned. "That was fast."

"I don't feel like going slow." As if to prove his point, Adrian pushed Greg's thighs apart, swooped down and swallowed his cock to the base.

The combination of Adrian's mouth—well, his throat, if you wanted to be accurate, damn—and the determined blast of power penetrating straight through to Greg's bones almost sent him over the edge then and there. He screwed his eyes shut, dug his unbandaged hand into the crumpled sheets and hung on for all he was worth. No way in hell was he letting himself come *this* fast. Even Adrian, the nicest person on the planet, would be obligated by the guy code to give him a hard time about it.

A few seconds spent frantically making a grocery list in his head settled Greg's teetering control enough to let him enjoy both Adrian's oral and psychic talents without worrying about embarrassing himself. He opened his eyes and watched Adrian suck him. One of Adrian's hands lay splayed on Greg's belly, the light brown a wonderful contrast against Greg's paleness. The other hand grasped the base of Greg's cock, thumb caressing his skin in tiny circles. Adrian's eyes were closed, lashes thick and dark against cheeks flushed pink, his expression blissful.

God, I love him so much. The sudden strength of the feeling dug into Greg's heart and yanked hard enough to hurt. His eyes stung. Aching inside and unable to say a word, he buried his uninjured hand in Adrian's hair and pulled.

Luckily, Adrian got the hint. He let Greg's cock slip from his mouth and moved up for a kiss.

This one was slow, deep, full of all the love and want and fear Greg couldn't have put into words even if his voice would've worked. Adrian tasted like salty skin and precome spiced with the faint coppery tang of his power, and fuck, it was so *good* Greg though it might break him. He locked his legs around Adrian's hips and did his best to crawl inside Adrian through his mouth.

Adrian shifted without breaking the kiss. Lifted one arm, then the other. Shook off Greg's grip and raised his hips. Greg didn't get what was going on until Adrian rested his bare chest and groin against Greg's and squirmed in a way that ground their erections together.

"Impressive," Greg mumbled against Adrian's mouth. "You usually mojo *me* naked, not yourself."

"Yeah, well." Adrian shook his left leg. A quiet *whump* followed. Adrian's jeans and underwear hitting the floor, Greg assumed. "I didn't want to get up." Adrian grinned, looking dazed, mussed and completely gorgeous.

Greg grinned back, his heart full. "C'mere."

More kissing. Harder, hungrier, more urgent. Greg thrust his groin against Adrian's, meaning *hurry up and fuck me.* His body still pressed tight between Greg's thighs, Adrian shifted his weight enough to lift a hand. Greg heard a *smack* as the lube hit Adrian's palm.

A shiver ran through Greg's body. "God, that turns me on."

"Lube?" Adrian trailed his tongue along Greg's jaw to the sensitive spot on his neck and planted a soft kiss there.

Greg snickered. "How you got it. Your mojo." He arched against Adrian with a low moan when the kisses turned into gentle nips. "Lube means you're gonna fuck me, though. So, yeah."

"Smart boy." Mouth still fastened to Greg's neck, Adrian rolled sideways, flipped open the lube bottle with his thumb and tilted it over Greg's crotch. Greg squeaked at the odd sensation of unseen fingers lifting his balls out of the way followed by slick liquid trickling down between his butt cheeks. Chuckling, Adrian clicked the lube bottle shut and tossed it away. "You ready?"

"What do *you* think?" Greg pulled his legs up and spread them wider. "In me. Now."

Adrian didn't say anything else. He raised his head and held Greg's gaze while he positioned his cock and pressed into Greg's body.

Greg fought to hold eye contact while Adrian pushed inside him. It didn't hurt, exactly—as often as Greg took it up the ass, he didn't need stretching anymore—but a tiny thread of pain wound through the pleasure, just enough to tear a sharp cry from Greg's throat.

He clamped his legs around Adrian before he could get the wrong idea and stop. Greg didn't want to stop. He wanted Adrian to fuck him hard and fast and deep. He wanted to still feel the lingering soreness tomorrow. To have a tangible reminder of Adrian while he was off battling demons.

Greg didn't want to think about that. Not now. Not with Adrian's cock filling him up and Adrian's wide-open eyes shining with everything they felt for each other.

"Oh God." Adrian's eyelids fluttered and settled at half-mast. "Close."

"Yeah." Greg always knew when Adrian was about to come. Knew the way his face softened, the hitch of his breath, the way his cheeks went pink. Greg had memorized the signs long ago and cherished each one. He curled his hand around the back of Adrian's neck. "Harder."

Adrian obliged, pounding into Greg hard enough to hammer his gland with every stroke and send him spiraling toward his own release. Grunting with the effort, Greg dug his heels into Adrian's back and did his best to get some friction on his cock without losing the perfect angle Adrian had going.

As usual, Adrian knew exactly what Greg needed. He let out a totally unmanly whine when Adrian took his prick in a firm grip and started jerking him off just the way he liked. The hot, electric buzz of Adrian's power flowed from his palm, took his touch to the next level and worked Greg's cock in a way no human hand could by itself.

When Adrian's orgasm hit, bringing an intense rush of power along with the tortured, transported expression Greg loved better than anything in the world, that did it. Greg came so hard it hurt, the spunk pumping out of him in violent pulses. He clung to Adrian, shook and moaned along with his man and wished it never had to end.

Nothing that good lasted forever though, and eventually Adrian carefully pulled out, pried Greg's legs off him and collapsed sideways. He laid his head on Greg's chest with a happy sigh and cuddled him close. "Wow."

"You said it." Greg rested his cheek on Adrian's sweaty hair. "Let's just stay in bed, okay? Everybody else can get along without us for the rest of the day."

Adrian lay silent for a minute, absently stroking the gelling semen on Greg's belly, and Greg knew what his answer would be. Sure enough, when Adrian pushed up onto his elbow and looked Greg in the eye, the *no* and the apology for it were written all over his face.

"You know I can't do that, much as I wish I could. We need Len's permission to go to her place and try this whole thing, and we need to get that today." Adrian's voice was soft but determined. He touched Greg's cheek. "I'm sorry. You can stay here. I know you're tired, and you're still hurting. I'll go talk to Len."

If Greg wasn't half-drunk with orgasm, he would've bitten Adrian again. As it was, he still felt irked enough to manage an eye roll. "Jesus, Adrian, don't be dense. You know that's not my issue."

To Adrian's credit, he didn't deny it. Scooting upward, he leaned down to kiss Greg's lips. "I have to do this, Greg. I *have* to." He rested his forehead against Greg's, his hand warm and gentle on Greg's cheek. "Please understand that."

Greg wanted to say *no*. Wanted to talk Adrian out of it. He could, if he tried hard enough. Adrian loved him that much. But it wouldn't be fair and he knew it, because he *did* understand.

He made himself smile, though he'd never felt less like it in his life. "I do."

The relief in Adrian's eyes was worth it.

Len took the whole thing better than Greg thought he would've in her place. When Adrian explained that he and Sam had bound the entity back to the fan and now they needed permission to bring in a priest to exorcize it permanently, she didn't even seem surprised. She just nodded and told them to do whatever it took.

Of course, Greg figured Len having her first taste of freedom from the thing in weeks probably made her willing to do anything to get rid of the damn thing for good.

Len gazed up at Greg and Adrian with wide, haunted eyes. "Is it safe?"

Greg crossed his arms and raised his eyebrows at Adrian, who darted him a dark glance but answered Len anyway. "The priest we've contacted has experience with exorcism, and we're researching the topic as well so we'll know what to expect. We're doing everything we can to make this process as safe as possible."

Len wasn't stupid, and Greg saw her expression turn fearful as she caught the subtext in Adrian's words. "So it's dangerous, or can be. That's what you're saying."

Adrian raked a hand through his hair. He seemed stressed and more than a little upset beneath his surface calm. Feeling bad for him, Greg slipped his arm around Adrian's waist and squeezed, trying to show his support without words. Adrian gave him a grateful sidelong smile.

"Dr. Hudson—the priest—told us there's a possibility that the demon might seek out a human being to attach itself to once it's cast out of the fan. The people who are physically closest will be in the most danger, but it may look for you because it already knows you." Adrian touched Len's arm when she let out a frightened little noise. "We're going to do everything we can to avoid that and distract it away from you. But you need to know what the dangers are before you agree. It's not fair for you to give us the go-ahead on this unless you know what you're agreeing to."

Len shut her eyes. She still looked tired and battered, though not as bad as before. Greg's heart went out to her, but he kept quiet. Ultimately, this was her decision. He had no business influencing her.

Finally, she opened her eyes again and looked at Adrian. "I still want you to do it. I'm willing to risk it if it means getting rid of this damn thing." She pointed at him, her expression turning hard. "You guys had better be careful, though. I don't want it back on me, but I'd rather that than it attach to one of you instead. This is *my* problem, not yours. Okay?"

Adrian's back tensed under Greg's arm. "I can't make any promises about what's going to happen. But I *can* promise we'll do everything in our power to get rid of the entity for good and not allow it to attach itself to anyone at all. None of us want that to happen."

"Well, I guess that's the best I'm going to get." Her lips curved into a faint smile. "Thanks for everything, guys."

"We're happy to help, believe me." Adrian took her hand and squeezed it. "Can we do anything for you?"

She shook her head. "I'm fine. Sleeping now, finally, since that thing's not bothering me anymore." She reached for Greg. "Hug."

Letting go of Adrian, Greg bent down and hugged Len. "I'm glad you're feeling better, hon."

"Thanks." She smiled at him as he pulled away. "How about you? How's your hand doing?"

"All right. Doc says it's healing up fine, and it doesn't hurt too much anymore."

She arched an eyebrow as if she knew better, but didn't contradict him. "Good. I'm glad." She peered solemnly at Adrian. "Call me after it's all done, or come by and let me know how it went."

"We will." Adrian reached for Greg's hand and wound their fingers together. "Try not to worry. We'll talk to you tomorrow."

She nodded, but Greg knew she'd worry anyway. Just like he would.

Outside, he slid on his sunglasses and followed Adrian toward the parking garage. Apparently a burn on his hand made Greg an invalid, so they had to drive. "You didn't tell her what you and Sam plan to do."

Adrian didn't look at him as they crossed Manning Drive at the light. "There was no reason to tell her."

"No reason?" Greg stared at the side of Adrian's stubbornly forward-facing head. "I thought you wanted her to be fully informed."

Adrian shot him a pointed glare. "If you thought that information was so necessary, why didn't *you* tell her? You've never exactly been one to keep anything to yourself."

Greg opened his mouth to answer and realized he *had* no answer. He thought about it while they walked to the garage and took the single flight of stairs up to the level where Adrian had parked. It wasn't a long walk, but it was enough to make him realize he agreed with Adrian.

The realization pissed him off, but he couldn't deny it, and he *really* couldn't lie about it.

"You're right," he admitted after they'd both buckled in and Adrian cranked the engine. "I won't pretend I like it, because I fucking hate it. But you're right."

"I know." Adrian rested a hand on his thigh. "I'm sorry."

Maybe it was petty of him, but knowing Adrian didn't like it any better than he did made Greg feel better.

In the end, Adrian's dads both agreed that the wisest course of action was to restrict the participants in the exorcism to the two of them, Adrian, and the priest. Adrian knew by the thunderous expression on Sam's face when they arrived at the apartment the next day that he'd wanted Bo to stay behind as well.

Adrian would've laughed if he hadn't been so nervous, for himself as well as his parents. When his father put his foot down, no force on earth could budge it. Sam ought to know that better than anyone.

"I've already called Dale," Adrian's father announced without preamble as he and Sam walked in. "We're going to meet him at the church in fifteen minutes and he's going to ride with us to Len's apartment."

"All right." Adrian glanced from his dad's stubbornly blank face to Sam's forbidding glower to the unhappy frown Greg had finally stopped trying to hide. The tension in the room made him feel tired. "Look. Sam, you know as well as I do that Dad's going to be there no matter what we say, so we might as well resign ourselves to it right now." Turning his back on Sam's startled expression, Adrian went to Greg, sat beside him and took his hand. "We've already talked about this whole thing, so I really don't have anything else to say about it, except that I promise I'll do everything I can to come back to you safe and sound. Okay?"

"Okay." Greg gave him a sad little smile. "Call me, yeah? When it's done."

"I will." Adrian pulled Greg close and buried his face in Greg's silky curls. "I love you."

"I love you too." Greg pressed a lingering kiss to Adrian's lips, slid his fingers through Adrian's hair and caressed his neck. When he drew away, his gaze held Adrian's with near-painful intensity. "Please be careful."

Adrian squeezed Greg's hand. "I will. I swear."

Greg swallowed. Closed his eyes. Opened them again and visibly composed himself. He let go of Adrian's hand. "Go on, before I try to keep you here."

His tone was teasing, but the look on his face wasn't. Adrian nodded and rose to his feet.

When he turned, he was surprised to see his dads standing in the entryway in each other's arms, sharing a deep kiss. He looked away. It wasn't like he'd never seen them kiss before, but something about this felt different. Intimate. Like he was intruding on an especially private moment.

Sam drew back, both hands cradling his husband's face and a tender protectiveness shining through the lingering exasperation in his eyes, and Adrian understood. Neither of his dads was particularly happy with the other right now, but both understood the danger facing them well enough to put their argument in the past where it belonged and make sure they went into this thing each knowing they were loved.

Watching them whisper quietly together, Adrian was glad he and Greg had done the same.

Adrian's father turned toward them, his hand still clasping Sam's. "All right. Adrian, are you ready?"

"Yeah." He gazed at Greg, who'd risen from the sofa to stand beside him. "I'll see you soon."

"You'd better." Resting his hands on Adrian's shoulders, Greg brushed a quick kiss across his mouth. "Bye."

"Bye." Adrian smiled and felt better when Greg smiled back at him, even though it was a watered-down version of his usual bright grin.

"We'll look out for him, Greg." Sam squeezed Adrian's shoulder when he reached the spot where they waited for him. "Talk to you later."

"Goodbye," Adrian's dad called to Greg as they left.

Before the door closed, Adrian caught a glimpse of Greg's pale face, gray eyes focused on Adrian as if he could bring Adrian back with the power of his will.

They picked up Dr. Hudson and headed to Len's apartment with a minimum of conversation. The priest looked grim but calm, exhibiting none of the nervousness tying Adrian's stomach in knots. He wished he had his father's and Sam's confidence. He knew they were aware of the danger, but they didn't seem scared at all. Adrian admired that.

Len's place hadn't changed since they left the last time. The fan still lay on the floor of the laundry room where Sam and Adrian had dropped it before.

"Sorry about the location," Adrian's father said as he shut the apartment door behind the group. "But we didn't want to risk anyone touching it to move it after what happened the last time."

"I can understand that." Dale walked into the cramped little room and looked around, hands on his hips. "More room would be better, but I can work with this. It's certainly preferable to anyone taking the risk of touching the fan."

A thought occurred to Adrian. "Maybe I can use my psychokinesis to move it. That way I wouldn't have to touch it."

Sam grinned at him. "That's a terrific idea. I can't believe we didn't think of it before."

"I can. You'd both just fought off what seems to be a fairly powerful demonic entity, and you were pretty shaken up. I'd have been surprised if you *had* thought of it at the time." Adrian's father rested a hand on his shoulder. "Dale, what do you think?"

Dale shrugged. "I have no experience with any kind of psychic phenomena, so I couldn't tell you whether or not it would be safe to use these psychic powers to move the object. I wish I could."

"My feeling is that it would probably be all right," Sam said when Bo looked at him. "Adrian, Cecile and I have all had our psychic shields open to this entity without feeling any sense of being overwhelmed or overtaken by it. It was only when Adrian and I touched the fan that we got dragged in."

"This is true." Tightening his hand on Adrian's shoulder, Bo peered into Adrian's eyes. "Are you sure, Adrian?"

He nodded. "Moving the fan isn't a problem. I do things like that all the time at home."

"All right. Well, try to place it on the table, then, if that's all right with Dale." Bo raised his eyebrows in question at Dale, who nodded. "If you get the slightest hint that this entity might be trying to attach to you through the psychic link, break it immediately. Don't hesitate. Okay?"

"Okay."

Adrian stared at the fan, trying to get the measure of it. The now-familiar energy still poured off it in crackling waves, but it felt different. More contained.

Angrier too.

This was not going to be a fun day.

Adrian cleared his throat to dispel some of the tightness. "Y'all might want to give me some room. I have excellent control over my psychokinesis, but I don't know how the entity being attached to the fan is going to affect its movement, and I don't want it to accidentally touch anyone while I'm moving it."

"Good thinking, son." His father strode toward the living room, gesturing to Sam and Dale to follow him.

The three of them gathered beyond the sofa. "Okay, go ahead," Sam said. "And let me know if you need backup. I know I can't help you move it, but I can help with the entity if you need it."

"I will. Thanks."

Closing his eyes, Adrian drew a few slow, deep breaths. Once his mind felt calm, centered and focused, he opened his eyes and pictured his psychokinesis as a hand lifting the fan from the floor.

It felt like throwing a rock at a hornets' nest. The demonic energy swirled and buzzed in Adrian's head, the fury of it increasing as he floated the fan along from the laundry room to the dining area. He set it on the table as gently as he could, so as not to stir up the entity any more than he already had.

He withdrew his metaphysical grip on the fan and plopped into the nearest chair. "It's angry," he said before anyone could ask. "But it's very much tied to the fan. I felt no danger at all of being possessed or otherwise taken over by the entity. Not for lack of trying on its part, though. It wanted to get at me very badly, I could tell." He rubbed at the ache beginning in his temples. "Maybe we should give it a little while to settle down before we do anything else."

"It won't help." Dale paced toward the table, his gaze never leaving the fan. "It knows we're here. It knows what we want, most likely. Waiting won't help." He frowned at Adrian. "It won't hurt for you to take some time to recover if you need it, though."

Adrian shook his head. "No, I'm fine. I just have a little bit of a headache, that's all. Moving the fan didn't wear me down any."

Dale studied him in silence for several long seconds, then nodded. "All right. If everyone's ready, then we'll begin."

Sam kissed Adrian's father, touched his cheek and moved to stand beside Adrian at the table. Bo stayed on the other side of the sofa, his pod in hand. Whether to record the proceedings or call 911 if need be, Adrian had no idea. He didn't much like either option, to be honest.

"Wait." Ignoring the priest's curious gaze, Adrian strode over to his father and hugged him hard. "I love you, Dad."

His dad's arms went around him and squeezed tight. "I love you too, son." He drew back, smiling in spite of the solemn look in his eyes. "It'll be all right. I believe in you both."

Adrian returned his smile, grateful beyond words and trusting his father to understand. "Thanks." He went back to the table, his heart beating hard, and wrapped Sam in a tight hug. "I love you, Sam."

"Love you, kiddo." Sam returned the hug, patting him on the back. When he pulled away, Sam took Adrian's hand and gave it a reassuring squeeze. "We're in this together, Adrian. It'll be fine."

"Yeah." Letting go of Sam's hand, Adrian faced Dale. "Okay, I'm ready."

Dr. Hudson gave Adrian an odd look, as if wondering why he wanted to tell his dads he loved them before confronting a demonic entity, but kept his thoughts to himself. "Very well. I will recite the necessary prayers and demand that the demon leave this fan in the name of God. Whatever happens, whatever you might see or hear, do *not* let it affect you. Remain strong, and don't listen to the lies this agent of Satan will no doubt tell you. Do you understand?"

Adrian nodded along with his parents, biting the insides of his cheeks to keep from laughing out loud. If Dale only knew what the three of them had faced in the past—especially his father and Sam—he wouldn't feel the need to warn them.

Closing his eyes, Dale began reciting a prayer in rapid Latin. Adrian caught only about one word in three, but it seemed to his untutored ear to be a standard-enough prayer. As far as he could tell, the entity didn't react at all. He glanced at Sam, who shook his head.

Adrian wondered if that was a bad sign. If an exorcism was likely to work, shouldn't a demon fear the power of prayer?

You don't believe in prayer. So what does that tell you?

Nothing. It told him nothing. No scientist worth the title let his own beliefs—or non-beliefs—get in the way of his observations. He needed to wait, watch and keep an open mind.

Adrian recognized the moment Dale switched from prayer to the exorcism ritual. The stream of Latin continued unbroken, but he opened his eyes and held one hand palm open toward the fan. His voice took on a firm, commanding tone.

219

The entity reacted this time. Adrian felt it—a quickening in the angry buzz of the thing's energy. A swift glance in Sam's direction confirmed that he felt it as well.

It wasn't enough, though. Not nearly enough to kick the entity free from the fan. Adrian felt it strain at its bonds, felt its fury rise with every word Dale spoke, but the demon remained trapped.

For a moment, Adrian thought about leaving it that way. Maybe he could use his power to levitate the fan to the dumpster outside and they could forget all about it. His father would definitely back him up, and Sam would understand.

What stopped him from letting Dr. Hudson fail, using his mind to discard the fan and thus allowing them to wash their hands of it, was the mental picture of some unsuspecting person salvaging the fan from the dumpster, or even from the landfill. With the number of people who scavenged from trash and the dumps in this area—looking for castoffs such as this fan in particular—the risk of the demon attaching to another innocent victim was too high. If Dale couldn't cast the entity out, then he and Sam had to try.

He let the knowledge that he'd predicted this outcome slide through his mind without sticking. If they made it through this, he could think about it later.

Dale continued talking in Latin, his voice steady and resolute. Adrian caught commands to the demon to be silent, pleas to God to cast out the demon. All of which magnified its wrath to a frightening level, but none of which budged it from the fan. Adrian looked at Sam, who stood to his right. Sam darted a brief but pointed glance at the fan then met Adrian's gaze with a grim awareness in his eyes that told Adrian they were on the same page.

On Adrian's other side, Dale seemed to reach a crescendo. The fan vibrated on the table and Adrian heard a low growl, but the essence of the energy in Adrian's head remained unchanged.

The entity wasn't going anywhere unless he and Sam intervened.

Sam touched Adrian's hand. *On three*, he mouthed. Adrian nodded. He took a deep breath and blew it out, forcing his pulse to slow and his mind to focus. He sensed Sam doing the same beside him.

Catching Adrian's eye, Sam held a clenched fist beside his thigh. Adrian nodded again to indicate he was watching. Sam counted with his fingers—One. Two. Three. They lowered their shields together and hit the entity with the force of their combined power.

Chapter Twelve

It felt like a heavy door being blasted open. If Adrian had ever doubted what sort of entity they'd faced all this time, he didn't doubt it now. The fan shot up to the ceiling, spinning so fast it was nothing but a blur, and crashed back down to the table hard enough to crack the cage. An amorphous darkness rose from it. The lights flickered. The growl they'd heard before came again, louder and more menacing. Adrian thought he caught words in it, but he couldn't understand them.

The gist seemed clear enough, though. Hate. Fury. Bloodlust.

Adrian didn't need to look at Sam to know the next step. He focused his psychokinesis as hard as he could on forcing open an interdimensional portal, in spite of the less-than-ideal conditions. Sam did the same, the heat of his active power like an invisible sun at Adrian's side.

The shadow grew to swallow the room. Within seconds, Adrian felt cut off, cold and alone in a pitch-black bubble with nothing but a confusion of sounds to keep him company— Dale's shaky but fervent commands, his father's muffled calls, the demon's rising roar and his own pulse rushing in his ears. But the unmistakable sensation of reality twisting on itself cut through the chill, the fear and chaos, and Adrian knew they were close to defeating this thing.

Apparently the entity felt it too. It fought against Adrian and Sam's unified grip. Adrian concentrated and held on tight. Thought the thing toward the rift between dimensions. Felt Sam do the same.

Pain clawed at the inside of his skull. His vision bloomed with spots, gray on black. His lungs froze. Blinded and unable to draw a breath, he felt himself topple. He grasped at the table, his whole mind working to keep the entity pinpointed with his psychokinesis.

One hand scrambled at the middle of the table. The other missed entirely. His chin hit the edge, snapping his head backward. He fell, landing flat on his back on the floor. His head thudded and bounced on the hard surface. It ought to hurt, all of it—his chin, his neck, the rear of his head where it connected with the wooden boards. But his body felt numb, all sensation drowned out by the agony of metaphysical claws inside his mind.

Just when he thought he couldn't hold on to the portal and the demon any longer, he felt it shift. Felt a hard mental shove followed by an ear-splitting shriek, then a ringing silence as the rift slammed shut.

The force holding his body paralyzed dissipated. He drew a deep, grateful breath then blinked until the blackness faded to a washed-out gray. A shape leaned over him and said something he couldn't hear. His father. He smiled and tried to answer, but nothing came out. Thinking maybe he'd try again when he wasn't so tired, Adrian shut his eyes.

He wasn't sure what it said about him that the last thing he thought before consciousness slipped away was that he hoped he'd wake up eventually, because he was damn well going to tell everyone *I told you so.*

Greg didn't last five minutes after Adrian and his dads left before the inevitable restlessness and fear set it. Thankfully, Dean and Cecile showed up soon after to keep him company.

Not that it calmed his nerves all that much. He jumped up from the sofa, abandoning the mug of chamomile tea Cecile had made in an attempt to settle him, and began a pattern of pacing between the French door to the tiny balcony and the front door's peephole. As if that would bring Adrian home safe any faster.

Cecile intercepted him on the fourth or fifth trip to the window. "Greg. Come on." She slid an arm around his waist and steered him toward the couch. "I know you're worried and scared, honey, but keeping it all in isn't going to help. Let's sit down and talk."

Greg darted a pleading look at Dean. Predictably, he was no help. He scooted over to make room for Greg and handed him his tea as Cecile forced him to sit. "You're worried, huh?"

"Do you blame me? I mean, Adrian's off fighting a *demon*, for fuck's sake. If that's what it really is. And even if it isn't, it's still something bad." Greg slumped in his seat and took a sip of tea. It was good, with just the right amount of sugar, and he gave Cecile a grateful smile. "Sorry, y'all. I know you've been through all this shit before and I'm probably just being annoying."

"No, you're not." Cecile patted his knee. "Believe me, we understand what you're feeling. We may be on the other side of the fence most of the time, but we've been where you are before, and we know how difficult it can be to sit and wait and do nothing while someone you care about is in danger."

"Which doesn't make it any easier, I know," Dean added. "But we're here for you anyway."

Greg glanced from Dean to Cecile, saw the worry and strain on both of their faces and felt like the most selfish person on the planet. Sam's and Bo's lives were on the line as much as Adrian's was. Dean and Cecile had been close friends with both of them for most of Adrian's life. They must be as afraid as him, but they'd managed to stay calm and keep from acting like drama queens.

With a deep sigh, he leaned against Cecile's shoulder and rested his bandaged hand over Dean's. "Thanks, guys. I'll be okay once they get back, I swear. It's just this is my first time with Adrian going off without me to do something dangerous. I'm finding out I don't do so good with that."

"Understandable." Cecile kissed his head.

The lock rattled for a second, then the apartment door burst open. Sam staggered in, looking pasty and exhausted. Bo followed behind him, half-carrying an unsteady, groggy Adrian.

"Oh, my God." Greg leapt up, almost spilling his tea. He set his mug on the coffee table and ran to Adrian. "Shit, what's wrong with him?"

"'M fine." Adrian gave him a wan smile. "Just got a little beat up, is all."

"I'll say. Shut up now." Slipping his good hand around Adrian's waist, Greg helped Bo lead Adrian to the sofa. "Bo, what happened? What's wrong with Adrian?" He glanced at Sam, who'd collapsed into the nearest chair, and frowned. "And Sam?"

"They were able to banish the entity into another dimension, but the effort took a great deal out of them." Bo rounded the end of the sofa. He and Greg lowered Adrian to the couch. "Adrian fell at one point and hit his chin on the table. He also hit his head on the floor, by the way, so if you have better luck than we did in making him see a doctor, then that would be wonderful."

Cecile sighed. "I can't imagine where he got that from."

Bo shot her a dark look. She crossed her arms and raised an eyebrow at him.

"Shit, Adrian." Parking himself beside his stubborn boyfriend, Greg cupped Adrian's face in his hands and stared hard into his eyes. "Are you crazy? Why won't you go to the damn hospital and let them check you out? You look like hell."

Adrian was already shaking his head before Greg was halfway done. "I'm not hurt, I promise. It's just that thing. It was *strong.*" His eyes drifted shut. He swallowed. Yawned. Opened his eyes again. "The priest couldn't get it loose from the fan. Sam and I had to kind of take over and do it."

"Seriously?" One arm protectively around Adrian, Greg peered over at Sam, who looked almost as bad as Adrian but had a lot more experience in the paranormal field. "Sam? What happened?"

"What Adrian said." Sam took the glass of water Cecile handed him. Greg hadn't even seen her go into the kitchen. "Thanks, Cecile. Yeah, Dale started the exorcism, but it didn't seem to be doing the job as far as getting the entity out of the fan, so Adrian and I both turned our psychokinesis on it." He let out a sharp laugh. "*That* worked. The damn thing came loose like a fucking freight train. It took everything the two of us had to get it through the portal we'd opened."

Dean nudged Greg out of the way. "Sorry," he said in response to Greg's protesting glare. "I want to take a look at Adrian, since he wouldn't go to the ER like a sensible person."

Adrian put on his irritated face, but let Dean—with his years of experience as an ER nurse's aid—get on with the exam anyway. Which was a good thing because if he'd refused, Greg had every intention of throwing the stubborn ass over his shoulder and taking him to the hospital whether he liked it or not.

While Dean made Adrian follow a penlight with his eyes and asked him if he knew what year it was, Greg crossed to where Sam slumped in the battered recliner with Cecile perched on its arm. "You okay, Sam?"

"I'm fine. Just feeling a little like I've been hit by a truck." He glanced at Adrian. "He'll be all right. He just needs some time to recover."

Greg nodded and managed an anemic smile. He trusted Sam's judgment and couldn't help feeling better to hear that Sam thought Adrian would be okay, but he wasn't comfortable saying anything out loud in case he jinxed it somehow. Silly, but there it was.

Cecile, who'd remained in pensive silence since Adrian and his dads got home, rested a hand on Sam's shoulder. "Sam, I'm trying to understand how this whole thing worked, exactly. The other day, you didn't think you and Adrian would be able to remove the entity from the fan on your own. You were fairly certain, and Adrian wasn't too hopeful of it either. So, what happened?"

Honestly, Greg wondered the same thing. Sam rarely read a situation wrong when it came to psychic abilities, especially his own. For him to misjudge to this level the amount of psychokinesis needed for a task was, in Greg's experience at least, unheard of.

Sam shook his head, his expression thoughtful. "I'm not sure, to tell you the truth. But I'm inclined to say that our friend Dale actually *did* help, to some degree."

"I didn't feel it." Adrian rubbed at his eyes as Dean switched off his penlight and rose to his feet. "It felt to me like nothing he did made any difference."

Much as Sam's answer interested Greg—and it did—he cared a lot more about Adrian's health and well-being. "Is he okay, Dean?"

"As far as I can tell, yeah." Dean strode into the kitchen and opened the fridge. "I still wish he'd go the ER, just in case, but I don't actually see any reason to worry." Taking the orange juice from the refrigerator's top shelf, Dean set it on the counter and went to search out a glass.

"Good. Thanks, Dean." Bo handed Adrian one of the sofa cushions, then stood. "Here, son. Lie down. Greg, sit with him and make him behave."

"Gladly." Plopping onto the sofa, Greg manhandled Adrian's feet into his lap. "Sorry, Sam. I think you were going to answer Adrian and I got in your way."

Sam grinned, though it wasn't his usual bright smile. "No problem. But yeah, what I want to say is I felt the same thing, but when I dug a little deeper, I caught a thread of something unfamiliar. It didn't feel like the demon, and it didn't feel like any kind of psychic energy either. It was human, though, which means it could only come from one place."

"Dr. Hudson. It makes sense, I guess, since the entity *did* let go of the fan easier than I would've thought, considering how strongly attached it was." Adrian's forehead furrowed. "How, though? I mean, seriously, from a scientific viewpoint, *how* does that work? Because I don't think any of you believe any deity really did this any more than I do."

In the silence that followed, Dean walked over and handed Adrian a glass of juice complete with a bendy straw so he could drink without sitting up. "Maybe this is one of those *how*s we never learn." Dean pulled out one of the kitchen chairs, straddled it and folded his arms on top of the back.

"Maybe." Bo, pacing as usual, stopped behind Sam's chair and laid both hands on his husband's shoulders. "Personally, I've come to believe the human mind has its own power, regardless of any psychic abilities. Any strong conviction is bound to enhance that power."

"A conviction such as a priest's faith." Cecile nodded. "It makes sense."

"Well, Dale's nothing if not passionate in his faith, that's for sure." Tilting his head back, Sam smiled up at Bo. "You're sexy when you're smart like that." He laid a hand over Bo's on his shoulder.

At the table, Dean snickered. Cecile shot him a *be quiet* look, but smiled anyway. Adrian rolled his eyes. It made him look about twelve, and Greg grinned. He wondered if Adrian had always done that when his dads got affectionate.

Bo laughed. "I think I need to take you back to the hotel for a nap."

"A nap. Right." Dean peered over at Greg and Adrian. "Mind if I stay here for a while?"

Adrian groaned. "Oh my God."

Greg gave Adrian's leg a comforting pat and tried not to picture a Sam-and-Bo not-nap. Adrian would not appreciate him appreciating the mental image of Adrian's dads not-napping.

"A *nap*. Remember what he's just been through." The glare Bo aimed at Dean was marred by a smile trying to break through, but it was pretty good anyway. Dean grinned wider and waggled his eyebrows.

"I really do think we should go now. Sam and Adrian both need to rest." Rising to her feet, Cecile brushed back a lock of long, dark hair that had fallen over her shoulder. "Greg, call us if either of you need anything at all, okay?"

"Sure thing. Thanks." Greg moved Adrian's legs, jumped up and hugged Cecile hard, then went to give Dean a hug too. When Sam stood, aided by Bo, Greg hugged them both. "Thanks for everything, guys. Sam, I'm glad you're all right."

"Me too." Sam smiled at him. "Take care of our boy there. And yourself."

Greg nodded, his usual Sam-and-Bo-inspired blush heating his cheeks.

Bo squeezed his hand. "I know I've told you both this before, but I'm glad you and Adrian found one another. He's had a difficult life, and you make him very happy. He deserves that happiness. And so do you." He smiled at Sam, who nodded his agreement.

To his absolute horror, Greg's eyes burned with impending tears. Mortified, he blinked fast until they went away. "Thank you."

He wanted to say so much more, but his throat closed up and nothing would come out. Sam and Bo seemed to understand just fine, though. Bo pressed his fingers once more before letting go, Sam slapped him on the shoulder and the two of them went to Adrian's couch.

After giving Adrian hugs, cheek kisses—on Cecile's part—and promises to get together and have a proper celebration the next day, the group left and Greg and Adrian were alone.

Greg wandered back to the sofa, gave Adrian a nudge and settled himself in his usual corner with Adrian's head in his lap. "Well. You've had an adventurous afternoon, huh?"

"You could say that, yeah." Adrian shut his eyes when Greg ran his fingers through Adrian's hair. "Mmm. That's nice."

"I know what you like. Lucky for you, I like it too." Greg took Adrian's glass, which was listing dangerously to the right, and set it on the little wooden table beside the sofa before Adrian could spill juice all over the floor. "How are you feeling? Any better?"

"Yeah. Especially now." Adrian's eyelids opened. He stared straight into Greg's eyes. "Let's go to bed."

Greg gaped. "Um. Not that I don't want to, you know, I mean I'm always up for it, but...now?"

Adrian laughed. "No, not now. I don't really feel like it at the moment. I just want to sleep for about a year." He turned his head to nuzzle Greg's belly. "This is going to sound stupid, but I wondered if you'd come lie down with me until I fall asleep?"

Something in Adrian's voice sounded hesitant, uncertain and afraid. If Greg could've gone to wherever Sam and Adrian had sent that fucking evil entity and kicked its demonic ass, he'd have done it for making Adrian—*Adrian*, mister scientific logic himself—scared to go to sleep alone in the daytime.

Not that Greg minded holding Adrian while he slept. He loved that, in fact. It was the *principle* of the thing.

"You know I will." He bent to kiss Adrian's lips. "Come on."

He helped Adrian up, and they went to the bedroom arm in arm. In spite of his worry about the effects of the whole exorcism event on Adrian, Greg felt tranquil for the first time since all this started. The entity was gone for good, nobody was possessed, and Adrian had returned home safe. Everything else was just details.

Epilogue

When Harlan Osterberg lifted Savannah Blackwood—now his wife—into his arms and kissed her at the end of *A Tar Heel Born*'s final scene, the audience rose to its collective feet, clapping and cheering. The sound echoed from the walls and ceiling of the old PlayMakers Theater.

Len leaned over from her spot to Adrian's right. "What a wonderful play."

Adrian nodded, beaming. If every show turned out as well as opening night, they were in for an excellent run. "It is, isn't it? They've done a fantastic job."

To Adrian's left, Chelsea shot him a wide smile. "Did you see Theo during the final dance number? He was great, wasn't he?"

Adrian stifled a laugh. Theo had come a long way with his dance moves, according to Greg, though in this professional crew he ended up on the low end of average. Chelsea was always proud of him, though. Adrian liked that about her.

"Yeah, he was terrific. Greg too," he added, well aware of his own tendency to see Greg as perhaps more of a stage star than was truly warranted.

Or not. Greg really did possess a formidable acting talent. The Chapel Hill theater community had to wake up and realize it eventually.

A renewed wave of applause broke out when the actors lined up for their bows. Adrian clapped with enthusiasm for everyone, because the whole cast was wonderful, but he thought he could be forgiven for saving his most ardent applause for Greg. The familiar gray gaze swept through the audience and caught Adrian's. Greg winked, and Adrian laughed.

Afterward, the PlayMakers hosted an opening-night reception in the lobby. Adrian wandered around, pleasantly buzzed on four plastic cups of cheap wine, talking with various cast members and telling everyone how much he'd enjoyed the play. Noemi stood near the doors, surrounded by students, veteran theatergoers and various press members, holding a cup of red wine in one hand and the bouquet of roses the cast had given her in the other. She was smiling and relaxed as she gave an interview to an older woman in an obviously expensive suit. Adrian thought she looked as regal as a queen holding court.

"Dr. Dimension. How goes it, man?"

Adrian turned and grinned at Theo. "Good. Really good. Speaking of, you were wonderful in the play tonight. Everyone one was. Fantastic job."

"Thanks, dude." Theo eyed Adrian's near-empty cup. "Refill?"

Adrian thought about it, thought about how much Greg would tease him for getting drunk at a theater party, then remembered how those particular episodes usually ended. His grin widened. "Why not? C'mon, I'll buy you one."

"Awesome. Love it when guys buy me drinks that're free already." Slinging an arm around Adrian's shoulders, Theo led him to the bar.

Greg stood there in his favorite snug black pants and deep purple silk shirt, talking with Malachi, Omar and Len. Greg's eyebrows shot up when Adrian and Theo approached. "Theo, you trying to poach my man? Not cool."

"Hey, he said he'd buy me a drink. Not my fault men find me irresistible." Theo shook back his wild curls and ran a hand over the beard he kept trimmed these days mostly because Chelsea liked it that way. "If you had all this going on, maybe you could keep your dog in your own yard, pretty boy."

Len snickered into her beer. Mal whooped out loud, drawing a roomful of curious looks. "Cat fight!"

"Good grief." Shaking his head, Omar signaled to the bartender, who'd just handed an order to the women next to him. "Could I have another brown ale, please?"

She handed him his order. The next couple of minutes were a flurry of orders called and filled. The bartender seemed relieved to get away from them once they'd all gotten their drinks and moved back from the bar to make room for the increasing press of customers.

"It's too bad the BCPI gang couldn't hang around," Greg said as the group crammed themselves into a corner beside the doors into the theater. "I'd've loved for them to see the play."

"They wanted to. Especially Dean." Feeling demonstrative, Adrian wound his arm around Greg and kissed the side of his head. "But you know they didn't have an extra two weeks to spend here. They have a business to run, and they had a new case coming up."

"It really would've been great to see them again." Len looked a little wistful. "They're a wonderful bunch."

Adrian saw the gratitude in her eyes and raised his plastic cup to her. She returned his silent toast with a smile.

"Oh, hey, guys." Jon slipped through the crowd to join them. "It's great to see y'all. I hope everyone enjoyed the play."

Watching Jon's movie-star smile and sparkling blue eyes, Adrian could see why he'd been cast as the play's male lead. A handsome man who could act, sing and dance equally well couldn't be easy to find. "It was wonderful, Jon. You all did an amazing job."

"You really did," Len added. "You and your leading lady—Isabella, right?—you were fantastic together."

"Thank you very much." Jon's smile widened as he reached a broad hand across to her. "You work with Greg and Mal, right? I'm Jon Hudson."

"I know." She shook his hand, looking pleased. "I'm Elena Sims, Len to my friends. I'm one of the managers at DogOpolis, yes. Nice to meet you, Jon."

"You too." Letting go of Len's hand, he gripped Omar's shoulder. "I tell you what, Isabella and I couldn't do our job at all if it weren't for these guys, though. Greg, Theo, Omar and the rest of the folks in the chorus. Not to mention Malachi and Sandra running the sound and lights. Wouldn't be much of a play if it weren't for all of them."

"Thanks, man." Mal slapped Jon on the back. "I know I pick on you actor types, but this is a good group."

Omar glanced up at Jon with a shy smile. "I've really enjoyed working with you as well, Jon."

Jon's face lit up like a spotlight. Greg stared at the two of them for a moment, then smirked in a way Adrian had learned to dread.

Before Adrian could say a word, Greg tilted his head sideways and aimed his best, most innocent smile at Jon. "Hey, Jon, Adrian and I are going to the physics frat's charity bonfire and cookout on Tuesday night. You ought to come with us." His eyes widened as if a brilliant idea had only that second occurred to him. "Omar, you should come too. Weren't you just saying you wanted to go out more?"

Adrian stifled the urge to roll his eyes. He loved Greg more than life itself, but nothing was more obvious than Greg in Cupid mode.

Either Jon and Omar didn't notice, or didn't care, because they shared a distinctly interested smile. Jon nudged Omar's arm with his. "How about it, Omar? I can give you a ride, if you need it."

Greg darted Adrian a smug look. Adrian drained his cup.

They stayed until the party wound down to a few actors and their families plus the long-suffering bartenders. Adrian and Greg both took a moment to speak to Jon's parents before heading home.

Len and Mal left the theater with them. "Len, how's everything at your place?" Adrian asked once they'd walked out of earshot of any casual listeners. Unsurprisingly, Len and Greg had told Mal the whole story as soon as it was all over. "You haven't had any more...you know, *trouble*, have you?"

"No." She gave him a wry smile. "I'm still having trouble sleeping, but that's just the nightmares."

"I'm sorry, hon." Greg put an arm around her shoulders and squeezed her tight. "Anything we can do to help?"

"Naw, I'll be fine. My doctor gave me a sleeping pill, and I'm seeing a therapist." She brushed her bangs out of her eyes. "Y'all've already done way more for me than any normal people would've. I owe you."

Adrian shook his head. "No, you don't. We were just glad we could help."

Mal, who'd been unusually quiet, chose then to talk. "Wait, where'd you find a therapist who'd listen to what happened to you and not call the guys with the straitjackets?"

Greg let go of Adrian's hand long enough to shove Mal as they crossed Raleigh. "Geez, way to be sensitive."

"What? Most therapists would think something like that sounded pretty nuts. I mean, *we* know it's true, but other people don't." Malachi aimed a wounded glance at Greg. "I'm just saying."

A crowd of students strode down the sidewalk on the other side, huddled close together and talking too loudly. Headed back to their dorms after a Friday night on Franklin Street, no doubt. Adrian and the rest of their group had to part and step off the sidewalk entirely to keep from getting mowed down.

"Jackasses." Len glared at them for a moment before turning her attention back to Mal. "No, you're right. Most people really would think it was nuts." She sighed. "Truthfully? I messaged your stepdad, Adrian, and asked him if he knew how to get a hold of someone who could help me without thinking I was having a psychotic break or something. I figured he might know somebody, since I'd read that he only found out about his psychic abilities less than fifteen years ago. Thought he might've needed help coming to terms with it all and might know of someone who could point me in the right direction. He talked to some people down in Mobile for recommendations and gave me some names."

Adrian stepped sideways to avoid a man yelling into his pod and paying no attention at all to where he was going. The distraction provided a welcome few seconds for Adrian to pull himself together. Sam must've talked to the wonderful therapist who'd basically saved Adrian's sanity in the aftermath of the portal incident when he was eleven.

Len bit her lip, clearly nervous, and Adrian smiled at her. "Good. I'm happy he was able to help you. He's great like that."

They stopped halfway between the Country Club Road intersection and Franklin Street, where Adrian and Greg always cut across campus to get to their apartment complex. "Well, this is our stop." Greg hugged Len hard and kissed her cheek, then forced a hug on Mal before he could protest. "I'll see you Monday, Len. Mal, I'll see *you* tomorrow night."

"You know it, man." Malachi saluted Adrian. "See you around, A."

Adrian grinned. "I hope so, Mal."

Len hugged Adrian. "Night, guys. See you later."

"Good night, Len. Take care."

"C'mon, Len." Mal touched her arm. "I'm going right past your place, I'll walk you home."

She smiled, her gratitude clear as day. "Thanks, Mal. I appreciate that."

They set off down the sidewalk toward Franklin. Mal turned before they'd gotten far and pointed at Adrian and Greg. "You know what, y'all would be awesome at solving mysteries. Like the Scooby Doo gang, you know? That old cartoon?"

"Except these monsters are real." Len gazed at Adrian and Greg without a trace of humor. "Bye, guys."

Later, Adrian lay awake staring at the ceiling and thinking of Mal's half-joking words, and Len's deadly serious answer. It shouldn't bother him, because really, what were the odds of Greg and him stumbling across something like the demon fan again?

But what if you did? Could you leave someone to live with that, knowing you had the power to help?

Adrian knew the answer. Even Greg wouldn't be able to turn his back, no matter how much he might protest the potential danger to Adrian.

Adrian sighed. He wasn't getting anywhere thinking in circles like this. He'd cross that bridge when he came to it, if he ever did.

Not that he would. The odds against it were astronomical.

A ghost mystery, like Groome Castle, on the other hand...

Adrian grinned in the darkness. *That* could be fun.

About the Author

Ally Blue is acknowledged by the world at large (or at least by her heroes, who tend to suffer a lot) as the Popess of Gay Angst. She has a great big penis hat and rides in a bullet-proof Plexiglas bubble in Christmas parades. Her harem of manwhores does double duty as bodyguards and inspirational entertainment. Her favorite band is Radiohead, her favorite color is lime green and her favorite way to waste a perfectly good Saturday is to watch all three extended-version LOTR movies in a row. Her ultimate dream is to one day ditch the evil day job and support the family on manlove alone. She is not a hippie or a brain surgeon, no matter what her kids' friends say.

To learn more about Ally Blue, please visit www.allyblue.com. Send an email to Ally at ally@allyblue.com, follow her on Twitter @PopessAllyBlue or join her Yahoo! group to join in the fun with other readers as well as Ally http://groups.yahoo.com/group/loveisblue.

To get to "Love Me Tender", they'll have to shake things up.

Graceland
© *2012 Ally Blue*

Kevin Fraser has a good life—a good job, good friends and a nursing degree within his grasp. There's not a lot of excitement to be found in Asheville, but so what? He doesn't need excitement. Or love, for that matter. Until a big man with an Elvis fixation and the voice to match shows up in his ER and changes his point of view.

A diabetes diagnosis isn't the end of the world, just one more problem Owen Hicks doesn't need. It hasn't been easy finding his place in the Cherokee tribe, his family and the world at large since he came out. On top of that, learning to manage the disease that killed his mother is a daunting challenge. He counts himself lucky that the nursing student he befriended in the hospital is willing and able to help.

As their fast friendship deepens into something both of them want—yet fear—pressures from without and within stretch their bond to the breaking point. The only way to find the strength to love each other is to find the courage to let go...and hope love is strong enough to bring them together again.

Warning: This book contains medical drama, relationship drama, sex, silliness and a Cherokee Elvis. Sorry, no fried banana sandwiches. Thank ya very much.

Available now in ebook and print from Samhain Publishing.

Enjoy the following excerpt for Graceland:

Half an hour later, he'd finished the pizza, polished off the lager and started on another. A regular one this time. He'd decided he liked the taste of the non-pretentious ones better. He was lounging on the sofa, his regular-guy beer in his hand and his bare feet on the coffee table, watching ultimate cage fighting—or poor man's gay porn, as Andy called it—when someone knocked on the door.

Kevin scowled. "Just a sec!"

Setting his beer on the table, he pushed to his feet and shuffled to the door just as his unknown visitor knocked again. Or maybe *knocked* was the wrong word. *Pounded* would've worked, since the door vibrated in its frame.

"Okay, okay! Geez." Kevin unlocked the door, turned the knob and threw it open.

Owen stood on the other side.

Kevin gaped at him. "Owen. What—?"

That was as far as he got. Pushing Kevin inside, Owen kicked the door shut, pulled Kevin close and kissed him.

For a second, sheer surprise held Kevin motionless. Then Owen grabbed Kevin's ass with one big hand and slipped the other up the back of his shirt, and the rush of desire drowned everything but the need to get closer.

With a moan that sounded as desperate as it felt, Kevin plastered himself against Owen's chest and opened wide for his kiss. Owen made a soft, helpless noise when his tongue and Kevin's slid together. His fingers dug bruises into Kevin's flesh. Heart racing, Kevin used Owen's wide shoulders to lever himself higher. Just a little, just enough to kiss Owen harder, deeper.

Owen's grip on him tightened. His feet left the floor, Owen's hand on his butt urging one leg to angle up and around Owen's hip. Pressed groin to groin, Kevin felt the unmistakable hardness of Owen's cock through his jeans.

Owen rolled his pelvis. His erection rubbed against Kevin's. A flash flood of heat roared through Kevin's body, fraying his consciousness at the edges.

Fainting like a wuss was just *not* allowed to happen. Especially *before* sex.

With a monumental effort, he broke the kiss. "Bedroom." He gave Owen's shoulders a light smack. "Put me down."

Owen obediently set him on his feet, looking dazed. "Bedroom?"

Kevin nodded. "Lube. Condoms." Cupping Owen's groin in one hand, he leaned in and nipped at his chest through his ancient UNC T-shirt. "C'mon."

"Lube's good." Owen lifted Kevin's chin and kissed him again, a light, teasing kiss that made Kevin want to rip his clothes off and attack him right there on the throw rug in front of the door. "Do we *have* to use rubbers though? I don't have anything and I'm betting you don't either."

"I don't, but that's not the point."

"Hm." Owen trailed his lips down the side of Kevin's neck.

Shivers ran down Kevin's spine. "Shit. Don't make me go all medical professional on your hot ass. No rubbers, no..." He wracked his brain for something to rhyme with rubbers, but either nothing did or Owen was screwing up his ability to think straight. "Other...s. Other stuff. Dammit."

Owen snickered. "That sucks."

"Yeah, well, I hope you like sucking, because that's all there'll be without protection."

Owen drew back, his gaze heavy. "I guess we're using 'em then, 'cause I want you to fuck me."

Oh, God. Kevin's knees went weak. He licked his lips. "I want me to fuck you too. C'mon."

This time, Owen let Kevin take his hand and tug him toward the bedroom. Not that they managed to get all the way there without stopping for a kiss or three on the way. In fact, by the time they'd reached the short hallway leading to the two small bedrooms and tiny bath, Kevin had given up on walking like a normal person and turned around to move backward, the better to unbuckle Owen's belt as they went. He told himself it saved time.

He got the belt undone as the two of them stumbled through his bedroom door. Before he could start on Owen's jeans, Owen swept him into another mind-melting kiss. Kevin stood there, clinging to Owen for dear life while each curl of Owen's tongue around his sent a little more of his brainpower spiraling down into his cock along with most of the blood in his body.

"Fuck, you kiss good," Kevin breathed when he and Owen finally came up for air.

"I was thinking the same thing. About you, I mean." Owen grinned. "We're in your bedroom."

Kevin laughed. "So we are." Taking hold of the hem of Owen's T-shirt, he tugged it up until he hit arms. "Off."

The teasing expression vanished from Owen's face, replaced by the lust Kevin expected and a vulnerability that surprised him. Owen pulled off his T-shirt and let it fall to the floor. Kevin leaned in to suck up a purple mark on Owen's collarbone.

"Oh. Fuck. Kev." Owen tugged at Kevin's shirt, wordless but eloquent.

Shaking with eagerness, Kevin peeled himself off Owen's bare chest, tore off his own shirt and lunged forward again, intent on decorating that gorgeous expanse of bronze skin with more love bites.

Owen stopped him by grasping his shoulders. "Bed now. Go."

Kevin went, dragging Owen with him by the belt loops. They tumbled onto the bed with Owen on top. Kevin wound his fingers into Owen's hair and angled his head to kiss him again. He ran his free hand over Owen's back and shoulders, tracing the bulge of hard muscles with his palm. Hooking a leg around Owen's waist, he used all his strength to try to force the big, solid body down more firmly onto his.

Owen resisted, holding himself up on his forearms. "I'll crush you." His voice was a rough, strained whisper against Kevin's lips.

"Don't care." Kevin dipped his head to suck at the juncture of Owen's neck and shoulder. Owen moaned low and sweet, and Kevin committed that spot to memory.

"But... Oooh. God." A hard shudder shook Owen's body when Kevin dragged the tip of his tongue up Owen's neck and around the back of his ear, another fact Kevin stored away for later use. "Fuck. Sorry, but I'm not a patient guy, and you're seriously turning me on here. Can we fuck now?" Owen pushed back enough to look into Kevin's eyes. "There'll be plenty of other times for taking it slow, I swear."

Kevin stared at the sincerity in Owen's face, the brown eyes wide with a kind of solemn desperation, and had to laugh. "In that case, yes, let's fuck now. Horny bastard."

Owen's fake-stern face fell apart in a matter of seconds. Grinning like a demon, he sat back on his knees, bent and dug his tongue into Kevin's navel. Kevin dissolved into surprised laughter. "No, stop it!" He tried to push Owen away.

"You're ticklish?" Owen's grin turned sly. He held Kevin's wrists to the bed and traced his tongue in a feather-light circle over Kevin's lower belly.

Kevin pressed his lips tightly together, but it didn't do any good. His chest shook with stifled laughter, and he couldn't keep himself from squirming.

Which clearly delighted Owen. He snickered. "We are *so* playing with this later. Right now, though..." Letting go of Kevin's wrists, Owen untied the drawstring on the ratty sweatpants Kevin wore and eased them over his hips.

The way Owen looked at him then—like he was a long-sought treasure—made Kevin wish he could hang on to this moment. Keep it like a picture in his wallet.

Impossible, of course. The moment passed, as they all do. Not that Kevin could feel sorry about that, when Owen got Kevin's sweatpants off, spread his thighs and deep-throated his cock as if it was easy.

Maybe it is, for him, mused the tiny portion of Kevin's brain not caught up in the best blowjob he'd had in ages.

SAMHAIN
PUBLISHING

It's all about the story...

Romance

HORROR

www.samhainpublishing.com